Of Darkness and Deathless

By Timothy Monahan

No Frills
<<<>>>
Buffalo

2

Printed in the United States of America

Monahan, Timothy

Of Darkness and Deathless/ Monahan- 1st Edition

ISBN: 978-0615708010

1. Of Darkness and Deathless – Dark/Fantastical – Fiction. 2. New Author – No Frills – Biblical/Supernatural.
1. Title

No Frills Buffalo Press
119 Dorchester Buffalo, New York 14213
For More Information Visit Nofrillsbuffalo.com

For my Grandfather, Poppo,
the Greatest Storyteller I Know

"The soul who sins shall die. The son shall not suffer for the iniquity of the father, nor the father suffer for the iniquity of the son. The righteousness of the righteous shall be upon himself, and the wickedness of the wicked shall be upon himself" - **Ezekial 18:20**

Chapter 1

The Psychopomp

The moon was absent the night Dr. Samuel Fox was laid to rest. Despite his vast integrity and fame, only a handful of people came to pay their respects to the distinguished Professor. The small party, comprised of relatives and associates, huddled around his casket, consoling each other in what used to be the gentleman's favorite room in the house, the library.

Dr. Fox's world-renowned collection of artifacts and manuscripts was a well-kept secret from his son, 14-year-old Preston Scott. The late Professor never permitted anyone to set foot inside his private chambers, and over the years a legend about the mysterious room began to grow. The breadth of the interior exceeded even Preston's wildest imagination, and the cathedral-like ceiling, stained glass windows, and finely crafted stonework were even more magnificent than the stories described.

The Fox homestead was an illustrious construction with superb and attentive craftsmanship, but small rooms and cramped hallways limited Dr. Fox's ambitions. In order to transform the structure to better suit his needs, he remodeled and reconstructed the entire rear façade to resemble the interior of a nearby gothic church. He sought a grandiose space in order to display his collection – a myriad of stone sculptures, metalwork, and ancient scripts adorned glass pedestals decorated with bronze placards explaining their significance. There were no partitions or walls to speak of as every object in the room was placed conspicuously along the outer edge in order to conserve space. A spiral staircase in the far left corner crept up the wall like a growth of ivy, and connected to a steel catwalk on the second story. From there, a narrow walkway with tarnished decks and railings linked three adjacent walls of bookcases. To the far right rested a smaller area cluttered with chairs, desks, and cabinets. Bookcases lined the walls and stacks of paper carpeted the floor of the disheveled study.

Preston sat on a chair near the center of the room, dumbfounded by the extent of his late father's collected works. While taking in his surroundings, he covertly listened to his relatives talk about his father, the past, and what was going to be served for supper. His cousin Pascal was most interested in the latter.

Despite a fight with his Aunt Charlotte, Preston was dressed in proper funeral attire – a black suit, white shirt, and a dark red tie with little black diamonds stretching from front to back. He greased and combed his short brown hair to the side like a businessman, and his Uncle Thomas even polished his shoes. Preston stared down at his feet and frowned at his reflection. Those black Dunboys were his favorite pair, meant for climbing trees and running through the woods, and had not been that clean since they came out of the box.

The setting sun forced tiny beads of sweat to drip from Preston's forehead; freckles on his face radiated from cheek to cheek, across the bridge of his nose, and flickered in the evening light. During the summer, Preston was the complete opposite of his winter persona; his hair was lighter, freckles blossomed on his face and arms, and his brown eyes burned brighter.

Preston scanned the room with his eyes but tried his hardest to avoid making contact with his father's casket. Instead, he saw what appeared to be drawings of dragons and medieval castles on the dusty jackets of his late father's books. A certain large volume dressed in dark crimson caught his eye, and he squinted in order to read the title – *The Modern Giant: Friend or Foe?* Upon further examination, many of the books nearby were also associated with the topic of giants, and Preston began to wonder why, if his father kept such a large collection of fantasy stories, he never read to him.

Not once.

A feeling of resentment rose to the surface of his emotions. Preston hated his father for as long as he could remember and every altercation seemed to revolve around the topic of his mother, but he never fully believed the stories that she had died while giving birth. It was an unspoken rule in the Fox home to refrain from talking about Preston's mother. Most family members always hinted that she had done something terribly wrong to become such an ethereal outcast, and his questions were always met with inconsistent answers, which in turn fueled his imagination. It was easier for him to envision that she was off somewhere living a life of vibrant joy, away from the dreary life his father lived, and that she would return to him when the moment was right.

"It is such a tragic loss," lamented Uncle Thomas, Dr. Fox's brother. "I always thought I would be the first to go. Samuel kept himself in the best shape possible, but now look at him. Charlotte, don't ever let me become one of those exercise obsessed."

Uncle Thomas took the prize for largest man in Preston's microcosm of a world. Every feature on his uncle's face was colossal in comparison to the average human being. His eyes, nose, and ears looked as though they were being viewed through a magnifying glass. Preston's Aunt Charlotte was as big and round as Uncle Thomas, but her feminine qualities granted her the honor of being 'fragile' and 'dainty'. She was two feet shorter than Uncle Thomas and the bushels of hair on her head more than made up for her husband's lack thereof. Her red, curly tresses fell below her knees and were the pride of her appearance.

Seeing Preston alone in his chair, Aunt Charlotte let out a long cry followed by an endless string of sniffles. She ignored her husband's commentary and instead conveyed her own emotions.

"I remember when Samuel was just a child and he and my Thomas had to stand at their own father's funeral," she said. "It makes me sad to think about what's going to happen to Preston. I'm sure he will impress the judges with his brains and the court will let him continue studying at Northrup, but I fear the dangers of being so alone. At least my Thomas and Samuel had each other."

She made the future sound very bleak for Preston, and though her words seeped with natural motherly instinct, the boy couldn't help but feel condemned to the fate.

"I am still astonished by Samuel's will," Mr. Tunnamore exclaimed, Dr. Fox's assistant and Preston's informal guardian since he was a child. "He must've changed the legal document after I transcribed it with him. Why would he only give me temporary custody of Preston?"

Tunnamore joined Charlotte in mourning the boy's unforeseeable future. Preston sat idle, recognizing the pretense in everyone's voices. He gazed into their eyes and saw nothing but a false sense of sympathy – sympathy for him and the lack of a father's love. A few other members of the crowd spoke about the prevalent issue, including Preston's cousin Emma.

She forced as comforting a smile as she could. Preston always liked his older cousin; both of them loved running through the woods, and both detested her brother Pascal. He smiled back and reminisced about the time they fed Pascal shortcake that Emma baked full of sardines. It was one of Preston's fondest memories because Pascal turned three shades of green after realizing what he ate and chased the two saboteurs through the woods for over an hour. Preston and Emma laughed all the while, and it was one of the only times during his childhood that Preston actually went to bed with a stomach ache from too much laughter.

Preston's eyes met once again with the lifeless body in the casket and sadness crept back into his conscience. He looked around at the present company and counted a little over ten tear-soaked faces. More people had arrived, but Preston did not recognize any of them.

"I wonder if he worked himself to death?" Uncle Thomas asked, without addressing any specific person in the room. "All those long days and nights might have finally caught up with him. I know they took a toll on me just watching him do it."

Everyone, except Preston, nodded in silent agreement.

Through all his contemplation, Preston eventually noticed the light outside the window beginning to fade into the distance. He longed to be outdoors and couldn't wait for the ceremony to end. Uncle Thomas and Aunt Charlotte continued their private conversation while Tunnamore made his way to the back of the room. During this time, no one, not even Preston, noticed a fresh presence in the Fox library. A dark, hooded figure stood in the back of the study. It was no wonder that none in attendance perceived the shadow sitting along the wall as it remained completely still and blended perfectly into the aged backdrop of the bookcases.

Tunnamore stopped short on his way to the doorway and tested the air surrounding him. He swung his head back and forth a few times, like a dog on the hunt, until he caught the scent of something nearby. Tunnamore made his way to the corner where the shadow sat and crept along the wall, trying not to make a sound. Preston watched his late father's assistant with intense focus. Uncle Thomas left the side of Aunt Charlotte and knelt down near Preston, obstructing the boy's view of the rear of the library. His uncle began saying something in a compassionate tone, but Preston heard not a word. Meanwhile, Tunnamore stretched out a long boney finger to poke at the wad of dusty robes. The shadow shrugged, making him nearly jump out of his skin. Uncle Thomas continued talking, and while Preston refused to give his relative any attention, the old man kept wasting his breath.

Turning to his Uncle, Preston said, "I have to use the bathroom, may I be excused?"

Uncle Thomas smiled warmly.

"Certainly you may, just be sure to make it quick."

Preston nodded, left his perch, and navigated his way through the gathered party, making a conscious effort to avoid making any eye contact that would result in being stopped. He dashed back and forth in-between relatives and friends alike without once alerting any of them to his presence. He overheard a few people mention his name, his father, and something about the University, but none of it was as important as what lay just ahead of him at the back of the library. When Preston reached the door to the outer hallway he made a sharp left turn and looked back to ensure his Uncle had not witnessed the detour.

Trying to get as close to Tunnamore and the mysterious guest as possible, Preston worked his way back into the library in order to spy on his quarry. He squatted down low among the stacks of books and papers and tried his hardest to blend into the shadows. After only a few seconds, Preston perceived a distinct aroma emanating from the two men. The smell was so intense it almost made him gag, and he had to cover his nose in order to focus on the conversation.

"...doesn't seem like the most proper way of conducting business, but then again, there are few dealings in today's world that are," Tunnamore said, with an air of curiosity. "However, I would ask that you wait until the service concludes, simply for the sake of my Master's distant relatives who would like to spend ample time saying goodbye."

A haunting voice responded, and when the stranger opened his mouth, a deep gurgle escaped from deep within his bowels. It sounded like phlegm rattling between his lungs and nasal cavity.

"I'm not here under any time constraints Mr. Tunnamore, but, if I may make myself very clear," the stranger stopped short to take an arduous breath, rattling all the while. "Your late master signed the proper documentation many years ago, and so, I have come to collect....Don't be fooled....I have not arrived early for the sake of trying my patience, I have had many years of practice for such trivial business already....but I am here to make sure the contract is honored.... and that my client gets what is rightfully his."

Preston was interested to overhear the exchange, but equally frustrated by the stranger's voice. He wanted to cough and clear his own throat in an attempt to signal that the stranger should do the same.

"I promise you that my Master left the contract for me to review, and yes, what you came for will most certainly be yours," Tunnamore replied.

"Have any others sought correspondence?" the stranger asked.

"No, you are the only non-relative in attendance this evening."

"I did not mean this evening alone....what about in the last few days, or even weeks?"

"I swear to you that no one other than yourself has addressed the contract to the likes of me."

By the time the verbal exchange came to an end, the stranger was struggling to catch his breath and Tunnamore appeared more agitated than before. Preston moved stacks of books out of his way in an attempt to crawl closer, but he soon realized that he was no longer the little boy that could sneak around the house without a sound. He was now in his teenage years and his body was much too large and awkward for a stealthy approach. As he tried to squeeze his hips through the maze of papers, he brushed up against a tower of crusty, yellowish leaflets, knocking it over. Tunnamore and the stranger both looked up in alarm, the latter jumping out of his seat, seemingly ready to defend himself.

It took the late Professor's assistant only a few seconds to isolate the source of the disturbance. He grabbed Preston by the collar, lifting him off the ground. The first thing Preston noticed was Tunnamore's black eyes, full of anger and a hint of fear.

"What do you think you are doing back here?" Tunnamore hissed. "You were told to stay put and refrain from snooping around your father's library. This place contains nothing of interest for you and I don't want your grimy little fingers, or your devilish little eyes prying into anything!"

Tunnamore exhausted himself while trying to keep his voice down, but Preston was not frightened. In fact, he wished Tunnamore had screamed so everyone in the room could understand how his caretaker really felt. That is why Preston was so disgusted when he saw Tunnamore sobbing with Aunt Charlotte; he knew very well that his late father's assistant could not care less about the Fox family. The man was more upset that Dr. Fox did not leave him the entire estate in the will like he felt he deserved.

"Who is this boy?" the stranger barked. "Tunnamore, I demand to know immediately who this is...and what he is doing snooping around in our business."

The color drained from Tunnamore's face and he turned steadily, struggling to get the words out of his mouth.

"This boy is Dr. Fox's son, Preston. He, uhh, was simply looking for me, but everything's okay now, right Preston?"

Tunnamore forced a nervous smile and stammered as he fed the stranger lies. Preston looked up at the man holding him and wanted nothing more than to kick him where it would hurt the most. They waited for a response from the dark figure, which was now working his way toward them. The stranger came closer and closer and Preston had trouble keeping track of the man in the darkness. The only reason he knew the stranger was too close for comfort was the rotten smell that invaded his nostrils. He cupped a free hand over his nose and mouth, and struggled to concentrate on the hooded figure now crouched in front of him.

"So this is the young boy that I've heard so much about," the mysterious man whispered. "So much for formal introductions, but now that I know your name...you might as well know who I am. My name is Arminius Blackwood."

Preston thought quickly about how he should respond, but could not bring himself to remove his hand from his face. He reached out with his free hand to shake Arminius's out-stretched limb.

"Pleasure to (cough) meet you Mr. Blackwood," Preston said in an attempt to be respectful.

The two shook hands and the mystery surrounding the strange guest became even more interesting. When Preston made physical contact with Arminius's hand he felt a wintry shiver shoot immediately down his spine. The man's hand was cold as ice and extremely brittle, ready to break off at the wrist and simply crumble in the boy's grip. Arminius felt something completely different. For the first time in almost half a century he felt a warm sting pulsing throughout his veins as they thawed from his fingertips down to his wrist. Both men retracted their hands and stared at each other with deep curiosity. Preston could not understand what happened, and he watched Arminius rubbing his hand profusely. The novelty and wonder that shined in Arminius's eyes left an impression on Preston and reassured him that the bizarre feeling was shared.

Uncle Thomas barged into the study, just as Arminius was about to speak. A look of desperation in his eyes revealed that he was on an intent mission, probably for Aunt Charlotte. The aging man also appeared to be out of breath, and with each intense heave of his chest he came closer to passing out in a pile of hardcover encyclopedias.

"I've been looking all over for you. Your Aunt Charlotte had a hissy fit when I told her I let you run off to the bathroom by yourself."

Uncle Thomas forced the last few words from his lungs and stopped in order to give his diaphragm a rest. Everyone stood in silence while he gathered his strength.

"It is time to say our last goodbyes," he uttered, a tear forming in the corner of his left eye.

Preston could sense that his uncle wished to say more, but the sudden onset of pain and sadness glued his mouth shut. With his bottom lip quivering, Uncle Thomas motioned for Preston to come along. Preston shot a glance at Arminius and Tunnamore, half expecting them to say something on his behalf, but the stern look on his caretaker's face revealed that he was alone. He lowered his head in defeat and followed his uncle.

Was it wrong that he found Arminius Blackwood more fascinating than seeing his father for the last time? Battling within his mind about what was morally right, he ultimately decided that it was his responsibility as a son to say goodbye to his father, regardless of past misgivings and resentment.

Preston followed his uncle back to the makeshift memorial at the far end of the library. A line of mourners, paying their last respects, moved quickly along the outer edge near the stained-glass windows. A string of endless sniffles, sobs, and coughs filled the thinning air while the sun continued its silent descent. Preston walked with his head bowed and his uncle's hand leading his shoulder. He kept telling himself that it was going to be quick and painless, and that he was not going to feel any sort of sadness in the least bit, but something deep inside kept gnawing at his emotions. What if he actually began to cry? Even with all his hatred directed at his father, death has a way of causing people to act outside of themselves.

"Come along Preston, we're almost to the front. I will give you plenty of time to say your prayers and say goodbye to your father," Uncle Thomas said, his voice undulating with every syllable.

To Preston's surprise, the expansive room became incredibly quiet when the honorable valediction began. It was so quiet that he could hear his heart beating through his chest. The constant thumping sent waves of heat and adrenaline throughout his body, causing him to become lightheaded and his limbs numb. It came down to just one person between him and the scariest moment in his entire life. Preston could see around those in front of him and observe the outline of the casket and the salt and pepper color of his father's hair. The little old lady in front of Preston picked up her head, wiped her eyes with a tissue clenched in her right hand, and headed for the exit.

Now the body of Dr. Fox lay in plain view, and a heavy weight dropped from Preston's throat to the tips of his toes. He became faint and found it hard to breathe under all of the pressure. He wondered why on earth the room would be spinning at such a time and wanted desperately for it to stop. Uncle Thomas gave Preston a light shove forward and the teenager put out his hands to stop himself from falling. Both palms rested on the edge of the coffin and he felt his knees give out and hit the floor with a soft, muffled thud.

The late Professor's hair was slicked back to reveal his slightly thinning hairline, a fashion choice he would have loathed if he were alive. His nose was smaller than Preston's and came to a point just short of his upper lip. Thin eyebrows splashed across his forehead, and his high cheekbones were a testament to his muscular physique. A scar stretched from the front of his right ear down the side of his neck, revealing a lifetime of mystery and adventure.

Preston heard the voice of a man, probably his Uncle Thomas, coming from all directions. The entire library seemed to be frozen in time. He gazed into the pale face of his father and saw nothing but 14 years of neglect and detachment. He saw a liar, a coward, and an all around horrid father; but it was the shape of the eyes that caught his attention. They were shaped just like his, and in that moment the pain and anger building inside of him came to a point and erupted from his eyes. Tears streamed down his cheeks and he cursed them as they fell. A barrage of memories and letdowns flew through his mind, whizzing above his head. Did he really hate his father so unconditionally, or did he simply long for the love of a parent? The realization that all of his unanswered questions about his mother died with his father caused him the most grief. Now he would never know the truth.

Uncle Thomas tightened his grip on Preston's shoulder and his voice gave way to uncontrollable howls. Preston gathered himself long enough to see his father's hand through the blinding, salty waterfalls cascading down his face. He reached out and placed his hand ever so gently over the top of his father's. They felt so cold, and Preston was reminded of the handshake he shared with Arminius Blackwood. The same icy jolt stung his hand.

"It's time to go Preston. It's okay to let go now," Uncle Thomas said. "It's okay."

Preston ceded and pulled his hand away from his father. In the very next instant, the once silent room filled with gasps and cries of horror and surprise. He watched Aunt Charlotte faint near the exit, falling flat on her face. Preston whirled around only to see his father half sitting up in his casket, eyes wide open.

Chapter 2

The Awakening

The next few hours passed in the blink of an eye. Preston sat on the front lawn with his knees tucked to his chest, eyes fixed upon the Great Lake stretched out before him. He observed a thunderhead rolling in from the west and tried to calculate how long it would take to reach the city along the northeastern shoreline.

Something poked him as he shifted his weight, and he reached into his pocket and pulled out the memorial prayer card from his father's wake. At the top it read, *In Loving Memory, Dr. Samuel Preston Fox, June 14, 1892 – August 29, 1939.* Preston kept reading until he came across the phrase 'loving father'. He decided to stop right there, skip the prayer and rip the card in half, tossing the scraps onto the lawn.

He looked at the driveway, the diseased and lifeless asphalt scar, and made note that it was filled to the brim with automobiles, including recent additions to the party; cars owned by his father's physician and multiple newspaper reporters. An ambulance, parked on the grass only a few feet from where he sat, completed the jumbled mess.

Apparently a person coming back from the dead was a big deal.

Dr. Fox had experienced a fatal heart attack only two days before. He was taken to the hospital where he was pronounced dead at exactly 11:42 pm on August 29. People did not simply come back from beyond the grave, especially not after two full days. Apparently, the experts on-hand came to the conclusion that it was some sort of toxic substance that Dr. Fox encountered while excavating north of the city that caused his heart to slow, giving the appearance of death. Preston did not believe a word of what they said, but he also noted the fact that those men were well-experienced medical professionals, and he was just leaving grade school. Even though the doctors' debate was entertaining, Preston could not withstand the commotion in the library and went outside for some fresh air. People shouted, cheered, and cried; many were elated to witness such an event, but Preston just wanted to be alone.

He lifted his left arm and pulled his shirt cuff back, folding it up around his elbow. He proceeded to do the same with his right arm and then unbuttoned the top four buttons of his dress shirt. His necktie, removed earlier, lay on top of his suit coat. It was nearing midnight, and yet, a thin layer of sticky sweat clung to every inch of his body.

Soon after Dr. Fox was deemed alive and well by his physician, the atmosphere in the house turned to all out celebration. Tunnamore opened case upon case of wine, and people shed their black clothes in order to properly celebrate the rebirth of their good friend. Dancing and music commenced and everyone appeared to be having a great time, except for Dr. Fox and his son. Preston noticed immediately that his father was withdrawn and not nearly as boisterous as the rest of the group.

A door opened behind where Preston sat and the sound of laughter and cheering exploded into the night air, shattering his tranquility. The sound quickly died and he heard soft footsteps in the grass behind him.

"There you are kid, I've been looking all over for you," Emma exclaimed in a jovial manner. "I figured you would try and get away, but I didn't think you'd actually come outside. You're the only person I know that would sit outside in the rain."

She pointed a finger toward a stretch of clouds hovering over the lake, plopped herself down next to Preston without asking permission, and reeled in her knees, mocking him. Preston smiled and gave her a nudge with his elbow.

"Why would I stay in there and watch them praise the almighty Dr. Samuel Fox," he said. "I swear, it's like the man has a cult following."

"You have to realize that he is an important man and that he has connections with some powerful people," Emma said with a comforting smile. "My father said that you're lucky Samuel came back from the grave because there is no telling what would have happened to you. At least now you can stay here and we'll still be able to see each other."

She forced a smile, but Preston was not paying any attention.

"You are thinking about her, aren't you?" Emma asked.

"You know me too well," Preston responded. "It is all just so frustrating. He's the only one that knows the truth and I thought that truth died with him. When I saw him sitting up in that coffin…well, you can imagine the thoughts going through my head."

"How can you be so sure that he hasn't told you the truth already?"

"Because no one has the same story. Some say that she died while giving birth to me, others say it was a car crash. How someone dies should not be a mystery. He is hiding something."

A flash of lightning struck the horizon and the cousins waited patiently for the roll of thunder. It was not long before they heard a low rumble and turned towards each other, smiling.

"7 seconds," Preston counted.

"I had 8 seconds, and since I am four years older than you, that makes me all the wiser," Emma replied, smiling ear to ear.

They both laughed and Preston was glad that he finally had some company; even though he wanted to escape, he never wanted to be completely alone. He was alone almost every minute of every single day. It was familiar, and many times he found solace in his isolation, but for once he really craved human interaction and wanted desperately to thank his cousin for joining him.

"You know what scares me the most about his whole ordeal?" Emma asked.

"That Pascal is still worried about whether or not someone is going to feed him?" Preston shot back, with a burst of awkward laughter.

Emma looked at her cousin and couldn't help but laugh, despite the pain she sensed behind Preston's attempt at humor.

"No, you goof," she said, as her laughter subsided and her cheekbones revealed pending seriousness. "I truly believe your father was dead. Deep down inside I think this was a surprise for everyone, *especially* your father."

"I think you're right," he said, in a hushed voice, barely audible over the grand piano and the string of thunder echoing over the lake. "He seemed out of sorts, as if he wasn't expecting it. He looked at me for only a second and then looked away as if he were afraid to make eye contact. People rushed the coffin and I was squeezed to the back of the library."

Preston grabbed a handful of grass and ripped it from the earth. He crumbled the green blades and tossed them in a fit of irritation toward his suit coat.

"Shows you how much people really care about my life. I get one day of attention and then here comes the great Professor Fox to take it all away. I mean, I like being left alone, but I have to admit that there is something nice about having people actually consider your feelings for once."

"Well, you wanted some excitement, didn't you?"

Preston was reminded of Arminius Blackwood and the conversation with Tunnamore. He almost forgot about his run-in with the hooded stranger and wondered if the man was still inside, hiding in the rear of the library.

"That reminds me. I met this very strange man talking with Tunnamore and–"

His words were cut short when the front doors of the house swung open with a bang and two drunken family members stumbled out onto the porch. Preston and Emma heard the sound of empty wine bottles clinking on the concrete walkway as their Great Uncle Pierce struggled to keep his balance. He peered at the two cousins through droopy eyelids and put a finger to his mouth, telling them to be quiet with a "shhh" that sounded more like a burp. His companion, unrecognized by Preston, burst into laughter, and the two men continued their drunken march down the driveway.

Returning his focus to the words on the tip of his tongue, Preston opened his mouth in order to tell his cousin about Arminius, but was interrupted again by more partygoers exiting the Fox homestead.

This time it was a complete exodus as more than fifty people filed out of the front door, many of whom were intoxicated. Most found it difficult to keep to the well-lit path and Preston heard a few men imitating farting noises and laughing uncontrollably. Preston never understood adult humor, or as a matter of fact he never understood anything about adult mannerisms. Maybe that was why he struggled to develop a relationship with his father.

"What were you going to say?" Emma, trying to make certain her words could be heard over the ruckus, yelled at the top of her lungs.

Preston just shook his head and motioned for his cousin to join him in returning to the house. Tunnamore came up to greet them about half way and informed Emma that her parents were looking for her. She turned and gave Preston a big hug and held him long enough that he felt compelled to put his arm around her and squeeze. Emma knew her younger cousin was shy, but she did not want him to forget how to love.

"Take care of yourself Preston," she said. "Think of it as a new start – for the both of you."

Emma adjusted his shirt collar and smiled. He nodded and could not help but give his cousin a smile in return. She had always been good to him and he felt comforted by her presence. She walked toward the driveway while Preston turned and faced Tunnamore.

"Your father would like to speak to you," Tunnamore informed, in a sour manner. "In the library."

"Am I supposed to be quiet about what I saw earlier?" Preston asked.

"That will be for him to decide, now *get* inside."

Preston moved quickly up the path and bumped Tunnamore's shoulder as a gesture of disgust. He entered the house, surprised to find it in complete disarray. Quickening his pace, Preston reached the library in record timing and found the door unlocked. He pushed it open with his right hand and stepped inside the massive space. Dr. Fox spun around in his seat to face his son while Arminius Blackwood turned in the opposite direction. Preston was surprised to see the strange man still there and even more surprised to see him corresponding with his father.

Arminius looked different from before, but Preston's father looked relatively the same, despite the fact that he was now 'alive'. His face was still devoid of color, youth, and his salt and pepper hair seemed to be saltier than before. His eyes were dark and heavy, an odd combination considering he had slept for two full days.

"Please Preston – have a seat," Dr. Fox requested, showing signs of great distress, his voice quivering as he spoke. "I understand that you've already met Mr. Blackwood."

Arminius shifted in his seat and looked at the boy. When Preston first met Arminius, the lighting in the back of the library was very poor and made it difficult to see the man's face. Now they were in the center of the room and the light from the chandelier shone brightly; his face was pale and gaunt, his eyes sunken into his face like little black holes, his lips dark blue, and his nose covered in dead skin, peeling in all directions.

"Good to see you again," Arminius gargled.

Preston nodded sheepishly and returned his gaze to his father.

Dr. Fox was completely out of sorts in the presence of his son. A distanced relationship fourteen years in the making was to blame, and one night of supposed miracles was not about to change anything for the father and son duo. Preston continued to stare at his father, hoping that he would not have to talk unless he was asked about Arminius and Tunnamore.

"There are some things – I need to say to you," Dr. Fox began. "And I want you to believe me when I say it is the truth."

Preston smiled derisively and laughed to himself. Who did his father think he was kidding? The man had never said more than five words to Preston at any time, so why the sudden change of heart? Coming back from the dead was an excuse, thought Preston, but he would need more evidence before he was fully convinced.

"Why should I listen to you?" he barked in defiance.

"You've never cared about me before. Why does it matter

what you have to say?"

"Because I never said anything to you before – before my death."

Preston was stunned.

"So, you mean to tell me that you really died?"

"Yes."

"But, what of the doctors? They said–"

"They said exactly what they thought science could prove, nothing more. A miracle occurred tonight, Preston. They don't come often, so I hope to make the best of it."

"But–"

Preston stared at the floor and tried to sift through all of the new information in his brain. If his father really died, then what happened that night was beyond the realm of possibility.

"I never had the chance to tell you how I felt or why things were the way they were," Dr. Fox said.

Despite the fact that he still had questions about his father's resurrection, Preston's anger surged once again as his father spoke.

"Never had a chance?!" he shouted. "Are you insane?! You had fourteen years, *fourteen years* father to say whatever you needed to tell me."

"I suppose chance is the wrong word then. I guess I never had the courage, or the decency to speak of the truth."

Burning with rage, Preston's face flushed scarlet and his hands balled into fists. Dr. Fox remained pale, his body worn thin, as sweat formed just above his brow. His son's words clearly hurt his confidence and it was obvious that this was an emotional, as well as physical, moment for the Professor.

"You just don't understand," Dr. Fox whimpered, slumping into a chair and burying his face in his hands. "I did what I had to do, you must know that much."

Dr. Fox no longer seemed to be addressing Preston as his words floated around the room in search of a distant, almost ghostly audience. The library became quiet again except for the sound of Dr. Fox's soft muttering. Preston thought about his relationship with his father and how much he detested everything the man stood for. He could not understand where any of this sudden attention was coming from, but he was interested to find out Arminius's role in his father's transition.

Dr. Fox, lifting his tear soaked face from his hands, looked pleadingly at Preston.

"Will you – at least listen to what I have to say?" he asked.

Preston was reluctant to sit and listen to his father's discourse, but he knew that the current confrontation would come to a close sooner if he obliged.

"I'm listening," he said sympathetically, more or less wanting his father to stop crying.

Dr. Fox took out his handkerchief and blew his nose like a trumpet. The sound reverberated throughout the library, and after wiping his eyes he stowed away the cloth in his pocket. Sharing a soft smile with Preston, the Professor rose to his feet and paced back and forth. It seemed like eternity before any words were exchanged, and Preston was sure that he was getting dizzy watching his father's scattered movement.

"I know this is the last thing you want to hear," he began. "But I want you to know that I am not ashamed of you as my son, but I've always wanted to protect you no matter the cost. My work, as you already know, is very secretive. Yes, I am a Professor at the University, but I am also an archaeologist of sorts. During my travels I have made many friends across the world, but I have also made a multitude of enemies. Many of whom are highly dangerous."

Preston was still hung up on the part about his father *not* being ashamed of him, but his brain quickly grabbed a hold of the phrases *"secretive...archaeologist...enemies"*. Dr. Fox couldn't stand still for more than a second and he continued glancing at Arminius from time to time, apparently waiting for some sort of signal. Preston had almost forgotten the man was still in the room with them and shot a pointed look in his direction.

"Your mother never cared for my work," Dr. Fox said, not missing a beat. "She felt that it took away from time that I should be spending with my family. In retrospect, I guess she was right, and I feel as though I have let you down – both of you."

Tears formed again in Dr. Fox's eyes and he looked straight into the face of his son without wiping away the pain. Upon hearing mention of his mother, Preston let down his defenses and opened his mouth as if to speak, but his father raised a hand in protest.

"Let me finish."

Dr. Fox's breathing became rapid and the weight from his sweat-stained shirt threatened to crush his fragile, recovering body. Preston's father looked at Arminius and took a deep breath, steadying his nerves.

"Can you please give us a moment alone? There are some things I wish to say to my son in privacy."

Arminius frowned and let out a long sigh. He coughed to clear his throat and shook his robes as he stood.

"Do not take long," he snarled. "I will return in *five* minutes."

He avoided Preston's eyes and dragged his feet, bumping and thudding out of the library. Preston caught a whiff of the same smell of decomposition he experienced the first time he met Arminius, only this time it was even more potent.

Dr. Fox waited until the door shut to start again.

"I want to tell you about your mother–" he stopped mid-sentence, troubled by the words in his throat. "Her name was – Allyson."

The Professor's mind felt like a beehive, humming with unseen dangers, but he was willing to endure the pain to make things right with Preston. He cleared his throat, smiled, and let the words make their own peace.

"I met your mother outside your grandfather's corner store downtown. She was on her break and I was on my way to the University, late for class. I was in such a rush that I had forgotten to tie my shoes, and I tripped and fell right at her feet, books and papers flying everywhere. She initially laughed at my misfortune, but fell silent when I shot her an appalling look. Years later she told me that I had the most mesmerizing eyes she had ever seen and that she was hypnotized from that moment forward.

"As I picked myself up and brushed myself off she insisted on helping me collect my books. Seeing as how she laughed at me, I was rude and told her to mind her own business, but your mother was stubborn. She waved off my insults and continued to grab my things, and that's when our hands met. Her skin was so warm and silky smooth that my entire body melted. When I finally looked into her eyes I realized that I was standing next to the most beautiful woman in the world. Her hair fell just short of her shoulders, and her almond strands shimmered in the sunlight. I couldn't get the words out of my mouth, but she must have read my mind because she told me her name was Allyson. Terrified and in shock, I ran off without ever telling her my name.

"It took me two whole weeks before I gathered the nerve to walk by the store a second time. I had dream after dream of her standing in the sunlight, smiling at me, and I gave up trying to get her out of my mind. I decided I had to act or I would never be able to sleep again. She sat on the steps outside as I strolled passed her father's store the second time, but this time I walked right up to her, handed her a bouquet of flowers and expressed my love for her. Oh thank God your mother was an understanding woman because she thought my nervous declaration cute and genuine. She laughed at first, again, but this time it was warm and inviting. Any other woman would have probably slapped me for being so upfront, but not your mother. She was different."

Preston saw a warm glow enveloping his father's eyes, and he could not help but laugh at the story. He always assumed his father was a big shot, egotistical brute, and maybe even a bully, but now he realized that he was just as awkward and confused as he was. Who knew embarrassment could be hereditary?

"We would joke about that day many years later," he continued, "and there were many times she would tell me that I even picked out her favorite flowers – lilies. You see, Preston, your mother was the greatest human being I have ever known. She was smart, funny, beautiful, and yes....she had little tucked back ears just like you."

Dr. Fox smiled. Preston smiled back. He tried to hide his emotion but it was too late, his father saw the expression.

"It wasn't supposed to be like this Preston," Dr. Fox said, his smile vanishing and his tone darkening. "Your mother was supposed to be here to take care of you when I wasn't able. When she died, everything became difficult to manage. I am not as strong as she was, I wish I were. I was overwhelmed and I know that I can never fully apologize for the ways in which I treated you."

Dr. Fox broke down and collapsed next to his son. Preston felt his heart beating through his chest. He was so nervous that he became lightheaded and struggled to make his next move. Then Emma's words echoed in his mind, "think of it as a new start." Preston reached out his arm and draped it gently over his father's shoulder. The old man leaned into his son and cried even harder.

Dr. Fox wiped his cheeks and coughed to clear his throat.

"I have to make everything right tonight. There may not be another chance. I have to leave and go with Arminius."

Preston jumped out of his seat, letting his father's weight slump to the floor.

"*What?*" he said, appalled at his father's callous nature.

"Preston, please calm down..." Dr. Fox said.

"You tell me you want to right your wrongs, and now you're going to just up and leave again?!?"

"You don't understand the situation."

"I have waited my whole life to understand the situation!"

"Not like this. Please Preston, don't make it happen like this."

"Then go ahead, father! You wanted me to listen to you, so here I am. Make me understand."

Preston sat down, crossed his arms, and distanced himself from his father, the fire growing deep inside his guts again. He wanted for his father to disappoint him one last time, so he would not feel guilty about running away.

"You really want to know the truth? You want to know about...*her?*" Dr. Fox asked.

Preston's thoughts lingered on his father's question, the particular emphasis plagued his mind with dread. It was his father's tone of voice that cued fear in Preston's spine. A cold shiver crawled along the edges of his bones and he came face to face with reality. What if the truth turned out to be more than he could handle? What if he was better off living his life sheltered and blind from the past? The air became so thick with anticipation that Preston felt pressured to make a decision. Claustrophobia set in, and three words fell out of his mouth, almost inaudibly.

"All of it."

Panic stricken, Dr. Fox rubbed his hands together with vigor, hoping that his brain would find the right words on its own. Sweat beaded along his neck and cheeks as his body tried to radiate the stifling heat. He began mumbling to himself. Preston waited for a coherent sentence, a phrase, or a single word, anything that made sense, but he had to settle for Dr. Fox's sudden psychosis.

Finally Preston heard a few words that he understood, but they only served to feed the shroud of mysteries his father continued to weave. He heard things like: "...*terrible choice...pure evil...forgive me...*" Preston also thought he heard his mother's name, Allyson, repeated multiple times. Tired of sitting still and watching his father struggle with diction like a child, he tapped his hand on his leg and opened his mouth to speak. Just then, a knock on the library door forced them both to jerk.

"Dr. Fox," Arminius's voice streaked from the other side of the door, "it is time to leave."

Feeling embarrassed and somewhat troubled, Preston challenged his father one last time.

"Not yet," he whispered, on the edge of his seat. "You can't leave now. I need to know. Please, it is the only thing I ever wanted."

"I'm afraid I've simply run out of time. When I return," Dr. Fox choked on his words, "we will have all the time in the world to talk. I promise."

"You never keep your promises."

Those words cut Dr. Fox like paper on flesh. The pain was immediate but the blood took its time to trickle. Preston's father turned aside and spoke to the wall, as if his son was on the other side of it.

"There is something on the kitchen table I want you to have. A sort of present that I hope will make up for some lost time."

"Now Dr. Fox!" Arminius demanded, revealing the limit of his patience.

Preston's father half-motioned for his son to accompany him out of the library, but did so without making eye contact. They opened the door to find Arminius and Tunnamore waiting, and together they traced the hallways of the house. Dr. Fox turned and placed a hand on his son's shoulder. He questioned whether or not the two had made enough progress to hug each other goodbye, but he was once again pulled back to earth by Arminius's unrelenting demands.

"I will not be gone long," Dr. Fox said. "Until I return, Tunnamore will be taking care of you as usual."

Realizing his words sounded too much like the father of old, he leaned toward his assistant and whispered, "Don't be too hard on the boy. Give him *some* freedom."

Tunnamore nodded in agreement and gave Preston a cautious stare. Dr. Fox took a moment to compose himself, emotionally and physically, and stepped out into the night air following Arminius along the winding path and driveway. It was not until the two men were out of sight that Preston opened his mouth.

"Goodbye," he uttered, not sure where the parting phrase came from.

It was probably a trick of the night, but Preston believed he heard his father respond in the distance.

"Well, now that that's over, I think it's time we both turn in for the night," Tunnamore declared, ushering Preston inside. "Come along."

Preston did not approve of the tone in Tunnamore's voice, but he was too exhausted to argue. His brain was overflowing with questions and thoughts and he would need a good night sleep to make sense of it all.

He almost forgot about the present left for him in the kitchen, and so he had to make a detour to see what his father deemed so special. Upon entering the kitchen he noticed a small rectangular package wrapped in tissue paper. He grabbed it and shook it once, nothing moved. Preston ripped open the parcel and was surprised to find that it was a picture frame. The photograph in the frame showed his father hugging a blonde haired woman. The caption on the bottom read, *Allyson and Samuel, Always and Forever*. Preston never saw a picture of his mother before and was stunned by her beauty. His index finger traced the outline of her face and rested upon her tucked back ears. He smiled, but the show of emotion faded almost as quickly as it had appeared. Preston had now been left with more questions than ever before.

Chapter 3

Sins of the Father

Wiping the tears from his eyes, Dr. Fox followed Arminius down the driveway like a loyal dog keeping at his master's feet. He was torn between going back to Preston and going forward with Arminius. He made the decision to leave on impulse, regardless of Arminius's advice, and while Dr. Fox hoped that leaving in a rash manner would ease the pain, it ultimately had the reverse effect.

He already regretted his choice.

Arminius's car was parked further down the lakeshore, and Dr. Fox was forced to walk the entire distance in complete darkness. Clouds over the lake were beginning to spread across the entire region and they slowly draped the moon in a shadowy veil.

"How much farther to your car?" Dr. Fox asked, after an enormous bolt of lightning struck the shoreline.

"We are getting close now," Arminius responded as he succumbed to a sharp cough. "Down the road."

They carried on down the hill until a large black shape protruded from the edge of the road. Arminius called out that he found the car and led Dr. Fox to the passenger side door. The first thing Dr. Fox noticed when he entered the vehicle was the stench of rotten meat. Arminius climbed into the driver side, coughing all the while, and turned the key in the ignition. The car started with a roar of the engine, and the headlamps pierced the darkness. He turned the car around and sped off northward, in the direction of the city.

The ride was relatively quiet, apart from a few bumps in the road. Dr. Fox was not sure where they were headed, but he understood what would happen if he did not comply. He folded his hands in his lap and let out a long sigh.

"Getting nervous yet?" Arminius asked.

"Should I be?" Dr. Fox countered.

He felt his stomach lurch and turned his thoughts to Preston and the discussion they shared before he left. If only he could return home and spend the rest of his life making up for all the mistakes he made as a father.

"Why are you doing this?" he thought out loud.

Arminius shook his head and kept his eyes glued to the road. He drew in a deep wheezing breath and hacked up another chunk of phlegm, or at least what Dr. Fox presumed to be phlegm.

"You ask as if you really want to know," Arminius said, eyes still focused on the road. "I'm telling you that there are times...that you do not want to know the truth."

Dr. Fox thought about his own situation and understood Arminius's words all too well. Preston desperately wanted to hear how his mother died, but nothing would be able to prepare the boy for the truth.

Nothing.

Dr. Fox looked out the window again in anguish and lowered his voice.

"Everyone has secrets. Everyone has a story that they don't want to tell, but a single tale can be liberating, maybe even defining," Dr. Fox said, his words intended more for his own personal reflection than Arminius's consideration.

"But you mistake me...for a man who reveals secrets. If you dealt with secrets every second of...every day, then you would understand my reservations."

"What if I told you my story?"

Arminius just smiled and leaned back in his seat, stretching his free leg and patting the steering wheel.

"I know your story well enough. There is nothing you can tell me that will come as a surprise. In fact, the only surprise in your story thus far occurred tonight."

The car took a sharp right turn and Dr. Fox felt his weight shift towards Arminius. For a split second, the two men were close enough that they could detect each other's emotions. Arminius detected desolation and fear, while the Professor sensed an aura of loneliness and confusion. Convinced that he was making progress in breaking down the strange man's defenses, Dr. Fox continued prodding and chose his next question very carefully. He felt his best weapon at the moment was the power of his rhetoric.

"What is your greatest fear Arminius?" he asked.

"Huh?"

"I mean, what are you most afraid of in life? There's no sense in beating around the bush any longer, we both know that I am frightened about my indefinite fate, but I want to know what frightens a man such as you."

"Nothing scares me."

"Nothing?"

"There is no longer anything for me to fear...I've passed through the darkness and returned in defiance of nature. If you're lucky...you might be granted the same gift."

A smirk flashed across Arminius's face and he fluttered his eyelids, attempting to refocus his attention on the road ahead. Debating his next move, Dr. Fox stared at the peeling skin on Arminius's nose and noticed a small chunk of skin missing from just behind the man's ear. The headlights of an oncoming car illuminated the cab long enough for him to analyze the rotten patch of flesh. Dr. Fox recognized a piece of smooth ivory, unmistakably part of the man's skull. In an expression of utter disgust, his eyebrows squeezed down over his eyes and his jaw fell open. Grunting and readjusting the collar of his coat, Arminius shot a pointed look at Dr. Fox and acted as though nothing was out of the ordinary.

"Is there something wrong?" Arminius asked with an air of agitation.

"Uh, no, I was just...I was just thinking about something."

"Or someone?"

Such a quick and offensive jab stopped the Professor's heart. What did Arminius mean by *someone*? Was he referring to Preston? Dr. Fox removed his gaze and took a deep breath to settle his stomach. Deciding to change the subject as quickly as possible, he looked outside to see if he could make out their location.

"You've told me very little about where we are headed. Can you tell me, or is that another one of your secrets."

Pointing his finger out the window, Arminius drove past a sign that read '*Briercliff – 2 Miles*'.

"I wasn't aware that he was so wealthy. What could he possibly want with me?" Dr. Fox exclaimed, with a hint of sarcasm.

"Don't humor me," Arminius snapped, "You know quite well that the business my client has with you doesn't pertain to money. You can't put a price tag on life."

The Professor started to hate Arminius with a passion. He thought about grabbing the wheel and giving it a sharp turn towards the side of the road. The chance of survival was slim, but at that point even the slightest hint of hope was a good thing. The only thing holding him back was Preston. Dr. Fox knew that if he did not obey Arminius's orders then Preston would be the one to suffer. Something about Arminius's tone made him aware that Preston may be in danger. The number one priority for Dr. Fox was to ensure his son's safety at all costs; even if it meant sacrificing himself.

Passing through the factory district, an orange glow filled the night air as the steel factories worked overtime in order to meet demand. Nova Steel Company was the largest in the Northeast and competing for the largest in the country. They produced steel for everything from cars and airplanes, to silverware and refrigerators. Lakeshore Drive continued north toward the main urban center of Briercliff, boasting population of more than 1 million people. The road curved like a blade along the Great Lake to their left.

Arminius rolled down his window and sulfur and ash spilled into the cab. Dr. Fox welcomed the outside air, for despite its toxic smell it was decidedly better than the putrid scent coming from Arminius. The car rolled by the factories and continued up the road until it was just inside the city limits of Briercliff. It was amazing how quickly the scenery changed when entering the wealthiest area of the city, South State, especially when it was located right next to the dirtiest and most polluted section.

Arminius pulled the automobile over to the side of the road directly in front of a large steel gateway that read, *PRENDERGAST ESTATE*. Completely puzzled and dumbfounded, Dr. Fox looked at Arminius for some answers. The driver grinned, pulled under the gateway, and headed up the driveway.

"You can't be serious," Dr. Fox joked. "You work for Prendergast, the steel tycoon? That is not the man I met, there must be some mistake–"

"Oh, there is no mistake, I can promise you of that," Arminius replied, cutting Dr. Fox short.

The Professor looked beyond his window and gazed up at the estate laid out before him. His home on the lakeshore was considered a mansion, one of the largest and oldest in the region; however, the Prendergast Estate rose like a castle in comparison.

"A king must live here," thought Dr. Fox.

It felt like an eternity as the car climbed up the driveway. They passed multiple smaller buildings, and even a tropical garden to their right. Large birds perched themselves on exotic tree branches just off the edge of the road. They were so still that Dr. Fox questioned if they were even real.

Behind one of the buildings on the left lay a massive chain link fence that looked like a cage for animals. Dr. Fox did not see any dogs, but the bones and chains strewn about the muddy floor of the cages hinted that some sort of large creatures lived there.

Further up the winding road another gate separated the actual living quarters from the rest of the estate grounds. Dr. Fox could not help but remain awestruck by the precise construction, maintenance, and detail of every structure. Even the blades of grass were cut at identical heights. It seemed too perfect, and he could not imagine how such conformity in a natural setting could be achieved.

Sprawling fields appeared as green carpets, soft and inviting, nearly making him forget about the cages and the bones. Under other circumstances, the Prendergast Estate might have been a nice place to visit. The entire property was lit by electric lamps towering over the grounds like beacons of fire. In the distance, the Professor traced the outline of a massive stone wall running along the perimeter.

The car jerked to a halt, catching Dr. Fox off guard. It was time to exit the vehicle and he realized that his chance of escape was long gone. He could only go forward from here on out and hope for the best. Two men with shotguns stepped forward and escorted Dr. Fox to the front door while Arminius followed behind. It was a long, grueling climb up thirty or more large marble steps just to reach the entrance. The main house was not unlike Buckingham Palace in size and grandeur. The front door itself was more than just an inanimate presence in the world. Standing nearly twenty feet tall and at least ten feet wide, the colossal wooden gateway looked as though it would keep King Kong from entering the home. Before anyone could reach the door, it swung open in a ghostly manner and came to a halt at a perfect perpendicular angle with the front façade of the house, never once making a creak. Dr. Fox held his breath and looked closely at the door and its hinges as he passed underneath the marble entranceway. There was not a crack to be found in the door, even though his archeological senses told him the door was at least 2,000 years old. He took a deep breath and tried to ignore the shiver that ran down his spine.

Once inside the main hall, Arminius took his place at the front of the group and ordered the two guards to return to their posts and assured them that Dr. Fox was not any sort of threat. Assuming that his presence was expected, the Professor stood quietly and waited. The main hall was divided by two spiral staircases that climbed to the second floor, connecting at the top to a balcony overlooking the front door and entire atrium. Standing at the edge of the balcony was a tall, well-toned man in his 30s, dressed in a pair of brown slacks and a white dress shirt with the sleeves rolled up. His face was smooth and void of any facial hair, while the hair on the top of his head fell to his shoulders. The purely masculine beauty of the man standing at the balcony captivated Dr. Fox. It was almost as if he was not human.

"Welcome to my home Professor Fox," the man said, with hands outstretched. "My name is Lastarr Prendergast and it is my pleasure to have you as my honored guest this evening."

Prendergast continued talking while he began his slow and methodic descent. He smiled wryly all the while, and Dr. Fox felt nervous in the presence of his host. The entire balcony and staircase were bathed in a delicate white light, but a darker shadow appeared to hold close to Prendergast, almost protecting him from the purely angelic rays.

"I hope Arminius did not frighten you. I understand he can sometimes be impatient and come off as a sort of demanding fellow, but he understands the manner of our business."

Prendergast neared the end of the staircase, but stopped momentarily to remain above his guest and to allow the Professor ample time to bask in all of his sincere power and beauty.

"You are not the man I met 15 years ago," Dr. Fox declared, eyes narrowed. "Arminius told me why I was to come here, but this is wrong. There has been a mistake and I–"

"The corner of 11ᵗʰ Street was seemingly quiet and lonely wasn't it?" Prendergast asked, a crooked smile sprawled across his face. "And I wonder Professor, how long did you expect to withhold the truth from your friends and family?"

Dr. Fox clenched his teeth and took caution not to lose his temper, not yet.

"You could have been told that information, you don't even know–"

"Her name? Allyson Fox. Even I will admit that she was quite beautiful," Prendergast smiled, "but you must understand that I prefer my women to be somewhat less eccentric. Would you like me to go on? I know much more than just her name, for example–"

"She is dead," Dr. Fox lamented with a whisper of defeat, folding his hands over his face. "Why am I even here if she is dead?"

Prendergast put his finger to his guest's mouth and gave Dr. Fox a fatherly "shhh".

"There is no reason to get all upset. I apologize for bringing up your painful past, but to be honest, eventually you will need to come to terms with what happened."

Both men were fully aware that Prendergast was teasing, and it frustrated the Professor to no end. Prendergast snapped his fingers and Arminius grabbed Dr. Fox by the arm, leading him down the hallway straight ahead. They passed underneath the massive balcony and followed the marble flooring along a frame of paintings and sculptures. The path gave way to a massive dining room, complemented by a redbrick fireplace and extravagant glass ceiling. Plants and flowers, exotic species similar to the garden along the road, were scattered throughout, and the entire room was bathed in a golden light; except for a lingering shadow that fell upon a second balcony. An upper circle capped the room, but was blocked from view by a large black curtain with silver lace trim.

"Please Professor, have a seat," Prendergast requested, motioning for Dr. Fox to sit at the end of the table in the center of the room.

The Professor sidled over to his intended place and fell into the chair. The seat felt much too large for his boney buttocks and he felt like a child sitting in a high chair. A picture of a horse was carved into the headrest of the chair and the armrests were ground around the edges with a peculiar bone-like shape. In a way, Dr. Fox felt very uncomfortable sitting in the chair. He thought that it would swallow him whole at any second. Prendergast took his seat at the opposite end of the table and motioned for one of his servants to pour Dr. Fox a glass of wine.

"I believe you will enjoy this Merlot, Samuel, it is from my personal collection I amassed while living in France."

The Professor stared at the still liquid. It looked so thick and blood-like that he was sure the only thing that could make it ripple was gravity. Prendergast cleared his throat, cupped his glass in his pale, delicate fingers and drained it. He smiled at Dr. Fox, reading the Professor's thoughts, and motioned a second time to the chalice. Dr. Fox was hesitant, but even he could not deny that there was something hypnotic about the wine. Against his better judgment, his fingers slid along the rim of the glass and lifted it towards his mouth.

He took a sip.

Swishing the juices around in his mouth, Dr. Fox tried to locate a hint of poison, but instead found it to be quite sweet and refreshing. He did not want to admit to letting down his defenses, but the warm syrup certainly calmed his nerves. In the meantime, Arminius walked over and whispered something in his master's ear.

"I apologize, but I need to speak with Arminius for a moment. Please, enjoy your wine and I will return in just a moment," Prendergast reassured.

The well-groomed gentleman rose from his seat and led Arminius out into the hallway, shutting the door behind them. "What is he going to tell him? What if he mentions Preston," thought Dr. Fox, and with his left hand impatiently shaking, he turned to the wine for comfort.

The room fell silent and he drank his wine in peace and tapped his fingers lightly on the table. With each swig of the liquor his body was revitalized; his mind was clear, his vision spot on, and even his toes felt warm for the first time in days. It was soon obvious that the wine itself was the only thing keeping him from scratching out his eyes or crawling out of his skin. No matter what he did, he could not sit more than a few seconds without taking a sip.

Dr. Fox turned his attention toward the door in which Prendergast and Arminius took leave only a short time before. He knew he would not be able to get out of his seat and eavesdrop without the servants saying something, but with the help of the wine he tried to hone his sense of hearing and narrow in on the hallway door. Like a radio searching for a signal, Dr. Fox was able to overhear bits and pieces of the conversation.

"What...tell me again...said...no, I want every detail," Prendergast demanded in his lofty aristocratic speech.

"A boy...Tunnamore...last one...son," came a voice that sounded like Arminius's labored tongue.

One of the servants suddenly appeared at Dr. Fox's side.

"Forgive me sir, but may I clean that up?"

Dr. Fox tilted his eyes toward the table and realized with horror that he had spilled his wine.

"Oh...oh my. I am terribly sorry, I um—"

The servant stared at Dr. Fox with squinted eyes and waited for the request that he knew was imminent.

"You don't think that...I could...that I could," Dr. Fox stammered .

"Have another glass?" the servant grinned .

Dr. Fox's eyes lit up and flickered with pure pleasure. He mumbled to himself and tried to overcome his sudden derangement while the servant retrieved more wine. "What is happening to me," thought the Professor, "what is that smell?" His senses recognized an odor coming from the direction of the servant, but he struggled to make a match. Somewhere deep in his mind he knew he needed to stop drinking the wine as soon as possible, but his body was beyond his control. His mind crawled deeper and deeper inside itself. "It is laced," he tried to scream, but the words echoed only in his head. He watched, helplessly, as the servant brought out another glass filled to the brim with the crimson liquid. Dr. Fox's conscience exploded in a torrent of protests and expletives as the servant placed a full bottle on the table, uncorked.

The conversation in the hallway continued, but the Professor was no longer able to listen. His mind was sharp, but his body was numb. "How could I have been so stupid," he thought. "All the training and practice over the years with poisons, and I just accept a glass of wine from a stranger who probably wants me dead?" He tried to focus and tried to think of how he reached the estate in the first place, but the panic from realizing the second glass of wine was already empty sent his brain into frenzy and he lost his train of thought.

Just as Dr. Fox was sure he was going to come apart at the seams, the door burst open and both men returned to the dining hall. Prendergast looked disheveled and a little worse for the wear, but he still took the time to adjust his shirt and sat down with a thud against the back of his chair. To Dr. Fox's surprise, his host's attitude transformed instantly and the man's eyes again became warm and inviting.

"Now, let's get down to business," Prendergast said, smiling in a buoyant fashion.

He looked at the half empty bottle of wine on the table and pointed a finger at the Professor.

"I told you that wine was delightful, didn't I?"

Before Dr. Fox could speak, or let alone refill his glass, a large piece of familiar paper materialized right in front of him, out of thin air. The title read 'Contract'.

"You are here tonight for business, Samuel, don't you remember? You signed that very contract sitting in front of you back when you first started at the University."

Dr. Fox squinted, looking from the devilish bottle of wine to the parchment under his nose, and felt all his vital signs come to a screeching halt.

"You sold me your soul," Prendergast sneered, "in exchange for Allyson's life."

Chapter 4

The Darkness

"I want you to look at that document and read aloud Clause Number 4," Prendergast ordered. "It is the one that starts with 'Upon death, the signee shall forfeit–'"

Dr. Fox's eyes glanced down under their own power as words and punctuation swam across the page. He narrowed his eyes and found the part Prendergast referred. He cleared his throat and began reading.

"Clause Number 4 of this contract regarding Soul Possession," his voice quivered as he spoke. "Upon death, the signee shall forfeit all rights, internal and external, to his or her soul in exchange for the agreed upon article–"

After stumbling through the first few phrases, the Professor stopped mid-sentence in order to wet his tongue. He took another deliberate draught of his wine and smacked his lips; his hands, mouth, and eyes, all moved on their own accord.

"If the signee is proven to be deceased, but then returns from the dead, thus retrieving his or her soul, this contract is invalid and all agreements are considered null and void."

He looked up from the contract and stared at Prendergast. Darkness crept into his peripheral vision, and he could not help but feel as though someone was watching him from above.

"I'm sure Arminius has already told you about that last little nut of information," Prendergast snickered. "When you came back to life, you voided that very contract, along with everything that you benefitted from it."

"I already told you, my wife is dead!" Dr. Fox screamed, slamming his fist on the table. "You brought her back to life only to let her die!"

"I let her die? *I* let her die? Why do you insist on misplacing the blame? I brought her back to life, but there was never any guarantee that she would be able to sustain that life. It was a deal Samuel, one soul in exchange for another. You gave your soul willingly to me, and in exchange I brought your wife back to life."

"But she is dead! There is nothing left to take!"

"Oh, my dear man. You are a tragic thing for sure, but you misunderstand me. The very laws of nature bind this contract, things you can't even begin to comprehend. Your soul is mine for the taking; my end of the bargain was upheld while yours was not. If you do not relent, then perhaps we can strike another deal, but I promise you will not like this second option. Your wife is dead, yes, but I believe she was pregnant the night you signed that contract, was she not? One soul for another Samuel. Either I take your soul, or that of your precious son – decide for yourself."

"You leave my son out of this! He is innocent!"

"That is yet to be determined, but the same cannot be said for you. You haven't told him the truth, have you? Even in death Allyson was able to tell me the horrible details."

Dr. Fox's body began to shake in anger and he dug his nails into the armrests of the chair to prevent lunging across the table.

"You lie," he growled.

The room grew silent and the lights above flickered. The darkness surrounding Prendergast grew opaque and enveloped the edges of his pristine frame while his eyebrows bounced with Dr. Fox's question. The industrialist rose from his chair and began walking the perimeter of the dining hall. Dr. Fox found it difficult to keep track of his host. His eyes kept betraying him and instead searched the balcony for something or someone. The stone curtain kept still, but Dr. Fox was convinced he felt a presence above him.

"Who the hell are you that you can do these things" Dr. Fox started, withdrawing his hand from the bottle of wine. "Am I supposed to believe that you are – the Devil?"

Prendergast burst into laughter and shook his hand through the air like a conductor unimpressed with his orchestra.

"No, no, no! Even though all the evidence would certainly support your claim. No Samuel, I am not the Devil. In fact, the Devil wishes he were me. Who or what I am is no longer important to you."

Prendergast tortured his guest's mind with every word and every new detail. It was all becoming too much for Dr. Fox to handle and he began concocting a plan for escape with what little sanity he retained. If he could just catch his host off guard, then he was sure he could take care of Arminius and the servants.

"You have to understand a thing or two about souls before my reasons become clear," Prendergast began, circling the edge of the table and eying the near empty bottle of wine. "I am in the business of souls because of their vitality and their recollections. You see, when I take a person's soul, I also take their memories. I bear witness to the entirety of their lives. You, Samuel, have one very important memory that I have waited 15 years to see."

Dr. Fox's eyes stared at the glass ceiling while the flowers along the walls began spinning all around him. An unexpected feeling of drowsiness swept over him and his plan of escape looked as though it were in danger. He closed his eyes and leaned back against the headrest, hoping the sensation would subside.

"I admit that you have kept me waiting far longer than I anticipated, and I assumed that your wife's death would have tempted you to end your life, but you persisted. I counted the hours that passed by and waited for my time. Fifteen years is not very long when you live for an eternity. If it wasn't for that contract, I would have taken your soul a long time ago."

The Professor slumped forward in his chair and caught sight of the contract still on the table. He reached for it with his left hand while his right lunged for the wine, the uneven movement sent him off balance and he flopped onto the floor.

Prendergast and his servants laughed.

"Now that was just plain silly of you," Prendergast whispered as he crouched to the floor. "You were going to try and destroy the contract, weren't you?"

Dr. Fox pulled himself to the edge of his chair and watched in horror as Prendergast snapped his fingers, causing the contract to disappear.

"Your soul is mine whether you care to give it willingly or not," Prendergast said. The Professor mumbled a few words and began shaking as he stared, teary eyed at the wine and the place where the contract lay only seconds before.

"Ppp...poison...poison," he repeated over and over.

"Poison?" Prendergast asked, confused.

The entire dining hall erupted in howls of laughter.

"Poison? You think that the wine is poisoned?" Prendergast roared, wiping a tear from his eye. "It is poison, I guess, if you think alcohol is poison. Samuel, it is nothing more than wine! I simply planted the thought in your head that it was calming your nerves so that you would drink it, and you ended up downing almost an entire bottle in a matter of minutes! You are not poisoned, you are drunk!"

The realization struck Dr. Fox in the chest, stopping his heart. Poison would have killed him, but alcohol would incapacitate him, the perfect condition for Prendergast to take advantage of him.

See how easy it is? A demonic voice echoed throughout Dr. Fox's head. *I can plant even the simplest idea in your mind and let it flourish. I only need your thoughts, not your body, so I could not risk destroying your conscience.*

Laughter erupted again throughout the hall and more servants crawled into the Professor's view, or were they illusions caused by the wine? He wrestled with the onslaught of hallucinations and tried hard to locate Prendergast but could not see any shadows nearby, only flashes of light. Dogs started barking and birds chirped as all manner of noise surged throughout the dining hall. The sounds appeared to be in the distance one second, and then right behind him the next. Dr. Fox pulled his knees close to his chest and closed his eyes, trying to avoid the swooping figures with flashing red eyes darting left and right.

It is terrifying, isn't it? The voice resounded in his mind once more, but this time it was more sinister, and penetrated every ounce of the Professor's being. *Even animals in the wild play with their prey before they feed.*

More laughter and the sound of glass shattering on the floor. "The wine," thought Dr. Fox, "it is just plain wine, fight it and pull yourself together! None of this is real!"

The Professor screamed at the top of his lungs as he fought the pain clawing at the base of his skull. Something cold grabbed hold of his arm and lifted him off the ground. In a flash of clarity he saw one of the guards helping him to his feet. He swung with his right fist and prayed that he would not miss. His knuckles connected with flesh and tore it from the man's face. Dr. Fox stared at the bloodless mess and collapsed again to the ground. The guard, trying to hold the skin from his cheek in place, pointed and laughed.

"What...but—" Dr. Fox stammered as he rolled over onto his stomach and vomited.

His body convulsed with every retch, and he could not help but stare at the pool of red liquid spreading across the floor and think that he was bleeding to death. He closed his eyes once more to make the room stop spinning and crawled without knowing any direction or reason. A dark, icy presence shattered the adrenaline flowing in his veins as a serpent-like hand clasped around his throat and lifted him off the ground. The lack of oxygen forced his eyes to flutter, and the only thing he saw was a shadow, and Prendergast's radiant blue eyes shining at the center. The laughter and all other sounds in the dining hall drifted into nothingness. Prendergast squeezed with brute force, causing the Professor's mouth to snap open.

Dr. Fox felt the sting of frostbite begin at his toes and work its way up to his eyes. He felt as though he was stretched and pulled in every direction. A blue mist emanated from his lips and it shone brighter and brighter with each passing second. He tried to fight back, but the strength to resist had already left his body. He could hear his heartbeat slowing as cloudy images swirled back and forth in his mind. For a split second Dr. Fox thought that he was drowning. Everything was quiet and he was hastily slipping out of consciousness. The last thing he saw was Prendergast's eyes as the blue ethereal mist of his very own soul drifted toward the ceiling.

Prendergast removed his hand from the Professor's throat and allowed the lifeless body to strike the floor with a loud thud. He staggered backwards for a second and then he too collapsed. Dr. Fox rolled over, blinked his eyes twice and licked his lips.

"Who...what...where am I?" he asked.

His soul hovered above his head and then drifted towards the balcony, passing through the curtain without resistance.

Take this one to the hold, ordered the evil voice from Dr. Fox's head. *Do it before he starts to stink like the rest of you.*

Arminius and the others grabbed the body that was once Dr. Fox, dragged him away from the table, and carried him out the door.

Arminius returned moments later and bowed before his master, awaiting orders.

I want you – The voice stopped short with a deep breath. *I want you to bring me the boy.*

Arminius smiled and nodded his head.

Chapter 5

The Next Day

Preston stood in the pitch-black atrium of the Fox estate, feeling for the staircase with his hands. He grabbed hold of the mahogany railing and pulled himself up to the second floor, one step at a time.

When he reached the top of the stairs he noticed that his bedroom door stood open, a white light glistening like the morning sun just beyond the frame. He raised a hand to shade his eyes and walked cautiously towards the light. He stopped short and discovered that the light seeping through the crack was impenetrable by the human eye, and that it appeared to be as solid as the door itself.

He pushed softly on the handle and it slid open without effort; the light inside the bedroom exploded and disappeared almost instantly. Someone laid in his bed, but a sense of happiness, not dread, swept over him. He stood in silence, leaning his shoulder against the doorway, and stared at the sleeping figure.

The covers of the bed shifted and the face of a young boy came into view. It was Preston who was in the bed, fast asleep. He was staring at himself.

Preston rose from his slumber and choked on the stale air in his bedroom. Coughing uncontrollably, he crawled out of bed and reached for the glass of water he set on his nightstand the night before. He leaned against his mattress, draining the glass, and reflected on what he had seen. It was a dream he reassured himself, but whose eyes did he experience it through? He looked outside and saw that it was morning already, albeit a cloudy and rainy one.

Waking up proved a difficult task for Preston. He was overtired from the previous night's surprises and the steady rain that arrived in the middle of the night lulled him to sleep. He set down his glass and looked at the picture of his mother and father. He smiled and said "good morning" with a groggy gesture, more so directed at his mother more than his father. Throwing on a plain white t-shirt and a pair of blue jeans, he looked in the mirror and combed his hair. He did not plan on going anywhere, but he still took pride in his appearance. He gave himself the seal of approval and went downstairs to get some breakfast. Tunnamore was sitting at the dining room table with a large cup of coffee on the table and the morning newspaper covering his face.

"Did you sleep well?" Tunnamore asked, without removing the paper from view.

"Okay, you?" Preston replied, trying to be as civil as possible.

"You left your suit coat and tie on the front lawn last night. They are covered in grass and mud, but don't worry, I picked up after you as usual, and yes – I am 'okay' as well."

Tunnamore grunted, reached around his paper to grab his coffee, and continued reading. Preston recognized the bitter sarcasm; he stuck out his tongue and went about his business. He grabbed a Danish and poured himself a glass of orange juice. Carrying both items close to his chest, he headed toward the library. When he reached the large double doors, he looked around to make sure Tunnamore was not watching and turned the handle.

Locked.

Tunnamore must have locked the doors after Preston went to sleep. Disappointed but not defeated, the teenager decided to sit on the back patio underneath the canopy of oak trees. The rain continued to fall and Preston sat alone eating his Danish, listening to the sound of water droplets dancing on the leaves. He tried to make sense of his father's speech from the previous night, but the only answer he scrounged up was a nagging headache. "Why was he so afraid of the truth," Preston thought. "Does that mean I should expect the worst?"

Instead of racking his brain, Preston decided he would spend the day trying to break into the library. He finished the last bite of his breakfast treat and washed it down with the last gulp of juice. A gust of wind swept in, soaking Preston. The cold shower felt like new life when it splashed against his face, and his body absorbed the water becoming rehydrated, refreshed; however, the fountain of youth turned with the intensity of the storm, and soon the deluge became too much for Preston and he retreated indoors.

Out of breath and soaked to the bone, he made the long trek back to the kitchen to deposit his empty juice glass in the sink. When Preston entered the room, Tunnamore was in the exact same place and reading the exact same page as before.

"Do you even know how to read?" Preston mocked.

"You watch your mouth boy," Tunnamore threatened.

"You're not my father. Besides, you heard what he said last night. I can do whatever I want until he returns."

Tunnamore put down his paper and shot Preston an evil glare. He leaned forward and lowered his voice.

"Your father is not here, which means *I'm* in charge. You don't like it? Then try me."

He returned to his paper while Preston left the kitchen.

"Who does he think he is making threats like that," Preston thought. "I'll show him."

He navigated his way back to the library and further analyzed the door. It seemed like a basic lock, small and fragile, but he was not familiar with the art of lock picking. Then it dawned on him. The back wall of the library was covered in large stained-glass windows, some of which were open during his father's wake. Maybe they would open wide enough for Preston to squeeze his awkward body inside. He realized that option meant going outside in a torrential downpour and trying to maneuver through the hedges along the back of the house, but he felt he had to try. He ran upstairs, grabbed a jacket, and put on his black Dunboys; there was no doubt his shiny shoes were going to get extremely muddy, but he felt he owed it to them after they were put through shoe shine torture by Uncle Thomas.

When Preston reached the front door it became clear that he needed to be careful about his next move. If he exited through the front, then there was a strong chance that Tunnamore would hear the door close and would come looking for him. Therefore, the back door to the patio seemed like the best possible choice. He ran through the house like a cat on the prowl, without ever making a sound, and arrived at the back door. He opened and swung it close all in one motion. Preston was free at last and burst into a sprint across the back yard. Rain fell harder and faster than before, pelting his denim jacket like hail, and he found it difficult to trudge through the swamp-like lawn. He reached the back of the house and recognized the stained-glass windows of the library, though they appeared dull and lifeless from the outside. He pressed his hand against the cold glass and began feeling with his fingers for some sort of crease or ridge resembling a hinge. Nothing. Frantically now, he placed both hands on the windows and began feeling up and down, left to right, across the whole side of the house. Nothing again. In a fit of annoyance and irritation he smacked the wall of windows with his right palm, and to his surprise, a rusty hinge creaked and an opening appeared. He moved closer and pushed harder, but the plate of red glass would not budge. The opening was only large enough for his hand to fit and it did not seem as though it opened any further. This was the end of the line.

Preston pulled his hand out of the hole and squished his face against the glass, eyes lined up perfectly with the opening. It was difficult to see anything in the room due to the cloudy skies and the lack of light on the inside, but he was able to see the outlines of a few objects. The wind howled and a flash of lightning streaked through the sky behind him. In that instant, the entire library lit up and Preston saw that it was exactly how it had been left the night before and that everything was indeed real. "Three seconds," he counted subconsciously as thunder boomed across the surface of the earth. The brunt of the storm was getting closer.

Wishing to avoid becoming a veritable lighting rod, Preston pulled the collar of his jacket up over his head and ran as fast as he could for the patio door. He pushed it open and slammed it shut, sending a slight rumble throughout the silent corridors of the house. Breathing heavily, he sat on the floor. Thoughts about Arminius Blackwood, his mother, and his father's secrets crept back into his mind. The sound of heavy footsteps echoed the dark hallway and Tunnamore's spectacled, narrow face shown in the doorway.

"Where on earth have you been? Are you insane?!" he bellowed.

"Calm down, I was just outside enjoying the weather," Preston teased.

"Don't you dare get smart with me young man, you're in big trouble this time."

Preston stood up and started walking away, but Tunnamore grabbed his arm and squeezed.

"Oh no, not this time, you're not walking away from me when I'm talking to you."

Tunnamore tried to adjust his grip, but Preston pulled free and sprinted down the hallway for the front atrium.

"Get back here!" Tunnamore screamed as he proceeded to chase Preston.

The teenager reached the top of the stairs before Tunnamore even turned out of the hallway and he made a b-line for his bedroom; slamming the door and locking it, Preston reached for his baseball bat and held it up high. The adrenaline in his body told him it was the right move, but his brain saw through the madness.

"This is insane," Preston said, out of breath and staring at the bat in disgust.

Was he really planning on defending himself and hitting Tunnamore, his father's scrawny little assistant, with a wooden baseball bat?

He flung the bat against the wall and sat on his bed with his head in his hands. The last twelve hours had been an emotional train wreck and he was not sure how much more he could possibly take without going crazy. Tunnamore's footsteps finally reached the top of the stairs and he threw his body against Preston's bedroom door.

"Open this door immediately!" he demanded.

"I'm not opening this door until my father comes home, and if you come in here I'm going to crack this bat over your head!" Preston screamed, looking at his bat on the floor.

"Fine! Fine! You're finished, you hear me! Stay in there and starve for all I care!"

Tunnamore stomped his feet as he retreated from the bedroom door and Preston could hear him mumbling something like "Good for nothing," and "After everything I've done."

Preston stripped off his wet clothes, lay down on his bed, and pulled the covers up over his head. The last thing he saw before the blanket shrouded him in darkness was his mother's smiling face on his nightstand. He wiped the moisture from his eyes and fell into a deep sleep.

Chapter 6

A Man and His Dog

A crack of thunder punctured the stillness of Preston's bedroom during the early evening hours. The elemental force sent shockwaves throughout the foundation of the house until Preston woke. His bedroom was painted in shadows and it took him a minute to find the switch on his bedside lamp. The light bulb hissed to life and burned with a fire that blinded Preston, sending his head into a carousel of blurry visions.

The doorbell rang and a dog barked twice underneath his window. Preston climbed out of bed and wondered whether it was the thunder or the doorbell that woke him. He pulled back the curtains and strained his eyes to make shapes of the darkness outside. Raindrops traced the edges of the windowpane and wind howled as it passed through the hinges. Preston scanned the area beneath his window and finally caught sight of what appeared to be two shapes, one erect and one hunched to the ground.

The doorbell rang again and this time Tunnamore's voice erupted from somewhere deep within the house.

"I'm coming already!"

Preston unlocked his bedroom door and slinked down the hallway. He stopped a few feet from the foyer balcony and fell to his hands and knees. Tunnamore had the eyes and ears of a hawk when spotting Preston, and so the boy took every precaution to stay out of sight.

Thunder exploded nearby, and the pounding on the front door turned furious.

"I'm coming!" Tunnamore shouted as he reached for the door handle.

While peeping over the ledge, Preston noticed his heart thumping against the floor like a drum. He grabbed his chest and tried to dampen the noise for fear that Tunnamore would hear. His caretaker checked the front door to make sure it was locked and then proceeded to address his visitors through the mail slot.

"What do you want? State your business immediately!" Tunnamore hollered. He battled against the wind and rain, and hoped whoever was on the other side of the door heard his demands. A hand reached through the mail slot and tried to grab Tunnamore by the shirt. Tunnamore squealed in fear, fell down, and crawled away as quickly as possible.

"Let us in for heaven's sake before we drown!!"

The hand stuck inside the mail slot tightened into a fist. Water poured through the opening and created a puddle on the floor that continued to grow with each waning second. Tunnamore stared in horror and could not gather his senses quick enough to respond.

Preston bolted down the staircase and pushed his father's assistant out of the way. He unlocked the door and pulled it open despite Tunnamore's protests. The large gate-like door swung open in a rush of wind, rain, and darkness. The owner of the hand lodged in the mail slot slumped forward and rolled across the threshold. An enormous beast lunged from the shadows and ran for cover in the dining room. Preston gathered his strength and stood erect against the gale force winds. He grabbed the door with both hands and pushed with every ounce of his being, trying desperately to get it closed. Giving one final shove, the mechanism clicked and sealed the elements outside.

Preston watched as Tunnamore and the visitor tried to untangle themselves from each other. The former kept crying out in fear while the latter shouted, "Stop whining like a little girl and hold still while I unhook my coat!"

Preston could not help but laugh. The two men finally separated and Tunnamore reached for an umbrella near the closet, holding it up like a sword.

"Who are you?!" he demanded.

Turning to Preston, he elevated his voice even higher.

"What were you thinking opening the door when a stranger is trying to break in?! Hurry up and call the police while I keep this intruder in his place!"

The guest stood slowly and raised his hands. His hood sagged over his face and Preston thought for a moment that it might be Arminius.

"Please, sir, I assure you that calling the police will not be necessary," the stranger replied. His voice was strong and steady, proof enough that he was not the previous night's guest.

"I apologize for the manner of my entry," he explained, "but you can't even imagine how bad the storm has gotten. We nearly got lost coming up the driveway and I was afraid we would end up walking off the cliff and into the lake!"

"I don't care about the weather!" Tunnamore bellowed. "Who are you?! The next word that comes out of your mouth better be your name or else I'm running you through with this umbrella! You...you...wait...we?"

Preston heard clicking, and turned to see a giant Labrador retriever enter the room. The animal was black as night and stood nearly three feet tall; its head, for its size and shape, looked entirely out of place. Preston was sure that he was not looking at a large dog but instead a small bear. Licking his chops, the black Lab tilted his head and looked quizzically at Tunnamore.

The stranger laughed and pulled back his hood. What little hair was left on his head was gray, and he had tiny eyes that disappeared when he smiled. Preston noticed immediately how healthy the man looked, even though he appeared to be much older than his father. A light brown mustache hung down over his top lip and he wore a very welcoming smile. There was an aura about him that washed away all of Preston's doubts and fears. Even Tunnamore began to lower his umbrella when he looked into the stranger's eyes.

"My name is Benjamin Cain," he explained. "Professor Benjamin Cain from the University, I am a friend and colleague of

Dr. Fox, and that over there is Errol, my best and most loyal friend in the whole world."

Professor Cain continued to smile and pointed over at the dog standing in the doorway. Errol barked and Tunnamore cringed, hesitating to say anything at all.

"Well, I guess I must apologize, Professor Cain," Tunnamore said, dropping his umbrella and taking a deep breath. "Your name does sound familiar. I believe Dr. Fox mentioned you a few times in the midst of discussing his work. You must understand that we've had a trying few days here at the Fox household, and I admit we've been a little on edge. My name is Robert Tunnamore, assistant to Dr. Fox, and this here is his son, Preston."

Cain lowered his arms and nodded to both men in a show of respect.

"But I am afraid to inform you, Professor, that my master is presently not home," Tunnamore stated. "In fact, I'm not even certain when I can expect him to return so I'm not sure how he may be of assistance to you."

Professor Cain looked at Tunnamore in a fit of confusion.

"Well of course your master isn't here," he laughed. "He's dead!"

"You...do not read the newspaper very often do you?" Tunnamore asked.

"Not on a regular basis, why do you ask?"

"My master is *not* dead. In fact, he is very much alive and well. The newspaper covered the story in-depth in this morning's issue."

"A shame, I must have missed that. So he's *not* dead?"

"Uhh no," Tunnamore stammered, taken aback by Cain's subtle reaction. "That is what I am telling you."

"Fascinating!"

Cain placed a finger on his chin and stepped towards Errol. The dog sat down and stared at his owner, waiting.

"I would love to hear every detail about Samuel's return, but I must first reveal to you my intentions for coming here this evening," the Professor said. "There are a few pieces in Dr. Fox's personal collection that he swore would be mine if and when he passed. I've simply come to collect those pieces. I would assume they would be in his library, and if you could show me the way–"

Tunnamore's cough interrupted Cain's directions and filled the atrium with a cloud of uneasiness.

"I'm sorry, but my master never mentioned any such things to me," he blurted out. "Believe me when I say that he entrusted everything to me, even his personal items, and that it is my duty to make sure nothing leaves this house without his consent."

"So what you're saying is that you're not going to show me to the library?" Cain asked, disappointed.

"I'm afraid I cannot, but I promise that the minute my master returns I will inform him of your inquiry and he will contact you as soon as possible."

Cain looked around the atrium and rested his eyes on Preston. The teenager was used to playing spectator when it came to his father's business, but he was surprised to see the Professor smile and wink at him.

"No problem Mr. Tunnamore," Cain sighed. "I do not want to get you in trouble with your master and I am a patient man. So, how about that newspaper? And maybe a cup of tea?"

"Oh absolutely, where are my manners," Tunnamore laughed, holding out his hand to show the way to the kitchen.

Professor Cain knelt down next to Errol and scratched behind the dog's ear. He whispered something and Errol took off through the dining room in the opposite direction of the kitchen.

"Oh, don't mind him," the Professor assured. "He's just an adventurous spirit and wants to do some exploring. I promise you he will be just fine."

"I bet he's looking for a place to go to the bathroom," Preston commented, not expecting the words to actually leave his mouth.

Cain laughed, but Tunnamore's jaw dropped.

"If he so much as–" Tunnamore started.

"Sir, I would never bring an animal into a friend's house without making sure he was housebroken first. In fact, Errol hasn't had any accidents in about four months so he should be just fine."

Both Preston and Cain laughed while Tunnamore scanned the dining room for any signs of disturbance. He was not exactly sure where the four-legged beast ran, but he knew he could not keep his guest waiting any longer.

Tunnamore led Cain into the kitchen and put on the kettle. Preston and the two men sat at the smaller of the two kitchen tables and discussed Dr. Fox and facts surrounding his death. Cain had some interesting things to say about his past, but even he could not determine what brought Preston's father back to life. For him, it was simply a miracle.

Preston wanted desperately to ask about his mother, but assumed Cain might not appreciate an interrogation, so the teenager sat in silence and listened to Tunnamore explain the prior evening's events. It only took about twenty-five minutes for the visitor to finish his cup of tea and read the newspaper article about Dr. Fox. Preston felt as though he had been sitting in the kitchen for nearly an hour when Errol galloped through the doorway and headed straight for his master. The dog buried his head in his owner's lap, and Professor Cain showered him with love and affection.

"Awww, that's a good boy Errol," he cooed. "Yes, you're such a good dog you are."

For a split second Preston thought he saw something in the dog's mouth. He strained to see clearly through all the hair and slobber, and saw Cain take the object and slip it into his coat. Preston glanced at Tunnamore, who was cleaning up crumbs from the table, and realized that he was the only one who saw anything strange. The Professor jumped out of his seat and shooed Errol away in the direction of the front door.

"I thank you very much Mr. Tunnamore for your hospitality, but I'm afraid we must be going," he said.

"That's too bad," Tunnamore responded, gawking at Errol in disgust. "I will tell Dr. Fox of your visit as soon as he arrives."

Cain hurried his pace towards the front door, placed his ear against the cold, hard wood and listened.

"Huh, the storm appears to have quieted down," he remarked. "Looks like we'll have a nice peaceful walk home Errol."

The furry behemoth barked and swung at the door with his gargantuan paw. Tunnamore winced and in grabbing the handle of the door he pushed his guest out of the way. He pulled open the door as fast as possible. Professor Cain bowed his head and shook hands with his hosts. Tunnamore waited just long enough for his guest's foot to clear the doorframe and then he slammed the entrance shut.

"Well that was interesting," Preston said.

"I'm just glad they are gone," Tunnamore sighed. "Now I have to make sure that stupid dog didn't ruin anything."

Preston spun around so Tunnamore would not see him smiling.

Meanwhile, Professor Cain and Errol made their way down the driveway, proud of their accomplishment.

"They have no idea what just hit them my boy," Cain exclaimed, reaching into his coat and removing a small, cracked stone. "I'll have to apologize to Samuel when I see him, but some matters cannot wait."

He tossed the rock into the air and caught it again, rubbing it like a fresh apple ready to eat. Errol let out a low growl, and the Professor stopped short of the road, surprised to find a group of six men walking towards him. He quickly shoved the rock back into his coat and brushed his mustache, trying to look presentable.

"Ahem, good evening gentlemen," he commented. "Good thing it finally stopped raining, huh? Now it is a beautiful night for a walk."

The six men scoffed at Professor Cain and Errol, and turned up the driveway. In passing, one of the men lowered his shoulder into the Professor, nearly knocking him to the ground.

"How rude!" Cain shouted, in utter repugnance.

The assailant turned and departed from his pack. He reached inside his jacket, ready to remove something with earnest, when another man interfered. They whispered back and forth while Cain dusted himself off and Errol continued to growl. The gentleman who hit the Professor rubbed his lips and decided to speak.

"Next time old man, you'd be smart to get out of my way," he advised, in a deep, husky voice.

The man turned and ran to catch up with his group.

"You're wasting your time! The master is not in!" Cain shouted after them. "He's not...oh, whatever."

Errol stopped growling and sniffed the ground. The man lagging behind waved off the Professor's advice and climbed onward.

Cain took a few steps and stopped, looked at Errol, eyes narrowed, and then glanced back at the Fox home.

"Do you smell that Errol?" he asked his companion. "Their attitudes are not the only thing foul and rotten."

Chapter 7

The Deathless

Tunnamore investigated the contents of his master's dining room and study, searching for anything Errol may have disturbed or, even worse, soiled. Meanwhile, Preston returned to his bedroom, jumped onto his mattress, and buried his face in his sheets. He tried to categorize Professor Cain as either a friend of his father, or a friend of Arminius Blackwood. The man seemed pleasant enough, and he was able to get Tunnamore to let his guard down, but since his father's wake, Preston was finding it difficult to trust anyone or anything. Perceptions and assumptions were now nothing more than childish imaginings in his mind. He needed cold, hard tangible truths in order to make sense of things. The mystery surrounding his father's resurrection was not helping matters.

Preston rolled over and looked again at his mother's photograph, marveling at her beauty for the hundredth time in less than 24 hours. He hoped the picture was enough physical evidence that she was real and that she was gorgeous. A tear formed in the corner of his eye and rolled down the contour of his cheek, falling onto his pillow. For the first time in his entire life he wanted his father to come home and sit on the edge of his bed, the two of them staring into Preston's mother's eyes. He did not need to hear his father talk, just look into her eyes and smile.

The doorbell rang and Preston heard Tunnamore groaning and moaning as he stomped towards the front door. Expecting to see either his father or Professor Cain, Preston leapt to his feet and ran for the foyer. The bell rang again and someone began pounding on the door from the outside.

"I'm coming!" Tunnamore yelled. "I hope you realize that your dog is not coming back into this—"

Tunnamore's warning was stopped short as he opened the door and found six menacing figures standing upon the threshold.

"Oh my, I apologize gentlemen," he said sheepishly. "Ahem, what can I do for you fine sirs this evening? I'm afraid it is awfully late for house calls."

Preston slowly backed away from the balcony. Something was not right about these men. They looked far too much like Arminius in dress, and he could also hear one of them struggling to breathe. The man standing closest to the door cleared his throat, reached into his coat pocket, pulled out a revolver and held it steady against Tunnamore's forehead.

"You can do plenty Mr. Tunnamore," the man said.

He smiled, revealing a dark chasm without teeth. Preston's conscience screamed for him to turn and run, but fear struck him from head to toe, his eyes and feet were frozen.

The other men squeezed passed the man with the gun and formed a perimeter around the foyer. Each removed some sort of firearm from their coats. Three of them carried revolvers, one a shotgun, and one held what looked like an automatic rifle. The man in charge kicked the door shut behind him and pushed Tunnamore forward with the barrel of his gun.

Tunnamore whimpered and fell to his knees, babbling like an infant.

"Please! Please don't...I..." he pleaded.

The man with the revolver smiled again and squatted in front of Tunnamore. He peeled a leather glove from his free hand with his teeth, revealing yellowish bones where fingers should have been. With this, Preston's eyes became more intense. The man reached out and cradled Tunnamore's chin in-between his skeletal forefinger and thumb. Lifting ever so slightly, he looked into the tear soaked face of Tunnamore and smiled with cold passion.

"Where is the boy?" the man asked. "Where is Dr. Fox's son?"

Preston's eyes widened with horror. Upon realizing that the men were there for him, he turned and scrambled to reach his bedroom. His knees thumped twice on the hallway floor; a muffled knock echoed through the silent foyer. He dragged his body through the doorway and pushed it shut with a soft click. Locking the door, Preston grabbed his baseball bat and stood near his closet.

"Now what," he thought. "You idiot, now you're trapped!"

One of the men heard Preston, and did not waste any time grabbing his boss's attention.

"Falon," he whispered. "Did you hear *that*?"

Falon, the man standing over Tunnamore, nodded his head towards the second floor and without saying a word, three of the men began their slow and deliberate ascent towards Preston's bedroom.

"I will only ask one more time," Falon said, keeping his voice low so only Tunnamore could hear. "Where is the boy?"

"I don't, uh, know," Tunnamore answered almost inaudibly, staring at the balcony in despair.

The men on the staircase moved closer and closer to the second floor, while the two remaining men in the foyer directed their eyes and guns towards Tunnamore.

"Fine then," Falon sneered. "I guess you really are a useless worm."

Preston recognized the sudden rise in the man's voice inflection, and knew something was wrong. He tightened his grip on the bat and backed up against the wall near his bedroom door. The men finally reached the top of the stairs and lifted their firearms like trained officers. Making slow and steady steps, they stalked the shadows and stopped at each closed door to listen.

Falon clicked the hammer on his revolver, causing Tunnamore to howl in fear. Preston reassured himself that Falon was bluffing, but his heart beat rapidly with the dread of uncertainty. He leaned his head against the bedroom wall and closed his eyes, praying he would not hear a gunshot. The intruders converged on Preston's door, fueled by the quiet drumming of the boy's heart against the wall. His eyes fluttered open upon hearing the floor creak in the hallway. One man took point in front of the door, while the other two took position on each side.

"You are pathetic," Falon snickered. "Nothing to say?"

Falon leveled his pistol with Tunnamore's forehead.

The three men upstairs cocked their revolvers and smiled at each other.

Preston turned, ready to fight to the death.

Then the doorbell rang.

Preston's heart jumped into his throat and he froze in place, while the three men outside his door all stared at each other in disbelief. Falon turned away from Tunnamore and growled in the direction of the front door.

The doorbell rang again.

The three men upstairs slowly moved away from Preston's bedroom and made their way towards the balcony. Falon motioned for his men downstairs to peer through the side windows and see who was at the door. Both men ran to the dining room and pulled back the curtains just enough to see the shape of a man and a dog standing on the front doorstep.

"It's the man and dog we met at the end of the driveway," one man said, returning from the dining room.

"Remember the one Karl knocked to the ground?" the other said.

Falon turned to Tunnamore and demanded to know the identities of the visitors.

"They are, they are Professor Cain and his dog Errol, friends of my master," Tunnamore responded, in-between cries of panic.

"Pull yourself together," Falon demanded. "You're going to get rid of them."

The other two men in the foyer lifted Tunnamore to his feet and wiped the tears and snot from his face. Upon hearing Professor Cain and Errol's names, Preston ran over to his window to see if it was true, and sure enough, there the two comrades were, waiting outside the front door.

Falon dug the barrel of his gun into Tunnamore's lower back and forced him toward the front door.

"Anything out of the ordinary and you're dead, you hear me?" he threatened.

Tunnamore forced himself to breathe, fighting the temptation to faint. He grabbed the handle, turned it, and opened the door about halfway. The light from the foyer illuminated Professor Cain's face and he offered a warm smile in exchange.

"Ah, Tunnamore, there you are," he exclaimed. "I'm sorry to call on you again so soon but I'm afraid I have left something of importance in your kitchen."

"It's alright Professor," Tunnamore breathed deep, staring at the ground. "What exactly did you leave? Maybe I, um I can get it for you."

"Oh no my good sir, I will only be a moment."

Cain pushed forward and stepped inside the entrance hall before Tunnamore could even suggest otherwise. Falon's men hid their firearms and acted as though nothing was amiss. Errol poked his head around the edge of the door and snarled at the men in the foyer.

"Hello gentlemen, it is certainly nice to see you again," Cain greeted, inspecting his surroundings. "I told you that the master wasn't home."

Falon, now agitated, decided to challenge the new visitor.

"We have *other* business here that doesn't pertain to Dr. Fox," he snapped.

"That sounds fascinating," the Professor replied, still looking around the foyer and analyzing the height and weight of each man before him. "I would love to hear what kind of business you have at the Fox home on a night such as this."

"Business that doesn't concern you. Now, Tunnamore, if you would please?"

Falon motioned for Tunnamore to order the Professor and Errol to leave, but he couldn't muster the strength to get the words out of his mouth.

"Okay, okay, I know when I'm not wanted," Cain acquiesced. "But before I go, we might as well make our introductions, no matter how short. My name is Professor Benjamin Cain. And you are?"

Falon hesitated to take the bait, but understood it would be the quickest way to get rid of Cain and his dog.

"My name is Falon, and that should suffice," he responded, tentatively.

"Thank you. A pleasure to meet you Falon," Cain said. "Now I must be going."

He turned for the front door, and the three men on the balcony crept back towards Preston's bedroom. Falon was convinced he had won until the Professor stopped and turned with a curious look.

"One last thing sir," Cain said, inquisitively.

He reached into his coat pocket and pulled out a Colt Revolver with unparalleled speed and delicacy. He clicked the hammer and pulled the trigger in one fluid motion. The bullet exploded from the barrel, deafening everyone within earshot and instantly blinding the other men in the foyer. Spinning through the air, the bullet hissed passed Tunnamore's ear and struck Falon in the jaw, completely severing it from the rest of his face. Before any of the other men could even draw their weapons, Cain grabbed Tunnamore by the arm and slid into the dining room. Just as the Professor's coat tails drifted from sight, a shower of bullets filled the room. Shards of glass from the chandelier cascaded over Falon while wood splinters bounced across the linoleum floor. When the smoke cleared, Falon stood alone in the center of the atrium with his hands covering his face. He peaked through his fingers to see if the bullet storm was over and discovered the bottom half of his jaw lying on the floor. Seemingly unfazed, he pointed to his men on the second floor and shouted something to them. The lack of a tongue made it near impossible to decipher the man's orders, but one word came in loud and clear – "boy". The three men turned on their heels and stormed down the hallway towards Preston's bedroom.

Preston was in complete shock after the hail of gunfire. He had taken refuge inside his closet and was now huddled under a pile of clothes, bat still in hand. Something banged against his door three times until there was a loud crack. The hinge remained intact, but one more swift kick would be more than enough to completely destroy Preston's last hope of protection.

In the foyer, Falon picked up his jaw and placed it in his coat pocket. He pulled out his revolver, checked that it was loaded, and motioned for the other two men to move to his position. The man holding the shotgun reloaded his weapon.

Cain, with the help of a hysteric Tunnamore, flipped over two tables and a couch in the dining room, and both men slumped down to the floor behind their makeshift cover. The Professor immediately began reloading his weapon while Tunnamore forced himself to breathe.

"Will you relax, I just saved your life," Cain groaned.

"But…but…you killed him–" Tunnamore stammered.

"If it were only that easy. Falon is still alive, I guarantee it, and if we don't think fast we won't be so lucky."

"How…alive?"

"I knew it the moment I smelled them coming up the driveway. Deathless Tunnamore, Deathless! In our city?! I don't know whether to be afraid or fascinated. Walking undead, right here in Briercliff!"

"Undead?!?" Tunnamore shouted in disbelief.

Cain quickly cupped a free hand over the man's mouth.

"Yes, *undead*, you idiot. Now keep your voice down."

"This is all too much!"

Tunnamore mumbled to himself and shook his head back and forth. His mind was too fragile to take any more fear or excitement.

"Do you know how to shoot a gun?" Cain asked.

Tunnamore stared at the Professor for a moment, trying to translate the question. He could not believe that Cain was asking him if he knew how to use a firearm. He was the kind of gentleman that was more familiar with a pen and ink than rifles and bullets.

"Do you know how to–" Cain reiterated, not wasting time.

"Absolutely not!" Tunnamore responded, offended by the inquiry.

"Well you do now."

Cain removed a second revolver from his coat, a little smaller than the first, and dropped it onto Tunnamore's lap along with a handful of bullets. Frightened and disgusted all at once, Tunnamore picked up the gun and looked it over. He slid his index finger along the trigger and touched the hammer with his thumb. A shiver ran down his spine as he cocked the firearm.

"I can't shoot a person Mr. Cain," he whispered.

"Well lucky for you, they're not really people," Cain replied. "In fact, we'll be doing them a favor. Rest in peace, if you know what I mean."

The Professor lifted his eyes over the edge of the overturned table and scanned the entranceway. He could hear whispers in the foyer and the crackling of glass. On the second floor, a string of loud thuds permeated through the ceiling of the dining room. Professor Cain turned his attention to Preston.

"Where is the boy?" he asked, grabbing Tunnamore by the collar in order to shake him back to reality.

"Oh!" Tunnamore responded in horror. "I…I am not sure. He was upstairs the last time I knew, in his bedroom."

Cain's smile disappeared, replaced by the stern look of a determined man. He seized Tunnamore's revolver, aimed it at the hallway, and unloaded it into the wall. Expecting his adversaries to be counting every shot he fired, he made sure that each of the six shots was loud and clear.

When the last bullet tore through the plaster about 30 feet away, the three men from the foyer ran into the dining room and started shooting at everything in sight. The man with the machine gun laid down heavy suppressive fire on the couch, but failed to hit the table. Cain reached over the top of his cover and fired three shots, hitting the man in the chest. The bullets tore through his rotten flesh and organs, leaving behind a trail of dusty remains, and while it was not enough to kill him, the force of the gunfire caused him to temporarily stop shooting. With three shots left in his revolver, Professor Cain was feeling lucky, but he did not expect the man with the shotgun to close on his position so quickly. The table exploded only a few inches from his face as the buckshot rained fire upon them. Cain laid flat on the ground, protecting his face from the flying timber, and began to doubt the possibility of success. Suddenly, the sound of a pistol interrupted the muffled blasts of the shotgun, and six shots brought the room to silence. Professor Cain looked up from the disintegrating cover, only to see Tunnamore holding a smoking revolver. He was not sure how or when Tunnamore had reloaded his gun and gained the courage to stand and fight.

The room fell quiet as both sides fell back and rearmed themselves. Cain took this moment to signal Errol. He whistled for the dog and told him that Preston was upstairs and in need of assistance. Errol barked twice and lunged across the foyer, climbing the stairs before Falon or any of his men could stop him. Once recovered, Falon and his men re-entered the dining room, but this time taking refuge along the kitchen entrance way, giving them plenty of cover to shoot from. Tunnamore could not believe his eyes when he saw the man with the shotgun standing again.

"How did he survive that?! I hit him with every single bullet!"

"They are already dead!"

"Then how–"

Falon began firing his revolver in the direction of Cain and Tunnamore. The two men rolled away from the first table and took cover behind the couch. The man with the machine gun shredded the first table in a matter of seconds, leaving nothing but wood splinters and bullet casings on the floor.

"There are three ways to kill a Deathless," Professor Cain explained, keeping his head down. "Number 1, you can set them on fire. Number 2, cutting off their head will sever the spinal cord and destroy all sensory connectivity between body and brain."

The machine gunner turned his attention to the couch and rested his cold finger on the trigger.

"And number 3, most importantly for this situation, a bullet to the head."

Cain jumped up from his hiding place and fired a solitary, well-placed shot right between the eyes of the man with the machine gun. Not taking any further risks, the Professor immediately dropped to the floor and hit the ground at exactly the same time as the lifeless body he put to rest.

Upstairs, the three men outside Preston's bedroom gave the door one final shove, completely obliterating the handle and lock. Pieces of wood and metal scattered across Preston's carpet. The room was shrouded in complete darkness, and the light from the hallway outlined the three men in shadows on the far wall. To Preston, they looked like giants, and his heart beat faster and faster. They spilled into the bedroom like water and explored every crevice in the blink of an eye. Preston tightened his grip on his bat and took a deep breath. One of the Deathless nearby stopped and sniffed the air, sensing the warm adrenaline coursing through the teenager's veins. Preston kicked open the closet door and swung with all his might. He struck the man on the wrist, shattering the bone and forcing the revolver from his hand. The other two men stopped ripping apart Preston's bed and lunged for the teen. Preston swung again, closing his eyes and yelling at the top of his lungs. He again heard the sound of bones cracking and opened his eyes, only to find his bat lodged in-between the ribs of one of his attackers. The man groaned and slumped to the floor. Preston let go of his weapon and tried to dodge the last man, but he lost his balance and slipped on a piece of the broken door. The man landed on top of him and quickly subdued Preston.

"You're going to pay for that!" yelled the intruder, struggling to keep the teenager pinned to the floor. "Come on, help me get him out to the car!"

The other two men stood up and checked their injuries. The man with the broken wrist shook the limp tendon a few times, shrugged his shoulders, and grabbed Preston with his other hand. The other man sat up and was shocked to see the baseball bat sticking out of his chest. He grabbed the handle and pulled with all his might. Removing the bat was strenuous work and did more damage to the man's insides than the initial blow.

Preston could not take his eyes off the hole in the man's chest. He stared at the ribs dangling from the gap and could not understand why there was not any blood, or why the man did not even show any signs of discomfort. Preston opened his mouth to scream, but he had lost the strength to speak. The three men hauled his limp body from the bedroom and carried it down the hallway.

Just as they cleared the doorway a horrifying growl pierced their nerves. Something was behind them, something that none of them expected. It was at this moment that they noticed the lights in the hallway had gone dark. The man carrying Preston's feet slowly put his load on the floor and reached for his revolver. In a flash of yellow eyes, teeth and golden hair, the man disappeared into the darkness of the hallway. The other two listened to his screams as they became distant.

"We need to get the hell out of here now!" one of the remaining men screamed, trying to pull himself out of a state of shock.

The two men grabbed Preston and dragged him towards the foyer, in a hurry to reach the shadow less section of the house, but before they could make it to the balcony, a giant paw reached out from one of the doorways and grabbed the man on Preston's right. The man squealed for only a second and then the hallway was again silent. Preston quaked with fear and was sure that whatever monster was in his house was coming for him next. He rolled over onto his stomach and tried to crawl towards the balcony. The Deathless began wheezing and stumbled as he tried to stand. He grabbed Preston by the shirt and dragged the teenager another few feet before he collapsed and began weeping. The same low, sustained growl they heard before echoed throughout the entire second floor. There was no way of tracing the source. The last intruder backed up against the wall and aimed his revolver down the hallway. He fired off one shot, wincing as the hammer ignited the gunpowder. The gunshot frightened Preston and cleared his senses. He turned and ran for the balcony as fast as the wind.

"Show yourself!" the gunman yelled.

He fired off another three rounds, spacing them so as not to empty the revolver too quickly. The beast's growl continued to echo and the man fired another shot. One bullet left. Hoping that the muzzle flash would illuminate the hallway, he searched for a sign of his attacker. Preston half ran and half fell down the staircase without ever looking back. When he reached the bottom of the steps, the man upstairs screamed at the top of his lungs. The final shot rang out and the ferocious bellow turned into a monstrous roar. Something very large trampled along the hallway on the second floor and Preston could hear the man's shouts turn into gurgles as they became quieter and quieter.

Falon saw Preston out of the corner of his eye and abandoned the dining room, leaving his last colleague to his own devices. Tunnamore had become an absolute marksman under the pressures of imminent death and was able to put a bullet through the man with the shotgun's brain. Professor Cain looked up from his hiding spot to see Falon heading directly for Preston. Fearing that his bullets would hit Preston, the Professor lowered his weapon and ordered Tunnamore to do the same. Falon grabbed Preston and held the machine gun to the boy's back. Turning on a dime, he began backing out the front door when he saw Cain and Tunnamore coming from the dining room.

"Stop right there!" he ordered. "You take one more step and I will kill the boy!"

"We both know that isn't true," Cain said, with a sudden calmness. "If those were your orders, then your men upstairs would have already done it. You need him alive, don't you."

"Shut up! Just, SHUT UP!"

Preston thought he heard thunder explode just outside the front door. Falon froze in fear while Preston peaked underneath his captor's arm and saw a pair of glowing yellow eyes in the darkness. A large paw reached across the threshold, grabbed Falon, and sucked him into the night. The Deathless was able to fire off a few bullets before being ripped to pieces. In the light of those gunshots Preston was able to make out the shape of a massive hulking beast the size of an automobile. It appeared to stand on four legs and had enormous white fangs that glistened in the rays of light coming from the foyer. Preston's fear became mixed with wonder and amazement as he realized that the creature was in fact protecting him.

Meanwhile, Tunnamore dropped his revolver and fainted on the floor. Professor Cain rolled his eyes and stepped forward, resting a hand on Preston's shoulder.

"Are you alright?" he asked.

Preston nodded, refusing to take his eyes off of the creature as it finished devouring its prey. The eyes of the beast met with Preston's gaze and seemed to glow even brighter. Tossing aside Falon's remains, the monster crept toward the doorway. It stalked in and out of the shadows until it was only a few feet from the doorway. Preston took a deep breath and reminded himself that there was no reason to fear the creature, especially with Cain at his side.

"Preston," the Professor said, smiling again. "I want you to meet the *real* Errol."

Just as the words evaporated into the night air, the glowing eyes disappeared, replaced by the dim shine of human eyes. They rose above Preston's eye level and the shadow around the creature became extremely tall and thin. A young man stepped through the entrance and shook the grass and mud from his coat. He drew his fingers through his damp hair and wiped his pointy chin with the back of his palm. Holding out the biggest hand Preston had ever seen, the man spoke with introduction.

"Nice to finally meet you Preston," he said, in a gruff voice. "I'm Errol."

Chapter 8

Moonlight Interrogation

Feeling confused and ultimately removed from reality, Preston stared in awe at Errol's outstretched hand. Cain smiled and gave the teenager an encouraging push, reminding him to be courteous and respectful. Preston observed as Errol's gigantic human paw engulfed his hand. He felt more like a child in that instant than ever before, and could not imagine any living man or woman being as big as Errol, not even Uncle Thomas. Every feature of the man's mythical stature was abnormally sized. He wondered if Errol would even fit through the doorway. Cain patted both Preston and Errol on their shoulders and then went to check on Tunnamore.

"He's certainly alive," the Professor commented, as he lifted Tunnamore's wrist and checked his pulse. "Although I don't believe he's very comfortable lying in a pile of broken glass."

"Well at least he's breathing," Errol laughed. "You all are."

"Always the optimist," Cain added. "At least tell me this, did you leave any of them unspoiled?"

"You underestimate me. What you're looking for is out back tied to a tree. At least, what's left of him."

Cain nodded his head in approval and lifted Tunnamore off the ground. Errol moved into the dining room and flipped over the couch with very little effort. Cain set Tunnamore down like a mother putting down her child for a nap. He then drew a deep breath and relaxed his aching muscles.

"Professor, may I have a word?" Preston asked.

Cain almost forgot Preston was in the room, and felt obliged to give the young man a moment of his time.

"Well I guess there is no harm in that, but I'm afraid there is no time to waste. We need to find out why these men were here tonight and more importantly, why they were after you."

Those last words left a sour taste in Cain's mouth and he looked uneasy as he stood in silent contemplation.

"I don't have a clue as to why they were looking for me, but I think I know who sent them" Preston said, timidly.

Cain arched his eyebrows upon hearing this new information. He motioned for Preston to sit next to him on the dilapidated sofa. In the background, Errol continued to reorganize the furniture and ensure that Tunnamore was comfortable.

"Who do you think sent them?" Cain asked.

"Last night, my father left here with a man named Arminius Blackwood," Preston said. "I have never seen a stranger man before in my life, and he smelled so foul that I thought I would vomit.

These men tonight smelled exactly the same. They even wore similar clothes."

"This is grave news indeed. Your father went with this Arminius fellow, and has yet to return? Did he say where he was going, or why he was leaving?"

"He uh…" Preston only remembered that his father's story was cut short by Arminius's insistence that they leave. "My father and I don't get along, Professor. Last night was the first time in years that we actually spoke to one another."

Preston wanted to ask about his mother, but was not sure if Cain would have any answers.

"I am sorry to hear that," Cain said. "Seeing as how I am a friend of your father's, it pains me to know that the two of you never saw eye to eye. In fact, I never knew he had a son until tonight. I guess we can take comfort in knowing that we at least have a name. Arminius Blackwood, hm? Can't say I've heard of him."

Cain scratched his chin and glanced around the room, obviously lost in thought, while Preston found his eyes glued to the lifeless body of one of Falon's men. The man's brains were spilled on the floor and a pungent odor rose from the wound. Preston noted for a second time the lack of blood.

"What are they?" he asked.

"Them? They are 'Deathless', or at least that is what the books say," Cain said. "They are undead human beings, walking the earth without souls. Unnatural if you ask me. Monsters. Some of my colleagues have done extensive research into the Deathless, but I myself have never seen one."

Cain conjured a handkerchief from somewhere deep inside his coat and pressed it against his nose. He squeezed the cloth and twisted his nose back and forth. Preston was not sure if the Professor was blowing his nose, or just taking thinking of what to say next.

"I am not sure how to tell you this," he began again. "I will give you the short version, but promise me that you will ask me later about the whole story, ok?"

Preston nodded his head without ever saying a word. He knew that he already liked Cain, but he hoped that the Professor would not leave him hanging on edge like his father; he did not know if his brain could store any more unfinished stories.

"Your soul is your life force, your identity," Cain explained. "Everything that defines a person, their memories, their family, it's all tied into their soul. Your body is nothing but a vessel for your soul. In fact, without a soul, you wouldn't be Preston. I wouldn't be Benjamin, and that wouldn't be Errol. We would be nothing more than the walking dead. There are dark things in this world, Preston, things that you think can only be found in nightmares. If a person's soul is taken from them, they become Deathless. They lose all sense of themselves, they lose their past, present, and future. Deathless have no purpose, except to walk the earth until they decompose entirely. Most Deathless only survive for a few weeks while their blood dries up, their organs turn to dust, and their muscles atrophy. Imagine a dead body in a grave, decomposing over time. The process is inevitable, and without a soul, the human body is nothing but a sack of meat. Falon and his men seem to be in good health, at least for being undead, which means they haven't been Deathless for long. I am convinced that we have stumbled upon something of great importance here. This many Deathless, this fresh? Definitely not a coincidence. Deathless are a rarity as you might have guessed, and usually their existence is a bad omen. Sadly, this whole thing might be far bigger than we imagine, and this Arminius fellow you mentioned, wanting to kidnap you, might only be a small piece of the puzzle."

Preston was at a loss for words. He thought about the man on the floor and who he was before someone, or something, took his soul. Did he have a family? Did he have a son?

"Somehow I believe you, but how do you know?" Preston said.

"During my years at the University I have encountered a multitude of things that would make you question reality, Errol being one of them," Cain said. "In my line of work, you never seek to prove if something is real. On the contrary, you always try to *disprove* its existence."

"Sadly, I believe your story more than I believe my own father's. Is it wrong to feel sorry for them?"

"For the Deathless? You shouldn't feel sorry for them Preston, you should have sympathy for the souls that were taken."

"But who would take souls from people?"

"That is what we will need to find out."

"And what about..." Preston hesitated to ask his next question. He glanced over his shoulder to see if Errol was paying attention.

"What is Errol?" he whispered.

Cain burst into a fit of laughter. The cloud of seriousness hanging in the room lifted and Preston felt warm blood course through his veins for the first time all night. He trusted Cain, and hearing the jovial Professor laugh left him feeling lighthearted.

"Errol," Cain called. "Preston wants to know what you are."

"Can't this wait?" Errol asked.

"Oh come now, humor us."

Errol shrugged his shoulders and dropped the end table he was carrying.

"Preston, what is your favorite animal?"

"I really don't know. I guess I like birds."

"Any bird species in particular?"

"Umm, I have only seen hawks and eagles, but I like hawks the best."

"Fair enough."

Errol closed his eyes and raised his chin. Preston knew the man was tall, but he was even more impressed when Errol's nose almost touched the ceiling. Suddenly, Errol's skin became dark and rough, like leather. His shoes spread thin across his shins and turned to scales. Then his clothing disappeared, replaced by large brown and gray feathers the size of turkey platters. His hair molded into the back of his neck and also turned into feathers. A long, razor sharp beak sprung from the tip of his nose, and his eyes grew in size and color. Errol's massive arms shriveled and his fingers came together to form what looked like flippers. As soon as the bones in his hands came together his arms ballooned out and became enormous wings. Fluffing his feathers, he spread his wings across the room, touching walls that were nearly 20 feet apart. When the transformation was complete, there stood a seven-foot tall hawk in the center of the room. Errol squawked at Preston and spoke, as clearly as if he were still human.

"Well, what do you think? I know the size might be a little extreme, but I have seen some extraordinary animals in my travels."

Preston's jaw fell open. He was in awe, and couldn't believe what he saw.

"Amazing," he said, his mouth wide. "I can't believe–"

"Errol is a Therian, and he just metamorphosed into a hawk," Cain explained. "He is human, in a sense, but he is able to transform into any animal that he touches. It's like having a zoo in your own home!"

Errol and Cain laughed, but Preston was too astonished to do anything.

"Listen, I know a lot has been dropped on your plate tonight, but we really must be moving on," Cain said.

Errol transformed back into his human form, and Preston noted how the process looked less painful in reverse.

"Feel free to ask any questions you have. Just know that you are safe with us," Errol said.

Preston blinked feverishly and shook himself back to reality.

"Uh, yeah, of course."

The three men navigated their way through the mansion on their way to Errol's supposed prisoner in the backyard. Along the way, they stopped a few times to check on Falon and a few of the other Deathless to make sure they were finished. Preston, Professor Cain, and Errol reached the back patio doors and stopped to make sure there were no surprises to be found around the corner. Once Errol deemed the coast clear, he opened the door and stepped aside, allowing his followers to step out onto the porch area.

The world around Preston began spinning. Everything he had ever known had been turned upside down in a matter of a few hours. He assumed that his father knew just as much as Cain, considering their collaboration at the University, and it made Preston red with anger knowing that he was fed so many lies in his lifetime. Regardless of where his adventure with the Professor and Errol would take him, Preston was happy that he was finally being fed the truth of the world.

He nodded and smiled at Cain, and the two of them stepped outside into the shadowy backyard. Errol was already checking on his prisoner when he turned to greet them.

"He appears to be no worse for the wear, even if he is missing an arm," Errol explained. "I think he might be sleeping, but it's up to you to tell me whether or not the undead sleep."

Cain stepped forward and analyzed the man tied to the tree. With his index finger, the Professor poked the man's chest a few times, and leaned in close to listen for any sign of breathing.

"He's still alive," he confirmed. "Or at least as alive as any undead person can be, but I believe fear and exhaustion have caused him to faint. We'll need something to wake him up."

Preston stepped forward and realized that the man did not look, or smell, as revolting as the other Deathless in the house.

"He smells fresh" Preston said. "Or, at least he doesn't smell all too bad and his face still looks warm."

Cain strained his eyes to see through the darkness and get a better look at the man's face.

"I believe you're right," he proclaimed. "Good work. Glad to see you listened to my little lecture."

Errol shook his prisoner and ordered him to wake up. The man's body remained limp, but his chest continued to rise and fall. Errol shook the body again, harder this time, but to no effect. Professor Cain cradled his chin and thought for a moment. Then, as if a light bulb went on in his head, he pulled back his arm and slapped the man's face with all his strength. The man's eyes snapped open as he squealed in pain.

"Owww!" he yelled.

Looking at Preston, the Professor smiled and gave Errol the go ahead to hit the man again.

"Stop!" the man screamed.

Errol stopped, cracked his knuckles, and waited for Cain to say something.

"Have you had enough?" Cain asked, his smile fading and his eyebrows furrowing. "I'm going to ask you some questions and you're going to answer them for me, and if you don't, then my friend over there will tear off your other arm and continue to beat you with it. Understand?"

The Deathless looked like he was about to cry as his lower lip began to quiver. Cain refused to budge and waited patiently for the man to respond.

"Oh...okay," the man muttered. "Just please don't hit me anymore. The pain in my shoulder is killing me already."

Cain dropped to one knee and pulled out a pipe from his pocket. He struck a match and stoked the tobacco until it ignited in a puff of smoke. Preston sat down on the wet grass, captivated.

"What is your name?" the Professor asked, in deep exhale.

"My name...my name is Arthur," the man responded, with trepidation.

"Why is it that you feel pain? We know what you are, but you appear to be different from the others. Why?"

Arthur hesitated to answer, but was mesmerized by the Professor's warm appearance.

"I guess...I'm new. I don't know how long ago it happened. They told me my body wouldn't start to rot for at least another week and I would still feel pain while I dried out."

"That seems logical enough," Cain exclaimed, pondering this new information. "Now here comes the big question. Why are you here and who do you work for?"

Preston leaned closer in anticipation while Errol closed his hand around Arthur's arm.

"I...I can't answer that," Arthur replied, lowering his head and hiding his face from his captors.

"I think you misunderstand your current predicament," Cain warned. "There is no *can't*. Maybe you *won't* tell me what I need to know, but there is no reason why you *can't*. My friend Errol will make sure of that."

Errol's gigantic paw began to squeeze Arthur's arm, nearly shattering the bone, and the prisoner winced in pain, crying out for mercy. Arthur screamed at the top of his lungs that he would comply and the Therian relaxed his grip. Errol grinned, obviously pleased with himself.

"I will tell you what you want to know, I promise, just please leave my arm alone," Arthur pleaded.

Professor Cain puffed on his pipe and nodded in agreement.

"Go on," he prompted.

Arthur took a deep breath and relaxed his shoulders in what looked like an act of defeat. The undead man's spirit was broken and he feared the consequence of his confession.

"I work for Lastarr Prendergast," he began. "And before you ask, yes he's the industrialist who owns Nova Steel. We were sent here tonight to kidnap Dr. Fox's son and bring him back to our master. No one really knows what Mr. Prendergast wants with the boy, I swear. We were ordered to bring the boy back to the estate, that's all. I swear. But you can't make me go back, I won't go back! Please help me. Please have mercy. I am not like the others, I swear!"

Arthur broke down and began sobbing, but there were no tears.

"Look, I can't even cry anymore!" he howled.

Cain showed no sympathy and continued his interrogation.

"You have to know what Prendergast wants with Preston," he demanded. "How does he even know who Preston is?"

"Because my master has the boy's father," Arthur replied, choking on his words. "Mr. Prendergast already has Dr. Fox, but he believes there is something special about Preston. He…"

Arthur stopped and glanced around the silent and empty backyard of the Fox household. Preston was ready to go crazy if he had to wait any longer for the truth he so desperately wanted to hear. He motioned for Arthur to continue, but the Deathless never saw him. Instead, Arthur's eyes continued to scan the darkness, trying to spot an assassin meant to keep him from saying what was on the tip of his tongue.

"My master believes Preston was the one who brought Dr. Fox back to life," the Deathless blurted out before he could stop himself.

Preston fell forward and almost landed on his face, while Cain turned slowly to face the boy. All three men were completely stunned by the news that Preston may have been the reason for Dr. Fox's resurrection.

"What? But how?" Preston asked, bewildered by the possibility.

"Arminius told my master about you and about what happened at the wake," Arthur explained.

"No," Preston scoffed. "No way. It doesn't make any sense. I didn't do anything, I swear. All I did was touch–"

"Mr. Blackwood mentioned something about a strange feeling he had when he shook your hand," Arthur said. "He said it felt like life was returning to his body."

Arthur's words trailed off into the moonlit fog. Preston remembered the moment in which he shook Arminius's hand. The Deathless had looked frightened, almost alarmed, and snatched away his hand all too quick. He must have felt something. Arthur's story confirmed Preston's fears.

"This is the same Arminius Blackwood that you told me about?" Cain asked.

"I think so," Preston replied, his mind elsewhere.

"Mr. Prendergast is fascinated by the chance that you have the power to bring people back to life," Arthur affirmed. "Is it true?"

Preston was at a loss for words, but deep down he knew there was a possibility that everything was true. He had never heard of Deathless or Therians before tonight, so maybe he was capable of extraordinary things.

"I can't answer that," Preston replied.

There was a moment of silence as the entire present company contemplated Arthur's story.

"I think we've heard just about enough for now," Cain said, interrupting the teen's train of thought.

He emptied his pipe, slipped it back into his coat, and snapped his fingers. Errol untied Arthur and grabbed the Deathless before he fell to the ground.

"What…what are you doing to me?" Arthur asked, terrified by his unexpected release.

"We're not going to do anything to you, as long as you cooperate," Cain explained. "You're going to tell us where Dr. Fox is being held and you're going to take us to him."

Arthur rubbed the empty socket where his left arm used to be. He looked shyly at Preston, wishing he could just touch the boy's hand.

"Why?" he asked, without looking at the Professor.

"Because we're going to rescue him from his undead fate, and have a word with your master."

Chapter 9

The Nova Steel Company

Errol and Professor Cain carried Tunnamore down the driveway in the direction of Falon's car. Hauling the load was an easy task for the two men, and Preston did not once feel obligated to lend a hand.

"So why aren't we waking him up?" he asked.

"I figure waking him up and explaining our plan will be time consuming, and we need all the time we can get right now," Cain said. "Besides, the less I have to hear him whine, the better."

Arthur opened the door to the backseat and watched Errol single handedly toss Tunnamore into the car. Cain told Errol to drive and requested that Arthur sit in the back, opposite Preston.

"I don't want you getting any ideas," he warned the Deathless.

Errol revved the engine and pulled onto Lakeshore Drive in the direction of the city. Cain elected to drop off Tunnamore at his

University apartment before going after Dr. Fox, and assured Preston that a note with a detailed explanation would be left in case his caretaker awoke during their absence.

"There is no way we could have just left him at your house," he clarified. "I'm sure someone will come looking for Falon's men, and God only knows what they would have done to Tunnamore. I promise he will be safe at my apartment."

Preston agreed, but could not believe that he was actually concerned. In a way, he felt the two were even after Tunnamore's courageous stance against Falon. Errol turned the car down the University Parkway and headed towards three towering brick buildings, the middle one housing Professor Cain's study and apartment. They quickly unloaded Tunnamore to safety and then climbed back into the car, anxiously unprepared for the unknown.

Cain made Preston sit in the passenger seat while he nestled himself next to Arthur. It was no secret that the Professor did not fully trust the undead man, regardless of any sympathy he felt. The automobile turned heavily down the highway and headed towards Briercliff and The Nova Steel Company.

"You'll need to stop on the side of the road about a half mile past the first factory house," Arthur directed.

Cain narrowed his eyes, questioning Arthur's motives.

"I thought your master lives in Briercliff? Why would we be stopping at the factories? I highly doubt a man of Prendergast's esteem actually visits his own place of business–"

"We're stopping there because Dr. Fox is *not* at the Prendergast Estate," Arthur replied, gaining confidence. "They take the new 'Deathless', as you call us, to The Hold, deep within the

Nova Steel factory houses. I've only been there once, but I remember the place. It was so hot, dark, and suffocating that I will never forget it. But we can't just go in through the front gate. We will need to park along the highway, scale the perimeter wall and make our way on foot."

"If that is the plan, then why do we need you?" Errol asked. "I thought the only reason we were bringing you along like a little pet was to have you get us through security."

"Well I am sorry to disappoint, but none of you will ever make it past the first checkpoint. The undead working there will sniff you out immediately."

"I trust him," Preston spoke up, trying to keep the peace. "He hasn't had a chance to let anyone know we are coming, right?"

Professor Cain scoffed and turned his gaze toward the lake on his left. The night sky became brighter and brighter as the car approached the Nova Steel factories. Heat stacks in the distance spewed flames into the atmosphere every few seconds. The interior of the car even reflected the orange glow, and Preston touched the dashboard with his hand, expecting it to be blistering. Driving through this part of town was like being on a highway to hell, and the silence in the car was a testament to the ominous feeling shared by the passengers.

Arthur leaned forward in his seat, but Cain instantly grabbed the man's chest. Arthur, putting up his one hand as a sign of no harm meant, pointed a finger towards the left side of the road and told Errol to pull over. The vehicle jerked left and came to a slow and steady halt just short of the *Briercliff Estates* sign. Preston turned in his seat and looked back at the steel factories. At that distance, he noticed a strange feeling of relief overwhelm him. Even the orange glow and the heat from the furnaces seemed to be out of reach. Cain ordered Arthur out of the car and told him to stand on the side of the road until he, Errol, and Preston were done conversing. Arthur did not seem pleased with the idea, but knew it would not help his case if he argued. Once out of the car, the undead man sat on the ground and pulled out his pocket watch, scratching his dying skin as he read the time – 1:36 a.m.

In the car, Professor Cain immediately pulled himself forward and rested his chin between Errol and Preston.

"So you don't think he can be trusted?" Errol asked.

"I never said that," Cain replied. "On the contrary, I think he is very trustworthy. I was simply testing him to see how loyal he is to his master."

"How do you know he is reliable?"

"Have you seen the way he looks at Preston?"

The teenager stopped staring in his mirror at the blazing infernal skies behind them and turned upon hearing his name.

"What have I got to do with this?" he said.

"Preston, Arthur is an undead man who thinks you have the power to bring people back to life," Cain laughed. "What kind of ideas do you think are going through his head?"

Preston searched for Arthur and found him sitting on the curb, staring at the ground. Deep down, he felt pity for the man.

"He believes that if he helps us, Preston will help him," Cain whispered. "As long as he believes that, then we can trust him."

The Professor turned in silence, pushed open his door and climbed out of the car. Errol winked at Preston and did the same. Arthur jumped up from his resting spot and stood at attention.

"I've been thinking," he exclaimed. "Once we get over the wall we will need to make our way to the Hold as fast as possible. There are constant patrols through the factory yard and the longer we take the greater the chance we'll be spotted."

"Security patrols in a factory?" Errol uttered. "Man, this Prendergast guy is something else."

"Are there going to be people working inside the factory house, or wherever the Hold is located?" Cain asked.

"There are plenty of men working around the Hold, but the overwhelming smell of toxins and steam from the minerals should make it harder for them to detect you," Arthur said.

"What do you mean *detect*?" Preston asked.

"You may think that I smell, but you lot give off a very distinct odor, which as far as I know only affects the senses of men like me. Your soul *smells*...wonderfully."

Arthur's eyes twinkled as he stared at Preston like a hungry dog. The teenager thought about the Deathless at his house earlier that night. He now realized the reason they converged on his bedroom so quickly; they were fueled by the power of his soul.

"Up you go," Errol said, nodding his head towards the wall.

He stood next to the wall and held out his hands, fingers locked together, awaiting the foot of the first brave soul. Cain stepped forward and climbed up Errol's makeshift ladder. With one solid shove, the Professor grabbed the top of the wall and rolled over the edge, disappearing from sight. Errol focused his eyes on

Preston and told him to hurry up. The teen climbed over the barricade in the same fashion as the Professor, and a moment later Arthur too came crawling over the pinnacle of the wall. Preston wondered how Errol was going to get over the wall. As soon as Arthur's feet touched the ground, a hawk perched itself on top of the wall, staring down at the three men. It was relatively smaller than the one Errol turned into a few hours before, but it still looked awesome and majestic. Arthur dusted himself off and cringed at the sight of the predator, expecting it to attack his rotting flesh. The bird glided to the earth and instantly took the shape of a man. Preston could not help but clap at the spectacle, and Errol was more than happy to bow in a show of respect.

"Absolutely incredible," Preston commented. "So, I was wondering, what animal were you earlier tonight?"

"Ah, I figured you might ask. That was one of my favorites from the zoo. A *lion*. Let's just hope I don't have to use it again tonight."

Arthur overheard Errol and Preston mention the lion and his body began to shake with horror. Taking the lead and trying to distance himself from Errol, the Deathless ran ahead toward what looked like the last building in the complex. It was located straight ahead of them, very near the lake, but appeared to be almost a mile or more from the highway entrance. He pointed towards the lights of the security checkpoint.

"See, that's why we didn't come that way," he whispered, keeping his voice down. "We would have never covered that distance without being caught."

Preston knew they were heading into danger, but the reality of the situation didn't hit him until Arthur mentioned being *caught*. Were they really in more danger now than they had been in the hands of Falon's men? The presence of Errol and Professor Cain was the only reason his mind didn't linger on safety. With those two men at his side, he didn't worry about a thing.

They ran until the massive doorway leading into the factory house was in sight. In that instant, the sound of an engine broke through the darkness. Arthur ordered everyone to hide behind a large gathering of brush nearby and Preston lay down on his stomach, completely hidden from sight. A few seconds later a truck appeared around the corner and bounced its way along the dirt path. The headlights were turned off and the back doors were open. As the truck came closer, Preston could make out the shapes of two men, one standing up and hanging onto each back door. With their headlamps dark and their eyes open, Preston assumed the men in the truck were security, trying to catch intruders off guard. Luckily for them, Arthur knew the inside workings at the Nova Steel Company. The truck passed without ever slowing down, and continued its trek towards the lakefront. Arthur breathed a sigh of relief and cautiously stepped out from the brush.

"That was a close one," he whispered. "Trust me when I say that those men were heavily armed and highly dangerous."

Cain pulled out his revolver and checked that it was loaded. Arthur's eyes widened when he saw the firearm and he began to panic.

"Oh calm down, I'm just making sure I'm ready in case things go sour," Cain assured. "You're almost worse than Tunnamore."

With the coast finally clear, they ran as quick as possible for the factory doors. When they were only a few feet from the main entrance, Arthur made a sharp left and crouched low along the left side of the factory house. He gave orders to stay low, and slowly crept along the wall towards the lakeside of the building. Once he reached the corner, Arthur stopped and told Professor Cain the plan of action.

"Okay, once we're inside I need the three of you to stay calm and walk behind me as if you're working for me. Don't say a word to anyone, and keep your head down as much as possible. Don't even make eye contact or else we might be exposed. The doorway to the Hold is located at the center of the warehouse. We go inside and head directly for that doorway."

"Is it guarded?" Errol asked.

"It's only guarded from the inside, which means once we get that door closed behind us things are going to get ugly. There should be at least three guards down there."

"I'll take care of them," Errol said, a big smile stretching across his face.

"Where exactly are they keeping Dr. Fox?" Cain inquired.

"After we get passed the three guards we'll reach a second door. That door requires a key from one of the guards, and on the other side is a hallway of caged rooms, like a prison gallery. Dr. Fox will be in one of those rooms."

"I hate to ask this question, because we've already made it this far, but once we find my father, how do we get out of here?" Preston asked, nervously. "Please tell me you've thought about that."

He looked from Errol's face, to Arthur's, to Professor Cain's, and saw nothing but blank stares.

"You have to be joking," Preston said, dumbfounded.

"Well—" Arthur started.

"I've only known you for a few hours but I'm already starting to like you," Cain said, looking at Preston. "It appears Preston may be the smartest of us all, or at least the most attentive. I say we go in, grab the Professor, and simply walk out. If no one stops us on the way in then they certainly aren't going to stop us on the way out. You just can't leave any survivors this time, Errol."

Everyone nodded in agreement. Arthur stood up, brushed the dust from his shirt and told everyone to follow him and remain quiet. He turned, opened the side door to the factory house and stepped inside. Preston was instantly struck by a blast of tremendous heat and toxic fumes. A loud hiss filled the entire space of the building while clouds of steam and exhaust made it difficult to see. Errol was surprised by the size of the structure, as the entire building was one room. All the machines and furnaces stretched from the floor to the ceiling and there were 50 or more men walking this way and that, working on a multitude of jobs. Arthur panicked when he saw his three followers frozen in the doorway, awestruck by the scene. He quickly ushered them inside and scolded them for not following his orders. The undead man began walking briskly towards the center of the warehouse.

Preston kept his eyes on the floor, but could not help sneaking a peek here and there at his surroundings. He was glancing to his left when he almost walked right into a man passing by with a large hammer in his hand. The man's body was covered in some sort of thick fire protective suit and he wore a massive mirrored faceplate to protect himself from sparks and other flying objects. From behind the mask, a grisly voice growled at Preston and yelled at him to get out of the way. The teen was ready to faint from fright, when Errol's massive hand grabbed his wrist and dragged him in the right direction.

"Stay in front of me," the Therian ordered.

Preston raised his head and proceeded forward. Arthur reached the massive doorway to the Hold and waited for the others to arrive. Seemingly agitated, he looked around the factory house and noticed a few workers watching him with curious eyes. Cain, Errol, and Preston finally reached Arthur's position. Just beyond the door, a staircase led underground and all four men quickly proceeded inside. The staircase became quiet, once the door was closed, and Preston felt a cool breeze blowing from somewhere beyond the dark void in front of him.

"I told you to stay behind me!" Arthur hollered. "I saw some men looking at me. I think they're onto us!"

"Then we don't have a moment to lose," Cain said. "Errol, you're up."

Errol winked at his friend and ran down the staircase, disappearing into the darkness.

"Now what?" Arthur asked, looking to the Professor for answers. "I thought you said we have to move quickly?"

"Errol needs to get rid of the guards first. We wait here for him to come back."

Arthur sat down on the staircase and again rubbed his shoulder. Peering through the darkness, Preston recognized the look of sadness on the man's face and sat down next to him. The Deathless was extremely nervous around Preston and his eyes began to shift back and forth.

"Hey, Arthur," Preston whispered. "You don't have to be afraid. I don't think Errol is going to hurt you again."

"Ha…well, if you say so," Arthur said, sniffling like a child. "I just…I just hope you can forgive me for trying to hurt you earlier."

Preston had almost forgotten that Arthur was one of the three men that broke into his bedroom.

"It's okay, I guess. You didn't have a choice, right?"

Arthur reached out to shake Preston's hand, but Cain interrupted.

"Don't even think about it," he cautioned. "I'm keeping a close eye on you."

Arthur retracted his hand without protest and rubbed his shoulder again, showing signs of anguish.

"Do…Do you remember anything from before you were made like this?" Preston asked, choosing his words carefully.

Arthur just shook his head and rocked back and forth on the step. Preston felt miserable. He did not know whether to feel sorry for Arthur, or for the man that came before Arthur.

"How does it feel?" Preston said.

Arthur's bottom lip quivered and he turned his head, embarrassed by his emotions.

"You know, they say it gets easier with time," he said. "They say that for the first few weeks you're still very much alive. You retain your emotions and even show compassion, but eventually all of that is replaced by emptiness. You lose everything. I don't want that to happen."

A gurgle and a whimper echoed from deep within the Hold. Cain stood slowly from his seat on the staircase and pulled his revolver from its holster. A soft clicking noise was coming towards them, louder and louder with each passing second. Professor Cain cocked his firearm and steadied it at the shadows. A pair of yellow eyes, low to the ground, came into view. Recognizing Errol, the Professor lowered his weapon and smiled. This time Errol did not hide in the shadows when he took human shape. Instead, he climbed the first few steps of the staircase so that they could see him. There, a few feet below Preston, was a long, slender panther. The animal's fur was jet black and so dark that it was almost impossible to see him if it were not for his glowing eyes. Errol turned back into a human and craned his neck. Arthur rose from his seat and reminded Cain that it would be smart to keep moving. Errol pulled a key ring from his pocket and led the way down the staircase and into the darkness. He cycled through the keys and tried to unlock the steel cage door blocking their path. Beyond the door, through the metal bars, Preston perceived a never-ending hallway lined on both sides with what appeared to be prison cells. The entire passageway was quiet, except for the hissing of the light bulb and the dripping of water somewhere nearby.

After only a few tries, Errol finally found the right match for the lock and pulled open the rusted door. Arthur stepped through the entranceway first, followed by Cain and Preston. Errol stood in the doorway a moment and stared back the way they came. He swore he saw something move in the shadows, but could not be sure. Sensing that something was wrong, he elected to remain by the door and keep an eye out for trouble.

"He has to be in here somewhere," Arthur exclaimed.

"There must be a hundred or more cells in here," Cain said. "How many undead does Prendergast leave rotting down here at one time?"

Arthur shrugged his shoulders.

Preston jumped back and forth from his left to his right, searching for any sign of his father. The first twenty or thirty cells he checked were completely empty, and the first two Deathless he came across were both women. Looking at them through the iron bars left a cold feeling in his heart. They just sat there, staring at the ground, completely lost in the world. He wanted desperately to save them from their fate, but knew time was running short.   He continued down the corridor until Professor Cain's voice rang triumphantly.

"I've found him!" he bellowed.

Arthur and Preston ran to his position, some 50 yards or more down the hallway, and peaked into the dark cell. There, huddled against the back wall, was Preston's father. He looked a little thinner and paler since the last time they saw each other, but Preston immediately knew it was his father; it was the shape of his eyes. However, there was something wrong with his gaze; it seemed empty, and almost as deep and dark as the Hold itself. Preston knelt down slowly and grabbed the bars of his father's cell with both hands, staring into the man's face.

"Father?" he asked, curiously.

Dr. Fox looked up and made eye contact with Preston. Without expression, he stared for a moment and licked his lips.

"Who...who are you?" he inquired, his voice weak and broken.

Cain wrapped his arms around Preston and pulled him away from the door.

"I got it!" Errol shouted, with exuberance.

The iron bars disappeared from sight, lost inside the Therian's gargantuan hands as he yanked the cell door open. Cain was the first to rush inside to tend to his cursed friend, Preston second, followed closely by Errol. No one paid any attention to Arthur as he stepped toward the door and hovered on the edge of the hallway, viewing the scene with a jealous eye.

"Samuel, for God's sake are you all right?" Cain asked.

"Who are you?" Dr. Fox demanded. "Where am I?"

Errol and Cain exchanged worried looks while Preston knelt down close to his father's feet. Arthur cleared his throat and said something about memories being erased, but his words fell on deaf ears.

Cain embraced Dr. Fox and shook the man in a fit of frustration.

"It's me, Benjamin!" he cried. "Don't you remember? The University, the museum?! Look at me!"

Dr. Fox's eyes began to bounce around the room without any show of life, or of concern. He looked as though he was in a drunken stupor.

"What about your son?" Cain continued. "Look here, do you remember Preston? This is your boy, Preston. Do you not even remember your own son?"

Dr. Fox's eyes rested lazily on Preston for a moment and a short smile broke across his face. The teenager mistook the smile as a symbol of recognition.

"Preston?" Dr. Fox said, struggling to say the name. He stretched his left arm and grazed the side of Preston's face. Once the cold finger touched the boy's chin, it fell lifeless on the floor once again.

"You – you were in my dream," he said. "I've seen your face."

Renewed with hope, the three men hurriedly lifted Dr. Fox from the dusty floor and brushed him off. He could not yet stand on his own, but Errol served as a dependable crutch.

"Well, go ahead Preston," Cain said.

Preston, taken aback by the request, had almost completely forgotten why they were there.

"What do you mean," he started.

"You have to have faith Preston. We won't know what you are capable of unless you try something."

"But I have no idea what to do or how to do it."

Preston's confidence was coming apart at the seams and the whole venture was in jeopardy. Errol groaned and grabbed Preston's hand forcefully.

"Just do what you did at the wake," he said calmly, though his vice-like grip sent a rather different message. "Put your hand on your father's and we'll just see what happens."

The world stopped and the sound of the factory machines overhead echoed into nothingness. Preston's eyes narrowed on the palm of his hand as he searched for any clue of an anomaly. It looked fairly ordinary to him; in fact, there was not even a callous to be found along the edges of his fingers. What could have possibly caused his father to rise from the dead? Dr. Fox rocked back and forth, uneasy on his feet, and his head swung from left to right like a baby, but for a brief second Preston believed he caught his father's gaze and saw life in his eyes. With a deep breath, Preston took his father's hand in his and closed his eyes.

Chapter 10

Reunion

Preston felt the same cold sensation swell over his entire body that he experienced when he first shook hands with Arminius. His spine tingled and he was worried that if he held onto his father's hand any longer, that his entire body would become numb, and maybe even paralyzed. He let go just as his legs gave out and he collapsed to the floor. Cain and Errol were not sure which of their friends to attend to first, but the drained, pale stare in Preston's eyes frightened them most. Cain seized Preston's arms and helped him sit forward while he motioned for Errol to cradle the boy's head and neck.

"Preston!" Cain shouted. "Preston, can you hear me? Preston, come on boy!!"

Errol placed his massive paw on the teenager's forehead and began murmuring underneath his breath. Preston continued to stare coldly at the ceiling without any sign of life. Dr. Fox groaned and sat up only a few feet away, stroking his head as if suffering from a migraine. He dusted his shirt and coughed uncontrollably, retching the last bits of his dying lungs onto the floor. Clutching his chest, he drew in deep breaths that revitalized his body, mind and spirit. It took a few moments before he realized that he was no longer alone in the dark. In fact, he struggled to make out the figures huddled in front of him until he recognized Cain's voice.

"Benjamin? Is that you?"

Cain was shocked to hear Dr. Fox's voice and he nearly dropped Preston when he heard it.

"Samuel!" Cain exclaimed, abruptly. "Oh my, no time to talk, your son…I don't know what happened…"

Dr. Fox was just barely able to recognize his son's face in the darkness, but the realization of the situation struck him like a fist to the chest, and his heart skipped a beat. He slid forward, hands clawing at Preston's limp body.

"Preston…" he whispered, fear in his voice. "What the hell happened? What are you doing here?"

Cain sat silently, not realizing these questions were directed at him.

A flush of color spread across Preston's face like a tidal wave of blood and vitality. His eyes fluttered and he gasped for air as Errol patted him on the back. When his eyesight returned, the first thing Preston saw was his father. Embarrassment swept over him and he averted his eyes and pretended to be searching around the room for something important.

"Preston?" Dr. Fox asked in a hushed voice.

Cain smiled and put a hand on Preston's shoulder, reassuring him that everything was going to be okay. Preston nodded in the direction of his father and before he could open his mouth, Dr. Fox wrapped his arms around his son and squeezed, Preston could not even lift a hand in protest. His father began sobbing on the boy's shoulder, and with the slow serenade hum of the factory overhead Preston closed his eyes, smiled, and fell back into a dream state. He could not help it. For the first time in his life he was happy to be with his father; he was happy to have someone embrace him and hold on tight. Cain glanced over at Errol and the two men grinned. Errol clapped his hands noisily and stretched as he stood with his back to the door.

"Think hard Samuel – do you remember what happened to you last night?" Cain asked.

"I…" Dr. Fox racked his brain. "I…remember bits and pieces. I could see Preston. I could hear him. It was like I was here all along, just locked away inside my own mind. It was…I was in another place. I was far away, floating, disembodied as I heard his voice echo in a very dark space. I could sense him nearby. Wait, I know this place! This is the…"

He snapped his fingers, searching for the right name.

"The Hold! I remember Arminius talking about it. Oh God, we have to get out of here. We have to go now!"

"But we need to know–" Cain muttered.

"It can wait. This is too dangerous a place."

"We are not leaving until we find Prendergast."

"What?!"

The mere mention of Prendergast's name took the air out of Dr. Fox's lungs.

"No! No!"

He repeated over and over again in hysteria.

"Do not say that name! We are leaving now. I will explain when I can."

A screeching clang reverberated off the walls of the prison cell as the rusted iron door slammed shut and locked. The sound frightened the four men as they had forgotten that they were not alone. Arthur stood only a few feet away, seemingly quiet until now.

"What a touching moment," he said.

Preston spun around, half expecting the Deathless to be overjoyed by the success of their mission, but he instead found Arthur to be nervous and panting heavily with anxiety.

"Arthur –" Cain began, but the undead man cut him off and raised his voice.

"I helped you, now I want what we agreed on."

Everyone in the cell stared at Arthur, confused. He lifted his remaining hand and slid it narrowly between the bars, palm facing up, motioning towards Preston. Errol was not as stunned as the others. He stood erect, hands clenched and stepped towards the door.

"How dare you," he barked. "How can you possibly think this will make us help you? Open the damn door before I rip off your other arm!"

"Errol!" Cain shouted.

"No! I am not about to let this unnatural beast try and blackmail us. Open the door now, because I think we both know that those rusted bars will not keep the animal caged within."

Preston thought he heard Errol growl.

"I am not trying to make matters worse, I promise," Arthur said, now sounding desperate. "I just want to make sure things are right. I helped you because you said Preston would bring help me, and I promise that I will open the door when he has done just that."

"Now you are making me mad," Errol roared. "We never promised you anything. I think it's time that I finish what I started."

Before anyone could object, Errol grasped two bars from the door in his hands and began pushing with all his strength. Arthur backed away in fear and cowered against the prison cell across the hall. Both Cain and Dr. Fox tried to restrain Errol but their efforts proved futile. Something had awoken inside the Therian. Something dark and angry. The ceiling and floor where the iron bars were attached crumbled under the immense pressure and the door fell forward, nearly missing the spot where Arthur stood. The undead man squealed and ran off down the hallway at full speed, heading for the exit. Errol, with his animal instincts kicking into overdrive, transformed into the Black Panther and took chase. In the blink of an eye he pinned the Deathless to the steps leading to the factory house and had locked his jaws on Arthur's arm.

"Errol, No!" Cain shrieked. "We need him!"

Cain took flight towards the stairs, while Dr. Fox helped Preston to his feet.

"You came for me, why?" he asked his son.

"I will tell you, when you tell me what you couldn't last night."

"Fair enough."

Dr. Fox understood that this was not the time for father and son talk, so he proposed that they go and help their friends. When they arrived at the steps, they found Cain still shouting at Errol, who was now human again, and Arthur cowering in a damp corner. Dr. Fox tried to intercede, but Errol's anger was growing with each waning second.

"Back off Samuel!" he snarled. "We don't need that pile of death and decay to get out of here! Watch this!"

Errol, adrenaline surging through his body, threw open the doors to the factory house. He made for the top step, but froze in place, just short of the exit. No one else could see what he saw, but they could tell by the drastic change in Errol's mood that it there was trouble. The Therian grabbed the doors and swung them shut. He leapt down the entire flight of stairs and landed with a thud.

"We're not alone," he muttered, his demeanor quiet and reserved. "We're trapped."

The doors opened again, this time from the other side, and a large shadow stood alone at the top of the steps.

"Come out of there," croaked a grueling voice.

They all looked at one another. There was only one way out of the Hold, and it looked as though they would need to play by someone else's rules in order to escape. Cain seized Arthur from the corner of the room and shoved him up the stairs.

"You're going first," he said.

Preston could not see what was happening just beyond the doorway. Cain and Arthur blocked his view, and the narrow staircase allowed only one figure to enter or exit at a time.

"Bring out the rest," ordered the voice. "Nice and slow."

Arthur raised his hand in concession and Cain quickly followed suit. Errol clamped down on Preston's shoulder, reassuring him that everything would be okay.

"Just stick close to me," he whispered.

The group climbed out of the Hold in single file. A solid wave of hot air blasted Preston as he stepped back onto the factory floor. The heat was even more unbearable than before, and he noticed a drastic change in the level of noise. Men were no longer shouting, machines no longer clambering, and hammers no longer hammering. The only sound left in the metal enclosure was the hiss of smelting fires. Preston raised his hands without objection as he observed a throng of armed men opposite him, and he measured his steps towards Cain and Arthur. Errol shifted his weight so that he stood directly behind Preston, draping his coat over the young boy's shoulders, nearly smothering him. Last to exit the hold was Dr. Fox and while he raised his hands to shield himself from the hellish fires, he failed to see the loaded danger only a few feet away.

"Get back!" screamed one of the factory men as Preston's father stumbled out of line.

Samuel dropped his hands and lowered his head, realizing his mistake. Preston peeked from behind Errol's dusty coat and found his father slouched to his immediate left. He looked tired and out of breath. The five men stood in silence, waiting. One of the factory workers stepped forward and raised his gun to Samuel's chest.

"This one," he said.

Preston scanned the man's face for signs of decomposition, but could not find even the slightest imperfection. Could it be that

Prendergast also employed the living? A hand suddenly appeared like an apparition and landed on the man's shoulder. The man with the gun nodded his head without taking his eyes off Samuel, and stepped to his right, revealing a short, fat little man with glasses.

The owner of the ghostly hand smiled and stood in thought for a moment, measuring the weight and bravery of his prisoners. Molten iron flared like the sun as it bubbled and boiled in pits throughout the warehouse, and the short man's glasses caught every flicker of flaming light in reflection. Preston could not even see the man's eyes.

"It amazes me to think that you imagined escaping here with your lives," the man said. "You come with the intention of rescuing your friend Dr. Fox, only to find yourselves in a far more dangerous predicament."

"How so?" Cain spat.

"You dare speak? I was told that *you* would prove to be difficult," the man smiled again, curling his plump lips and oiled mustache. "And you," he turned his attention to Arthur, "what are you doing here helping them? This transgression cannot, and will not, be forgiven. You throw yourself in with the lot of them; you get the same treatment as well."

Arthur shook from head to toe as judgment fell upon him. He was clearly privy to information that the others were not.

"I had no choice Mr. Viddler," he cried out. "They threatened to kill me."

"You imbecile! You're already dead!"

The entire company laughed.

Preston struggled to lean forward and get a better view. Being a foot or two behind Cain, he watched as the Professor removed something in secret from his back pocket. Preston was reminded of the first time he met Professor Cain and Errol, and how he thought the two had exchanged some sort of object while in the kitchen. He wondered if this item was in fact the same.

Viddler began to pace back and forth, one stumpy foot in front of the other.

"Orders, orders, orders. We have orders to bring you back to the house. All *four* of you. We no longer need this one," he hissed, pointing at Samuel. "Kill him for me."

The man to his right still held his gun pointed at Dr. Fox, and upon hearing his cue he stepped back into formation and steadied his hands.

"No!" Preston shouted, lunging forward with his arms flailing for the gun. Viddler kicked Preston's leg mid-stride and sent him tumbling to the floor, but Preston turned over in a flash and clawed at the shooter. Viddler planted his foot on Preston's back and pinned the boy to the floor with all his weight rested on one heel. There was no way Preston was getting up, and the warehouse once again filled with laugher.

"Ah this is the son, is it not?" Viddler asked in a mocking tone of voice.

"Screw you!" Preston hurled back.

"That's right, give me your best shot. Be the big man."

Viddler continued to taunt Preston as the boy wrestled to free himself. Laughter echoed throughout the room, and no one but Preston noticed Cain slip away from the scene. The Professor sidled over to the nearest slag pit and tossed something small into the pool. Realizing that his resistance was causing a distraction, Preston lashed out with renewed ferocity and screamed at the top of his lungs.

"If you kill him, I swear that I will rip out your heart! Do you hear me?! I will tear you to pieces!"

"Let me do you the favor," Viddler laughed. He buried his hand beneath his coat and twisted his wrist. Wrenching his arm up and down, he freed his heart from his ribcage and held it out for Preston to see, cold and lifeless. A few of the factory workers dropped their firearms as they were overcome with uncontrollable fits of laughter.

Preston was not amused. He kicked harder and harder until he freed himself and crawled to where his father stood.

"Are you mad?!" Samuel yelled. "You could have gotten yourself killed!"

"Touching that you would risk your own life to save your father," Viddler said, wiping away an imaginary tear. "Now will you kill him already."

The executioner shook himself into focus and steadied his aim, placing his finger gently along the curvature of the trigger and measuring it for bounce. Just a slight pull he told himself. At that exact moment a fastener bolt from the trigger wriggled out of its socket and plopped onto the floor. Even though the bolt was an inch in length, everyone noticed it lying there, glistening in the light of the furnace. The man tried to ignore the bolt and convince himself it was just a trick of the mind. He pulled the trigger but nothing happened.

Out of curiosity, he bent down and saw the bolt on the ground. Preston narrowed his eyes and took a step forward. The laughter in the warehouse disappeared, replaced by hissing and bubbling. As the man reached for the bolt it began to slide along the ground at a snail's pace. No matter how much steam or how much soot filled that warehouse, no one could deny what they saw. The man shook his head, scratched his chin, and watched the bolt move away from him, leaving behind a trail in the dirt floor.

The bolt's pace quickened and then it bounced and jumped until it reached the edge of the nearest smelting pool. Preston may have been the only person to recognize that particular pool as the one in which Cain made an offering a few seconds before. With everyone watching in awe, the bolt hovered and waned along the rim, and then toppled. Like a monster eating its prey, the pit let out an instinctive burp as it devoured the steel pin. Preston stepped back until he brushed against his father's arm. Errol slid his massive hand along Preston's lower back and whispered in his ear.

"Get ready to run."

The man with the gun stared, astonished, at the fiery pit. The light from the molten iron seemed to burn brighter than before, and a dull pulse reverberated beneath their feet. Another small bolt removed itself from the man's gun and slid across the floor, and into the pit. Then another. And another. Soon the trigger itself broke free and caromed through the air, as if thrown, and landed in the pit.

Raised voices could be heard as more small metal objects marched their way to an infernal death as if possessed by some mystical force. Viddler's glasses began to wobble, and he only saved them at the last second by clasping his hands over his face.

Men shouted to one another and somewhere a pistol shot rang out. Everyone ducked, but Preston held his ground and saw the gun sliding along the ground and disappear into the pool, which was now glowing brighter, and burning hotter. Chains clanged against machine trucks and hammers bounced their way along the rafters. Steel rafters above them groaned under pressure. The throbbing under their feet became faster and more intense. The scene turned to pure chaos as factory workers dropped their guns and ran for the exits.

"Run, now!" Cain yelled.

Errol slumped Preston over his shoulder like a sack of flour and took off running. A man to their right clutched at his waist and fumbled as he tried to undo his belt buckle. His heels dug into the floor as he resisted, but slowly he began to slide across the floor like the bolt from the trigger. Men screamed and grabbed onto each other as they tried to remove their tool belts and clothes. The magnetic pull was gaining strength with each and every second, and each tool that passed Preston was bigger than the last. He glanced over his shoulder and saw a steel table hurtling right towards them. Errol diverted the table's direction with his free shoulder like a linebacker, and it looked like tumbleweed as it rolled past and became one with the inferno.

With each lunge of Errol's mammoth stride Preston's body bounced up and down. The scene was bedlam; a mass of bodies silhouetted in the burning night, doomed to the magnetic volcano threatening to swallow them whole. The entire warehouse was caving in on itself. Beams and tiles from the ceiling bowed under pressure; bolts ripped themselves from structural supports. An enormous sheet of steel tore itself from the wall to Preston's left and took off like a kite towards the far end of the factory. It flattened two men and cut another almost in half along the way, and Preston had to shut his eyes to avoid the details. He kept his eyes closed until he felt a rush of cold air scramble across his neck. They were finally outside.

Upon opening his eyes, Preston was surprised to discover that they were still in danger. The entire ceiling and half of the eastern wall of the warehouse were gone, but he could still see the flaming eye of the storm 100 yards away. He even felt the heat.

Cain yelled something while Arthur tripped over a downed tree. Their voices were muffled beneath the pulse of the smelter. It continued to drum so loud and so hard that Preston felt as though his eardrums might burst. Errol flipped the boy over and tossed him to the ground. He pointed over to Samuel and screamed something to Preston. The boy could not hear the order, but he could read lips.

Run.

Errol ran back to help Cain, while Preston attended to his father. Rocks, pebbles, and shards of scrap metal streaked past and showered down from above like rain. Dr. Fox used his coat to shield Preston's face while the two ran towards Lakeshore Drive. Even at a few hundred yards away Preston felt the magnetic pull. Looking back, he witnessed a solitary automobile park just outside the factory house. The poor fools had no idea why the place was falling apart. The car lurched forward and rolled right into the fire. Professor Cain and Errol were now only a few paces behind, but Arthur was nowhere in sight. Dr. Fox seized his son's arm and motioned for him to keep going.

Just then, the pulsing stopped and silence fell upon them. Preston heard his father trying to catch his breath.

"Don't stop!" Cain bellowed. "It's going to–"

Preston never heard the rest of what Professor Cain shouted. A blast with the magnitude of a thousand pounds of dynamite struck the shoreline. Pure white light scorched his eyes and lit up the entire night sky for miles.

Chapter 11

The Great Escape

Preston was not sure how long he had been unconscious, or how far the force had thrown him from his feet. The dust was still settling when he woke. He was alone. With his ears ringing and his brain disoriented, Preston tried to gain his bearings. He pushed himself off the ground with his fists, only to collapse back to the earth face first. The wind stopped, but now the world was turned upside down. Preston rolled onto his back and blinked his eyes until they focused. The night was black once again, and a dark cloud of smoke, dirt, and soot blocked out the moon and stars. He pushed himself onto his knees and caught his breath. He felt something warm and wet on the side of his face. Blood.

Voices echoed in the distance, but he could not focus on their exact location. Preston wiped the dirt from his eyes and realized that his efforts were in vain. The cloud of smoke was as dense as black paint, and he could not see more than six inches in front of his face. A cool breeze swept across his neck and caused the fog to swirl around his body. Footsteps crunched somewhere nearby. Preston crouched, hiding himself below the cloudy veil as he could not be sure if the person nearby was friend or foe.

The footsteps stopped only a few paces away.

"Preston, is that you? Samuel?"

It was Professor Cain's voice, although rustier than usual.

"I'm here, right here," Preston answered, lifting his head above the crest of the settling dust.

"Thank God, are you hurt?"

"I am bleeding, but I don't know where from. Where are the others? Where is my father?"

There was a pause before Cain's next words.

"You're the only *living* thing I've found."

Preston sensed something for the first time in the Professor's voice – fear. Ever since their first meeting, Professor Cain had been a symbol of confidence and sound judgment. Now he seemed disoriented and weary. Preston staggered to his feet and rubbed his knees.

Now he could better assess the damage with the smoke finally clearing. A large crater stretched across the piece of land that was once Prendergast's makeshift prison. Debris and bodies lay half buried in the earth and sand for yards in every direction. The smelter still burned and its light beckoned amidst the darkness. Preston noticed that they were the farthest from the explosion, and that being the sole reason why they were still standing.

"Did you know that would happen?" he coughed.

"I had an inkling of what might happen, but seeing as how that was the first time I experimented with meteor ore, I will admit

144

that even I had no idea that it would be that catastrophic. The extreme heat of the smelter must have increased the magnetic force beyond my calculations."

"Was that what you stole from my father's study, meteor ore?"

Professor Cain stopped short and winked at Preston.

"You are a clever boy."

"And you are a thief."

"We need to find the others. Your father was nearby when the explosion happened. If we're here, then he has to be alive."

"What about me?" a voice sounded behind them.

It was Arthur, and he looked no worse for the wear. Part of his left leg was missing, but an injury like that would only slow down a Deathless such as him.

"You bastards left me back there!"

"Oh hush now, we were trying to get the hell out of there. In case you didn't know, warm blood still courses through our veins! I was not about to risk my life for something that isn't even alive!" Cain barked.

"Did you see my father anywhere? Anyone alive?" Preston prodded for information.

"He and Errol are over in that direction, moving fast," Arthur said. "We don't have much time. Security is coming in droves and will be bearing down on us any second."

All three men broke into a run toward the direction Arthur pointed. Preston was surprised at how quickly Arthur moved with his handicap. The air cooled and the smoke cleared as they ran. Soon Preston spotted lights from the main factory houses and

Lakeshore Drive. His father and Errol sprinted ahead of them without looking back.

"Why didn't they try and find us?" Preston shouted.

"Look!" Arthur belted.

Errol and Dr. Fox were illuminated in the landscape as two automobiles sprang into view. Headlights were centered on the two men and the dust trail behind meant the trucks were moving fast. Gunshots rang out and Preston saw flashes of light from just above the cab of the truck on the left.

"Let's go!"

Preston lowered his head and dug his toes into the dirt. He no longer cared whether Professor Cain or Arthur could keep up with him. He needed to get to his father as fast as possible. More gunshots resonated across the open field. Preston's eyes remained fixed on his father's location, but he knew he would lose track of them once they crossed over into the train yard. There were train cars and countless storage crates littered about; he would never find them in that maze.

Preston stopped to take a deep breath when Cain called his name. Preston quickly scanned to his right and then to his left, and found the Professor and Arthur in the distance.

"This way!" the two men shouted almost in unison.

They took off again, running towards the Northern end of the complex. Preston was confused by their decision, until he observed the trucks turn around and head in the same direction.

"What the hell," he growled to himself and broke into a sprint.

Three more gunshots severed the night. Preston entered the train yard, weaving in-between and around large crates and train cars. He kept his eyes on the brake lights of the trucks and the trail of dust their tires kicked into the cooling air. Surprised that he was gaining on them, he let up on his pace and stopped again to catch his breath. Just then a large hand seized him by the collar and threw him to the ground, pinning him. He tried to scream but a second hand swallowed his mouth and half his face along with it. The size and shape of that hand was familiar. It was Errol.

The hulking man released his grip on Preston's collar and pressed a finger to his lips. Dr. Fox crouched a foot away, peaking around the corner of the brown storage crate. He nodded towards Preston and smiled.

"More are coming," he said.

As the engines from the two trucks faded in the direction of Arthur and Professor Cain, the rumbling of three more roared from the south. Errol lifted his hand from Preston's face and peered over Dr. Fox's shoulder.

"How did you guys end up here?" Preston asked, breathing heavily. "Why did you stop?"

"If we kept running out in the open they would have eventually caught us," Errol whispered. "In here, we can take them close quarters. We have the advantage."

"We can't let them get Arthur and the Professor." Preston pointed his finger in the direction of the original trucks. "They will never make it," he lamented, lowering his hand.

Headlights from the automobiles to the south now bounced into sight. Each truck carried a cabin full of armed men. The vehicles stopped and the drivers assessed the situation, looking for a clue of where to go next. Wind carried the sound of a train whistle to Preston's ears. Errol stripped his coat and kicked it across the dirt.

"Listen to me," he said. "The Professor is always one step ahead of me. He knows what he is doing; we don't have to worry about him."

He glanced around the edge of the crate and counted his adversaries.

"The two of you are going to make a run for that train. They will try to follow you, but I will make sure they don't get far. Just keep your heads and down and your legs moving."

"Are you crazy?" Dr. Fox said. "We can't leave you here by yourself."

"You can, and you will. Trust me."

Dr. Fox grumbled and shook his fist. He nudged Preston and motioned for him to go, but the boy stood still.

Errol turned his head and stared back into the Preston's serene face. The Therian's eyes were black and his teeth were larger and sharper than normal for a human being.

"Get out of here!" he growled.

Preston turned and together, he and his father ran towards the screech of the train's whistle and brakes. As soon as they cleared the edge of the crate, the men in the trucks shouted, the engines sputtered and kicked into gear, sending each vehicle ahead with a jolt. One of the men opened fire. He squeezed his trigger and sent bullet after bullet exploding into the night. Bullets snapped and hissed all around Preston and his father as they ran, but they bobbed and weaved using the crates as cover. Preston knew that the more objects they could put between them and the gunmen, the safer they would be. One of the trucks pulled ahead while all three headed straight for the crate where Errol hid. They would reach the corner and then bank east in the direction Preston and Dr. Fox ran.

Suddenly, a brutal, inhuman roar erupted from somewhere in the train yard. Preston heard it, but he kept his head low and his mind on the objective. The crate where Errol stood lifted from the ground and slammed into the hood of the first vehicle, stopping it in its tracks. The gunman in the bed was ejected and landed on his head in a pile of railroad ties. Screeching to a halt, the other two trucks stood idle a good twenty yards away from the crate. With headlights on the lead truck, the gunmen and drivers stared in disbelief. A massive black shape hurdled the wrecked automobile and landed on the far side, sticking to the shadows. The driver side door of the damaged truck was ripped from its hinges and thrown in the direction of the other trucks; next the driver and the two passengers, flying through the air like rag dolls.

Shouts of "Shoot" and "Fire" rang out among the men still standing. "Shoot what?!" screamed one of the men as he saw nothing but darkness. Before anyone could respond, one of the men opened fire. The rest followed suit and emptied their chambers in a matter of seconds. As the men started to stop and reload, the lead truck, leaking oil and gas, lifted off the ground and took flight. A few of the security guards tried to leap out of the way, but the truck came crashing down, flattening the second truck and squishing three men in the process.

The beast was now in clear sight; it was Errol as a savage gorilla.

He stood ten feet tall, maybe more, and gnashed his teeth and beat his chest with enormous fists. A few of the men took flight while the others opened fire. Errol barreled down on them and dispatched those remaining with one fell swipe. He lifted the last truck like a child playing with a toy, and smashed it into the ground. He beat his chest and let out a frightening howl. The train whistle seized his attention; he turned and lumbered across the tracks heading north.

Preston and his father cleared the final row of train cars, and to his surprise he could now not only hear the train, but also see it with his own eyes. It was a large steam engine used for the transportation of coal, steel, and other resources. Just as Errol imagined, the train was leaving the station and appeared to be their ticket out of the complex.

"We're nearly there, come on!" Preston shouted back to his father.

Dr. Fox was slowing down. He was weak when they first found him in the Hold, and the events since then had taken a harsh toll on his body.

"You have to go, you can't wait for me," Dr. Fox huffed as he collapsed.

Preston returned to his father and knelt at his side.

"I am not leaving you. Get up!"

"I...I can't Preston..."

"I said get up!"

Preston lifted his father to his feet. The wretched man was now deadweight and Preston found it near impossible to carry him. After only a few steps the two fell to the ground, exhausted. For the first time all night Preston gave in to fatigue and closed his eyes.

He was not sure if he were dreaming, but he felt his body lifted with ease by clouds of black smoke. He and his father hovered above the ground and glided towards the oncoming train. They were set down inside a passing train car with as much care as they were originally lifted from the ground. The floor beneath his head felt warm and soft, and Preston felt as though he could sleep forever.

The train whistle blew, startling his fantasy.

Preston shot straight up and found himself inside a dark, damp train car, and his father unconscious to his right. He steadied himself as the train gathered speed, and he swung his legs out the doorway. He gazed across the train yard and perceived a shadow moving fast along the tracks, headed for the trucks in the distance.

It was Errol, and he looked terrifying.

Preston recognized the shapes of Arthur and Professor Cain near the front of the train. They were trying to reach up and grab onto an open car, but the locomotive moved much too fast. Arthur latched onto a handle with his free hand, but lacked the strength to pull himself up. He fell backwards and landed in the arms of Cain. Both men tumbled to the dirt.

The train charged ahead, faster than the trucks, and Preston saw that the security guards were almost within firing range of the Professor. Preston heard Errol roar, and one of the trucks flipped forward, landing on the roof. The driver of one of the other trucks kicked the gearshift into reverse and slammed the gas pedal to the floor. Two gunshots rang out as the passenger fired his pistol. Errol shrugged off the advance, and seized the truck by its headlights. He brought both of his fists high above his head, snarled, and slammed down with all his might on the front of the car. After a few more strikes, there was nothing left that resembled an automobile.

Preston passed by and called out.

"Errol!" he shouted. "Errol! Come on!"

Panic set in as Professor Cain and Arthur came into view. Preston lay onto his stomach and reached out with both hands.

"You better hope this works," he told himself. "Professor! Grab on!"

Cain looked up and was surprised to see Preston hanging out of the oncoming train car. He gathered his strength and broke into a run. Trying to keep up with the train, he reached out and slapped at Preston's hands.

"It's moving too fast!"

"Just grab on! Jump!"

Cain attempted a leap of faith, but he could not keep pace and plummeted to the ground swallowing a mouthful of sand and grit.

"No!" Preston screamed.

Arthur came up behind Cain and helped him to his feet. Countless headlights bounced along the landscape; the entire force of Nova Steel's security would be on top of them any minute. Two sets of headlights were suddenly blacked out as a massive shape catapulted itself towards the train. Errol moved even faster than before.

"Come on Errol, you can do it," Preston whispered.

Errol scooped up an unassuming Cain and Arthur and continued at breakneck speed. They were gaining on Preston's car when bullets skipped across the tracks. Sparks showered Errol from above.

"They are gaining on you, it has to be now!" Preston shouted.

With only a few more feet to go, Errol flung Arthur towards Preston. The undead man screamed and clawed with his hand as Preston leapt out of the way. Arthur landed with a thud on the floor of the car, but slid too far towards the door on the opposite side. Preston scrambled to grab hold of Arthur's arm and pull him inside.

Preston turned back to Errol and saw that he was losing pace to the train; now he was two to three cars behind them. Each foot that Errol lost was gained by the trucks in pursuit. They were running out of time. The train was heading towards downtown, and the walls of the complex were a few hundred yards away. Errol must have noticed this as he closed his eyes and drove his body beyond its limits, exerting all the rest of his energy. His muscles burst forth and his lungs expanded and contracted simultaneously.

Preston screamed as Errol came closer and closer. Then more gunshots. A bullet tore through Errol's shoulder, showering the ground with a blood offering. He grunted, clenched his teeth, and kept forward. They were close enough now that Preston could reach out and help grab hold of Professor Cain. Errol gave a shove and the Professor's body floated through the opening. He landed on his feet with the help of Preston.

"Now you're next!" Preston shouted as he beckoned Errol.

Errol, heaving with each breath, looked ahead at the wall of the compound.

"Go! Get out of here!" he roared. "Help your father!"

He was beyond exhausted, that coupled with his injury, and his body was shutting itself down. The effort he made to throw Cain into the car was his last. He fell further and further behind until he went from running, to galloping, to walking. The trucks bore down on him as Preston lost sight of him.

"No!" Preston squealed. "No! No!"

"Get in here!" Cain growled as he snatched Preston's arm and yanked him inside the car. Just then they passed into the tunnel at the edge of the compound.

"What happened?!" Preston demanded.

Cain slumped to the floor and buried his head in his hands. "He did what he could," he muttered.

Preston wiped the tears from his eyes, and fell in beside the figure of his father lying on the floor.

"He gave his life to save you," he whispered. "Why the hell are you so important?"

Dr. Fox rolled over and took his hand from his face. He struggled to get the words out of his mouth.

"He wasn't saving me," he mumbled. "He was saving you, Preston."

They exited the tunnel, and the darkness of the car broke as the moon faded with the night. It would be morning soon. Preston looked into the faces of his fellow travelers and saw nothing short of sadness, disappointment, and exhaustion. Even Arthur looked distraught. Preston closed his eyes and hoped to never open them again. He heard something flapping and opened his eyes. The sun was rising beyond the open door, and he shielded his eyes from its stoic rays. Something small was silhouetted in the doorway and while it remained low to the ground, it stood erect. It was a hawk.

The bird flapped its wings again and squawked.

"You all counted me out, didn't you?"

The shape of the bird shifted and contorted, and the outline against the sun grew larger and thicker. Errol stood in the open doorway; dirty, bruised, and holding his shoulder. He was smiling.

Chapter 12

The Eternal Sorrow of Preston Fox

"You need to keep pressure on the wound to stop the bleeding," Cain advised, as he held a rag against Errol's shoulder.

"I will live," Errol said. "I think the bullet went straight through."

"You're lucky then. All that gunfire could have killed a dozen men."

Preston sat against the wall of the train car and continued to gaze out the open door. He watched as houses, buildings, and grain elevators flashed by. The sun kept rising higher and higher in the sky, and its rays began to creep across the floor in front of him. Like a pool of oil, it spread towards his feet. He subconsciously pulled his legs against his chest, wanting to stay in the shadows for as long as possible.

"So, Samuel," Cain said, still holding the cloth against Errol's shoulder. "Are you going to tell us where we are going and what we are supposed to do?"

Everyone was silent, and the only sound they heard other than Errol's heavy breathing was the screeching of the train on the tracks. Preston was the only person not looking directly at his father.

"We need to go to the University," Dr. Fox said , softly. "I must speak with Grishkat."

"Grishkat? Grishkat the old bat? How in the blazes is he tied into this," Cain said.

"Prendergast is looking for something," Dr. Fox stopped, uneasiness spreading across his face. "He's looking for a key of some sort. I have no idea what he plans to do with it, but I do know that he has waited a very long time for this opportunity. He isn't normal, as you can already guess. I don't know who or what he is, but he isn't human. This key is his focus and Grishkat is the last person to see it."

"Well if he is looking for a key then I think we should be more concerned about what the key opens," Cain said.

"I don't know anything about the use of the key."

"So, why did Prendergast come after you?" Errol asked.

"He wanted Dr. Fox's memories," Arthur interrupted, his monotone voice tumbling across the floorboards without life. "Dr. Fox knew where the key was last seen. My master needed to look deep into his memories. Nobody except Dr. Fox knew Grishkat had the key."

"Is this true?" Cain said, as a look of concern spread over his face.

158

Dr. Fox simply nodded his head. He started scratching at the floor, tracing the knicks and marks cut deep into the timber.

"When he consumed my soul, I was given a glimpse into his own mind," he started. "It was brief, but the things I saw were disturbing. I saw storm clouds rolling across an open field, and a white castle rising towards the skyline in the distance. Then I saw the same field littered with the dead. Men. Women. Children. They were cold and rotten. It was horrific."

His lips froze and he looked as though he was going to cry. Just then, a twinkle of light flickered somewhere deep inside his eyes. Preston noticed that those amber globes of pain and sorrow were instead reflecting hope for the first time all night.

"That's when I saw the key," Dr. Fox recalled. "It was white, small in size, and looked almost unworldly. A shadow hugged close wherever it went. I saw the key twisted between two fingers. Then I caught a glimpse of Prendergast, and he was asking someone about the key. I could see him getting angry as he described it to him. The man didn't know what he was talking about. He...He killed that person; slit the man's throat right there. Finally, I saw him poring over newspapers and books, trying to locate the key, and that's when he found it. He saw an article in the University Times that recorded my discovery of the key, showing a picture. However, the reporter never made mention of how I gave the key to Grishkat for study and safe keeping."

Everyone remained still and let the details of the Professor's story settle like pixie dust. Preston, however, felt compelled to snap out of the trance and be the first to speak.

"Why didn't he just ask you where the key was?" he asked. "You said he killed another man for not telling him. So, why didn't he threaten you?"

"My master was weak back then," Arthur said, sounding as if the words coming out of his mouth were not under his own volition. "He needed to be careful. He was willing to wait, as long as it meant that Dr. Fox's soul and memories were guaranteed."

"I am curious as to why you didn't tell us this before," Cain said, staring at Arthur. "You mind explaining that to me?"

"I heard the other men talk from time to time," Arthur muttered, snapping out of his hypnotic state. "It must have slipped my mind."

Cain kept his eyes fixed on the Deathless, not willing to look away just yet. He wanted to make sure Arthur knew that this new information had jeopardized his trust.

"Prendergast is being careful," Dr. Fox continued. "He needs a contract to take a soul, that much I know. I signed my contract 14 years ago, and he waited all that time for the smallest bit of information. Even all the Deathless that work for him have bargained with him one way or another. It's odd, but I feel like he didn't have a choice. Something frightened him after he slit that man's throat. He could no longer take any risks. Ever since then the laws of nature held within the soul contracts bind him. But I think that will all change when he retrieves the key."

Preston froze when he heard his father say '14 years'. He was born 14 years before, and he had always been told that his mother died around the same time.

"What do you mean, *14 years ago?*" he asked, his words seething with fear and anger. "*What* did you trade for your soul?"

Dr. Fox felt caught between a rock and a hard place. He closed his eyes, clenched his teeth, and tightened every muscle in his body like a steel trap. It was a defensive strategy he learned years before whenever his son asked about Allyson, but this time his efforts were in vain.

"Your mother's life," he whispered, withdrawing into the shadows. "I traded my soul for her life."

"But...I don't understand," Preston muttered, shocked by the possibility. "She is dead, isn't she? If you traded your soul for her life, then why is she dead?"

"She became ill while pregnant with you," Dr. Fox said, leaning slightly forward and emphasizing every word. "A man came calling the night that she collapsed in the street. I was stricken with panic, but he seemed so calm, so collected. The stranger was tall and thin, pale and sharp, and he wore a top hat and a fine suit made of black silk. It was an upscale part of town, so he didn't necessarily look out of place. His smile was cold and narrow, and now that I think of it, I never saw his eyes. The shadow from his hat shielded the top portion of his face from view. He told me that she would die unless I did something, and I tried crying out for help, looking for anyone else on the street, but we were eerily alone. It seemed as though time stood still. Her breathing became shallow, and she was slipping away from me with each passing second. It felt like a nightmare, but I couldn't wake."

Preston's eyes locked onto his father's. He refused to blink and instead stared deep into his father's soul. What he saw was a man full of terror and sadness, but what he heard was even more troubling. This was the moment he dreaded most, but he needed to know the truth.

"The man told me that he could save her. I know now that he was Prendergast. Maybe not the exact man I met tonight, but a version of him. He said, 'I will give you her life, her health, in exchange for yours.' He assured me that I would still live a full life, and that only upon my death would he take what was rightfully his. He promised that she would be healthy, and that she would never remember a thing about that night. You might wonder how I could believe him, but you weren't there, watching her suffer, lying on the cold pavement with our unborn child. I broke down and couldn't control myself. I signed the contract without ever reading a single word. The man rolled up the piece of paper, tilted his hat and said that we would meet again. He vanished into the night, and soon the world began spinning again. I hadn't noticed that the streetlights had gone dark until they flared up, forcing me to shield my eyes. When I ventured a look, Allyson was sitting up, brushing the dirt from her dress. She thought she had slipped and fallen and was laughing about it. She never saw the tears in my eyes, and I was so happy to see her up and well that I never gave it a second thought. I looked up and down the street and saw dozens of people out for a stroll, but I couldn't find the stranger. Believe it or not, I figured that maybe it really was a nightmare. How wrong I was."

Preston still could not blink.

"How…" he said, choking on his words. "How then did she die?"

A weight fell upon Dr. Fox's shoulders and his face saddened. Cain cleared his throat and ventured an interruption.

"Preston...are you sure this is the right time?"

"I am sure," Preston shot back, his words slicing through the dense morning air like a hot knife through butter. "I need to know why I never had a mother. This coward has kept me in the dark for my entire life, and I want to know why he is so afraid of the truth. You have told me how she *almost* died once before, fine, but I want to know what happened to her after that."

Preston shook with anger. His heart skipped a beat and he closed his eyes to keep from being sick. Dr. Fox could no longer control his emotions. His eyes were puffy and red from all the tears, and his lower lip trembled as he tried to speak.

"There was nothing...I could do," he stammered. "Preston, you have to forgive me. I tried...I tried to save her. Prendergast is to blame, it's his fault!"

Dr. Fox was now shouting, lashing out at a distant foe. Preston was shocked by his father's outburst, but he could not give in, not yet.

"Why didn't you tell me?" he asked.

"I still haven't come to terms with it," Dr. Fox said, his voice now hoarse. "Fourteen years later and I still can't believe she is gone. I chased her..."

Dr. Fox paused again, stricken with grief. He clasped his right hand over his mouth and pinched his eyes, tears streaming down the sides of his face.

"She was too close to the edge...it was a windy day and the gusts were the strongest I'd ever felt...she tried to hang on...but she fell…I couldn't reach her…she fell over the cliff…into the water and…and…drowned…"

Preston only heard bits and pieces of the story as his father tried to breathe in-between fits of crying. He forced himself to look down and away from his father. The morning sun was disappearing behind distant clouds and the light on the floor of the train car was instantly extinguished. It was as if all of Preston's hopes and dreams were dashed in the moment when he thought the truth would finally liberate him.

"How was I supposed to tell my son that I watched his mother die?" Dr. Fox said. "I don't. That was the answer I came up with. The guilt has been killing me ever since and I wish Prendergast had taken me sooner. I have lived with this burden for too long, and now you know why I could never face you."

The atmosphere in the train car was so tense that Preston forgot that he and his father were not alone. Errol and Cain were completely silent during the entire conversation while Arthur blended into the wooden planks along the back wall and disappeared from sight. Preston, upset that this was the forum in which he finally learned the truth, started to cry.

"I have never wanted your love, or your generosity," he said. "But I see how things could have been different if you had told me from the beginning. If you loved her so much, then why did you lie to everyone?"

"No one would have understood," Dr. Fox said.

"You think this is what she wanted for us? To hate each other?"

"I never hated you, Preston."

"But you didn't love me. If you did then you would have told me the truth. She was *my* mother."

"And she was my wife, and I loved her with all my heart."

Preston was beyond exhausted, and his body could no longer keep up with his quarrel. He rubbed his eyes raw and tried to slow his heart rate. It seemed forever before someone finally moved. Dr. Fox rolled over and lifted himself onto one knee, then, with both hands he pushed and pushed until he was standing. The train rocked back and forth and the Professor found it difficult to remain poised. He shuffled one foot in front of the other in Preston's direction, while Preston continued to stare at the black floorboards, refusing to look up. Preston was overcome with panic and found it impossible to catch his breath. His chest kept rising and falling, faster and faster, but he wasn't getting any oxygen. Something fell down around his shoulders, some sort of weight. The floor around him became darker as a shadow loomed over top of him and the world became blurry. The weight on his shoulders shifted and something grabbed hold of him. A warm, soft fabric drifted across his face and wrapped him up like a child. His body melted into his father's embrace before he knew what was really happening. Preston was completely bushed, and could not even open his eyes if he wanted, let alone talk. He heard his father muttering "I'm sorry" over and over. Preston believed him for the first time in fourteen years, but his strength was gone. Sleep took hold and he fell prey to his dreams.

Chapter 13

The University

Preston stood on the porch of his home on Lakeshore Drive. He scanned the horizon, nervously looking for something or someone. The sky was dark and tiny droplets of rain fell to the earth all around him. He looked left, then right. He took a few quick steps forward and looked again. He raised a hand to his mouth and yelled. The noise was loud, blood curdling, but the words seemed to be lost, indecipherable. Suddenly, something caught his attention. A rustling of leaves and bushes in the woods to his left. He broke into an immediate sprint, screaming unintelligible words. He reached the woods and the smell of fresh water, cold and deep, filled his senses. He ran and ran without looking back. He pushed small branches out of the way with his limber arms, and blocked his face with nimble hands. A thick branch broke his defenses and jabbed him in the cheek. He felt the pain, the sting of lacerated skin and blood trickling down his chin, but he did not let it slow him down. Whatever he was after was too important to stop now.

Finally, he navigated his way through the brush and fell onto the sparse floor of the forest. The trees stood five or more feet apart and their branches arched high into the atmosphere. He bent at the waist, hands at his knees, catching his breath. His cheek was numb, but the blood dripped like a leaky faucet onto his hands. He looked down and saw the scarlet liquid. It infuriated him, and he scanned the woods again with growing intensity. Snap. Snap. He darted in the direction of the sound, closer and closer to the lake. This time he kept his mouth shut. A figure snuck behind the trees ahead of him; he was closing in. He tripped over a rotten log and planted his face in a dense pile of dead leaves. The smell of dirt and decay made his blood boil. He looked up. There, standing only a few feet from the edge of the water was a blonde haired woman; her watery eyes and frigid stare proved to be the grim illustration of fear.

"Allyson," he said. This time he heard the words.

"Samuel, No!" the woman screamed in surprise and panic. "Don't...don't..."

Preston opened his eyes. He sat up, drenched from head to toe in a cold sweat. He was positioned near the back of the train car, isolated from the others. A dream, he reassured himself, it was just a dream, but that time it felt too real. It was another one of his father's memories, the one Preston wanted desperately to see, but now that he had witnessed the beginning of it, he was not sure if he wanted to know the ending.

Dr. Fox yawned and gazed tiredly into the morning landscape. "Why was she so frightened," Preston thought. She was not afraid of the cliff per se, but instead Preston's father. Dr. Fox had revealed that she fell over the edge and drowned, but the vision showed that she was safe. Surely she would not have taken her own life. Was there someone else there besides his father? The questions gave Preston another headache, and his body barely felt revitalized after such a short catnap. He felt it best to keep the dream to himself for the time being.

It was not until a large hawk landed on the edge of the train doorway that Preston realized Errol was absent. The Therian transformed back into a human and leaned against the open door.

"We are getting close," he said. "The tracks will pass within a mile of the University's south entrance. The train itself will not stop, so we will need to jump."

"Well then, I hope everyone is rested up," Cain said.

Dr. Fox stretched his arms towards the ceiling and tried to shake off his aches and pains.

"As ready as we will ever be I guess," he said faintly, averting his eyes from Preston's resting place. It seemed that the steady flow of truth over the last few hours had caused Dr. Fox to become even more nervous and embarrassed around Preston than ever before. Preston was learning that patience would be his greatest ally in his quest for the truth, even after 14 years of waiting.

Arthur steadied himself next to Errol and blinked at the rising sun.

"Is that where we are going?" he asked, pointing at two massive red turrets rising above the tree line.

"That's it, Briercliff University," Cain said. "The greatest post-secondary establishment this side of the Mississippi River, and

I am not boasting simply because I work there. Nope, it is common knowledge that those ancient stone structures are home to many of the greatest minds in all the world."

"And I am sure that you count yourself among them, eh?" Dr. Fox laughed.

"I would say myself, more so than you, my friend. Although Grishkat certainly far exceeds our talents and abilities. I just hope the old coot hasn't gone and lost all sense of his humanity. The last time I spoke with him was years ago, and he was under the impression that I was secretly a woman."

Preston could not help but laugh.

"It isn't funny at all," Cain said, laughing to himself. "He even tried to ask me to dinner."

Arthur burst into an uncontrollable fit of laughter, coughing in-between chuckles. Cain stared at him with a blank face, and then pushed him in the chest. The Deathless flipped out of the moving train car with a squeal and hit the ground tumbling head over heels.

"Time to exit," Cain announced, smiling as he leapt from the train.

Dr. Fox stepped forward and lined up his jump.

"Are you ready?" he asked his son.

Preston refused to look him in the eye; instead, he leaned closer to Errol and kept his eyes focused on the passing trees.

"I will take care of him, don't worry," Errol said, trying to mediate.

Dr. Fox nodded with disappointment and took his leave. Errol grabbed Preston around the waist and jumped. Both of the men sailed through the air and landed without so much as a crunch of gravel on the ground. Cain continued to brush himself off as Arthur stumbled up behind him, shouting obscenities and pointing his finger at the Professor.

"Oh shut up you dimwit," Cain snapped. "Maybe that will teach you to laugh at me again."

"Leave him alone," Dr. Fox shouted. "Let's get going."

The trek through the outlying brush was arduous, and it took the men nearly another hour to reach the border of the University grounds. The sun was now creeping further up the skyline, inevitably reaching for the heavens. Preston tried to guess at the time, but he was still too groggy to make such deductions. Errol took flight once more to survey their next move. It was mid-week, late morning, and many students and Professors were going about their business in the University Square. From his vantage point, Preston could make out four rectangular buildings encompassing the busy square. A large bell rang in the distance. The largest of the four structures contained a bell tower, which more than likely signaled the hour. Preston thought he saw Errol returning to their position, but the bell caused a flock of pigeons to soar high into the air. Preston lost sight of Errol amidst the retreating fowl.

"We cannot wait much longer," Dr. Fox said, unnervingly. "Prendergast's men already had the jump on us getting here. There is no doubt that we will come in second in this race."

"If so, they might be waiting for us to arrive to finish the job they started at the train depot," Cain said. "We need to make sure that there are no more surprises, and so we use Errol's sense of nature from here on out."

Arthur peeled a long piece of dead skin from just behind his ear. Grief overcame him as he stared at the crumbled flesh in his hand.

"Prendergast's men would not linger in a public place such as this," he groaned. "We Deathless are under strict orders to remain within the confines of the factory or, if we must, travel under cover of darkness, but only in the company of a Viceroy such as Arminius."

"Viceroy? What is that?" Preston asked.

"My mast...I mean, Prendergast's most trustworthy servants. They are the highest in the ranks and answer directly to him."

"So, what does that make you?"

"Bottom feeder if you must know. New recruits are treated with cruelty and disdain. Sadly, it gets only slightly better when you move up."

"How does one become a Viceroy?"

"No clue. I am not sure that one can even *become* a Viceroy. They have been and always will be. I heard rumors that Arminius has been a Deathless for over a decade. It seems impossible, when you consider the rate of decay we have to contend with."

Arthur scratched his neck and once more extracted a thin strand of dead skin. He whimpered at the sight of it.

"But there are strange happenings in the world. All I know is that Arminius is the top Viceroy, so if he came to your father's house the other night then this matter is of utmost importance to his master."

"Recruits. Viceroys. It almost sounds like Prendergast is building an army of Deathless."

Cain, listening covertly until now, turned and spoke directly to Preston.

"I think you may be onto something. It seems to me that Prendergast's business is bigger than we can even imagine; hundreds, if not thousands of Deathless under his thumb – sounds to me like he's planning something big."

Preston thought about his meeting with Arminius. Compared to Arthur, the man seemed like the typical Deathless servant, nothing about his demeanor suggested he held the power which Arthur attested. Errol landed behind them in the brush and took human form. He patted the dirt from his coat and cocked his neck, causing it to crack.

"Well?" Cain asked.

"The coast looks clear. Most of the students and faculty are in session. I did not *see* any Deathless, but they have most definitely been here. I was able to sneak into Grishkat's office through the high window you described. The place is a disaster. Someone or something has been there recently and turned the place upside down. The smell of decay is extremely potent."

"Dammit!" Dr. Fox kicked a rotted tree branch. He paced back and forth with his hand over his mouth.

"Now what?" Cain asked.

Dr. Fox stopped and seized his friend by the collar.

"Now what?! Now what?! I don't think you understand the gravity of this situation!"

Errol separated the two Professors with one solid chop of his right arm.

"They came and left," Cain said. "Experience tells me that they found what they were looking for, which means it is time to move on."

"We need to be sure," Dr. Fox whispered.

"Huh?"

"I said, we need to be sure. Maybe they left because they did *not* find it. Errol, you said yourself that the place was turned upside down, right? How bad was it?"

"Pretty bad. It would have taken quite some time to create a mess like that."

"Which means we have a good chance that they walked away with nothing."

"Forgive me, but I am having trouble following your logic, Samuel," Cain said.

"No time, we need to get into that office immediately."

Cain, flabbergasted and lacking the will to argue, shrugged his shoulders and spit into a puddle of water to his right.

"Errol, lead the way."

Together the five men stepped out of the brush and strolled across the University Park and entered the massive colonial square. They walked with earnestness, and showed no signs of tension. They carried themselves according to the decorum of the institution, but the dirt and grime caked on their clothes and skin gave a rather different impression. Thankfully, only a few stragglers congregated in the square, and most buried their noses in their books as Preston and his comrades hurried past.

Errol took a sharp right turn and headed towards the far end of the square. The building in front of them was labeled Beasley Hall. They climbed the massive stone staircase in mere seconds and entered the structure. Once inside, Errol pointed to a directory on the left-hand side of the doorway. There, Preston read the following in white block lettering pinned against a black background: *Grishkat, Herman, Professor of Antiquity, Room 609.*

"Looks like we have a bit of a climb," Cain said.

They continued up the staircase in front of them. The steps came to an end at a large landing and then proceeded left and right up to the second floor. Then from there they rose up through the center of the building and split a second time. Each consecutive floor was the same. Preston, Arthur, and Dr. Fox consistently took the left side of the stairs while Errol and Cain took the right. Preston began counting how many left turns he took. Eventually he lost count, and suddenly came to the realization that the 6th floor was the top as the staircase ceased to exist. Errol stopped and tentatively sniffed the air. Preston tried to catch his breath, but Errol did not linger long. He caught the scent he was searching for and took off down the hallway to their left. Beasley Hall was a perfect rectangle, and so each floor was nothing but one massive hallway. Preston cautiously glanced over his shoulder, but saw nothing in the hallway at the other end except for a few statues and paintings.

They finally arrived at room 609, the very last door on their left. Errol nodded and stood back to monitor the hallway. Cain stepped forward and put his ear against the door. He remained still for quite some time until he relaxed his shoulders and walked away.

"Sounds quiet enough," he said.

"I told you there was no one inside," Errol remarked.

"Well I thought it better to be safe than sorry."

Cain showed signs of agitation, and that surprised Preston. Professor Benjamin Cain had been the voice of reason since they met.

Dr. Fox cupped his hands together and placed them against the dark window of the door. He pressed his forehead against his forefingers and tried to see inside. Removing his left hand, he grabbed the handle and turned it. It was locked.

"You must be kidding," he said in shock. "Errol, you said that you went inside the office, right?"

"Yes, I flew right in, why?"

Dr. Fox clawed at his hair and clenched his teeth in anger.

"Did it ever occur to you to check the door? How do you presume we enter a locked door *without* drawing attention?!"

CRASH. The window shattered into a thousand little pieces. The sound made Preston jump. Cain removed the handkerchief from his fist and shook it in the air.

"Who said anything about not drawing attention?"

He unlocked the door from the other side and pushed it open. The Professor ushered everyone inside and quickly closed the door before they could be seen.

"Are you insane?!" Dr. Fox hissed in outrage. "Someone will have heard that!"

"Just like someone heard Prendergast's men tear this place apart?"

Dr. Fox raised a finger and opened his mouth, but he froze as he contemplated Cain's words.

"Logic, Samuel. I thought you were an expert."

Cain winked at his friend and started feeling for the light switch on the wall. The room exploded with light. They were standing in a small office, maybe 10 feet by 10 feet, with two doors; the one in which they entered the office, and a second set of large veranda doors to their left. Preston stood closest to the doors, and felt it his duty to take action. He pressed gently against the two walls of glass. They parted with ease, revealing a massive room, almost 5 times the size of the front office. Three small windows along the wall to his right only illuminated sections of the room. Dr. Fox entered behind Preston and flicked another light switch. The place was a disaster. Desks, chairs, cabinets, and bookshelves were broken and overturned at every angle. The floor was littered with papers – white, yellow, and grey.

"Now I understand your reasoning Mr. Cain," Arthur said as he crossed the threshold, staring at the mess like a child at the zoo for the first time. "This is incredible."

"This is just pure chaos," Preston said. "How many Deathless were here?"

Arthur shrugged his shoulders and began sifting through papers on the floor.

"Do you think they found it?" Cain asked.

Dr. Fox sighed heavily, his eyes searching for any clue as to the whereabouts of Professor Grishkat or the Key.

"Well, they were certainly looking for it," he said. "This place has been turned upside down. We may never know if they found it or even Herman for that matter. How would you even begin to decipher the wreckage? Was there a struggle?"

"There is no sign of any blood," Errol remarked. "I smell Deathless, but I do not smell anything else. Using the coats in his closet for scent, I can honestly say that the trail is cold. I don't think Grishkat has been here in quite some time."

Preston stepped over another overturned desk and began sifting through loose papers in one of the drawers. It was impossible to read the cryptic scribbles on the yellow paper. Preston himself was not even sure what he was looking for, but he wanted to at least give the impression that he was helping. He tossed the drawer to the side with an ear-splitting crack.

"Sorry," he said, embarrassed.

The others stared for a moment and then went back to their business as if nothing happened. Preston seized one of the larger, square drawers of the desk and pulled with all his might. Suddenly, the drawer let loose without so much as a soft squeak; it was empty. Preston shrugged his shoulders and laid it gently on top of the others, trying not to make a sound. Something rolled around in the drawer, clicking against the solid oak frame. Preston paused, his brow furrowing, and stared at the drawer. He glanced over the edge and peered inside. Empty.

He lifted the drawer and examined the weight. It was lighter than the other drawers, he was sure of that, but it was not as light as an empty drawer should have been. He tilted the drawer to his right; he heard the same noise and felt the same vibration. Still puzzled, he set the drawer on the floor and knelt beside it. He began pulling and prodding the edges, seeing if any of them were loose. Nothing. He then began tapping along the outside of the drawer, listening for any sort of change in tone.

Knock. Knock. Knock. Wonk.

He stopped. Slowly, he tapped it again. Wonk. And again. Wonk.

"It's hollow," he said out loud.

Errol heard him and stopped digging through a filing cabinet at the other end of the office. He held up his hand, signaling Dr. Fox and Cain, who were busy tearing apart a shelf on the wall. They ignored him and kept working.

"Quiet," Errol hushed them. They ceased their act of barbarism and looked up.

"What did you say Preston?"

Preston, still staring at the bottom of the drawer in-between his legs, responded automatically.

"It's hollow."

Errol and the others rushed to his side, moving broken furniture out of their way.

"What is it?"

"What did you find?"

"Where is the Key?"

The questions smothered Preston, taking the words right out of his mouth before he could catch his breath.

"I…Well…Maybe..."

One word at a time was all he could manage.

Errol seized the drawer and lifted it high above his head. He shook it up and down with dizzying speed, flexing his tremendous muscles in the process. The rolling noise returned.

"Something appears to be–" Cain started, but he was stopped short as Errol slammed the wooden box onto the floor. The drawer exploded on impact, sending shards of timber and brass flying in every direction. Preston shielded his eyes and face, praying that rogue splinters would not impale him.

"You are out of your mind!" Cain shouted. "You could have hurt someone!"

Errol ignored his friend and stepped forward to survey the drawer's remains. He slapped aside the smaller pieces with his giant paw like a bear fishing in a stream.

"There were other ways to do that you know," Cain said. He stood behind Errol, looking over the Therian's shoulder with intrigue. Dr. Fox joined him, and Preston followed suit. Errol picked up an elongated, rectangular piece of wood nearly two inches thick; it was the bottom of the drawer, still intact. Errol placed his ear against the side of the wooden slab and tilted it away from his body. Something rolled the length of the board and stopped.

Preston shuddered at the sound. What if it was the key? What if he had found the key by dumb luck? On the other hand, what if it was something else? Who would hide something in such an inconspicuous spot if it were not important? Errol clamped his hands on opposite ends of the board and applied pressure. Surprisingly, the piece of wood began to bend at the middle like a piece of rubber. Crack. Crack. Crunch! Small splinters split from the edges. CRACK! The board broke in half; Errol now held two equally sized pieces of wood in his hands. Preston saw the secret of the drawer almost immediately, the entire two-inch width of the board was hollow.

Errol shook both of his hands up and down. The slab in his left hand remained quiet, while the one in his right rattled. He flung the piece in his left hand against the wall; it lay amongst the rubble of the office as if it belonged there. Holding out his now empty palm, Errol tilted the piece in his right hand and a small, black marble rolled fell from the hollow space. Preston's heart sank. Errol, dumbfounded, let the wood slip unceremoniously from his grip. All four men stared at the tiny glass ball.

"That's it?" Dr. Fox asked, his voice sullen. "Who the hell would hide a marble?"

"Maybe we missed something," Cain said. "It cannot simply be a common marble, it must be something more."

"Is it? Grishkat was always quirky, but I didn't think that he had completely lost his mind!"

"Maybe..."

"Oh spare me, Benjamin. You and I both know, that thing is nothing but an ordinary glass marble. Don't be a fool."

"A fool? Are you sure you really want to go down that road Samuel. Let us compare our foolishness."

"Oh stop. If we keep looking, then maybe we can find you some jacks to play with as well..."

The two Professors continued bickering while Errol slowly sat on the floor against the far wall and closed his eyes. Preston read pain and exhaustion in his face. The distressed Therian rubbed his shoulder, wincing with every roll of his wrist. Preston altered his line of sight and stared at the black marble lying still on the carpet. He picked it up and let it roll around the rim of his cupped palm. It looked bigger in his hand, and somehow not as dark. In fact, Preston was sure that the color of the object was changing. One second it was black as night, solid and cold, and less than a second later it was cloudy and grey, full of visceral mist. Astounded, Preston stared motionless into the ever-changing glass orb.

"You would not even be here if it wasn't for me and Errol," Cain shouted.

The argument continued in the background, but Preston did not dare take his eyes off the marble. He watched as grey mist turned blue, and then red. Colors swirled in and out of view like smoke in the wind. Despite the sudden rise in Cain's voice, Errol drifted off to sleep. Cain removed his revolver from his coat and the shouting match came to an abrupt end.

"What...what are you doing?" Dr. Fox stammered. "Come now Benjamin. Surely you don't..."

Dr. Fox pleaded with Cain, thinking that their argument had suddenly taken a turn for the worse. Cain spun around, cocked his pistol and aimed towards the veranda doors of the office. Preston noticed the sudden drop in his father's voice, but he still was not aware of the drawn firearm hovering above his head. Something else caught his eye instead.

There was a dark figure standing in the doorway, breathing heavily. Preston raised his eyes, slowly. The shape blended with the shadows. A spark of light flickered in the dark hallway and a single flame floated in the air as if conjured out of nothingness. It was a lighter. The owner lit a cigarette and then snapped the lighter closed. He sucked on the smoldering paper and tobacco, the burning embers setting a faint glow across his face. The man had an eye patch over his left eye, and a long brimmed hat caught the smoke that concealed his face.

"You should be careful where you point that thing, Mr. Cain," the figure grumbled.

It was a Deathless. Errol's eyes snapped open and he shot up off the floor and grabbed Preston by the arm, pulling the young boy close to his chest.

"Not another word," Cain barked at the undead man in the doorway.

Errol held up his hand in warning.

"He is not alone," he said, sniffing the air. "Huddled in the hallway, five...maybe six."

"Why didn't you sense them sooner?!" Cain whispered to the side, angered by the mere fact that they were caught off guard.

"The entire place smells of rotten flesh from before we even arrived. It is kind of hard to distinguish."

Errol blinked uncontrollably, still struggling to keep awake.

"There is no need to be alarmed," the Deathless said, blowing smoke from his nostrils.

"I don't like to repeat myself," Cain shouted, repositioning himself for better accuracy.

Arthur, skulking in the back of the office until now, stepped forward. He blocked Cain's view of the doorway.

"He's not with Prendergast," he said.

"But, how can you tell?" Preston asked.

Arthur clawed at the edge of his coat and shook it hard and fast.

"His clothes are different.." he said. "And they are not covered in soot."

"That simple, huh?" Dr. Fox said.

Arthur nodded.

"Will you get out of the way," Cain growled as he shoved Arthur with his free hand. "Anyone can change their clothes you imbecile."

"Can I speak yet?" the Deathless asked patiently, his lips curling around his cigarette.

"Shut up!" Cain roared.

Dr. Fox clamped down on Cain's wrist and forced his friend to lower the revolver.

"That is enough Benjamin," he said. "We have been in enough danger for one night. I don't need you causing anymore tension with that damned pistol."

Cain's eyes boiled with anger and he hesitated.

"I saved your life tonight with *this* damned pistol!"

The Deathless in the doorway removed his cigarette and tossed it into the hallway. Cain, trembling with fear and an overwhelming feeling of insignificance, refused to take his eyes off of the Deathless. Dr. Fox moved more slowly this time, sliding his fingers along the edge of the revolver, prying his friend's fingers from the grip.

"That's it, good lad," he said, reassuring Cain that it was the right move.

Cain stopped glaring at the doorway and shook his head. It was as if he were hypnotized.

"I...I am sorry," he said, reluctantly, before turning to the side.

"You sure about this?" Dr. Fox whispered to Arthur.

"He is different, I am sure of it," Arthur said.

Dr. Fox took a deep breath, revolver pointed at the floor.

"I apologize for Professor Cain's actions, but we have had a trying night," he said.

"I quite understand," the Deathless responded, his arms folded across his chest. "That explosion at the factory was pretty impressive."

"Aha, yes, well it was unplanned as you can guess. My friend here seems to think that you are not one of Prendergast's men. I am inclined to believe him, but I will hold onto this revolver regardless. I hope you understand."

"Of course."

The Deathless lifted his arms and opened his hands in order to show the present company that he was unarmed.

"Right, now, since it seems that you know who we are, I think it is only fair that you divulge similar information."

"Only seems fair. My name is Franklin."

"Good. Good. Now, here comes the most important question, and the one that will determine whether or not I need to raise this revolver a second time. Why are you here and whom do you work for?"

Dr. Fox steadied himself, ready to act at a moment's notice; Errol closed tighter around Preston, making the young boy as small a target as possible; Cain, overcome by yet another trance, sat on the floor staring at nothing in particular; Arthur quietly took hold of a wooden cane from the wall and concealed it behind his back.

"We originally came for one thing, but it seems as though we have found more than we could have hoped for. We came to make sure that Prendergast's men were gone, and that they left empty handed. On the flip side, it is a good thing that we found you here."

"And why is that?"

"Because Herman Grishkat sent us, and he thinks it is time that the two of you have a little chat."

Chapter 14

Zoar Valley

The next few hours vanished before they could even be counted. Dr. Fox and Cain decided that they could trust Franklin, if even temporarily, and together they began the long trek south of the city to an area known only as Zoar Valley. The wilderness location, considered by many to be the Grand Canyon of the east, was a massive network of

river valleys, cliffs, and lush green forests, stretching for more than 50 miles in every direction. It was there that Franklin claimed Professor Grishkat had been in seclusion, hiding from Prendergast.

Franklin and his men parked their black sedans just off the beaten path, no more than two miles from the last General Goods store on Route 219. Everyone piled out and stretched their legs. Taking in the sheer beauty of the scenery, Preston sat down along the edge of the path and looked out over the Valley spread out before his eyes. A few of Franklin's men went ahead in order to make sure that the trail was safe. Errol took flight and performed his own reconnaissance, while Dr. Fox and Cain discussed a contingency plan. Franklin groaned as he crouched down across from Preston. He rolled a cigarette between his fragile fingers. Flakes of dead skin stuck to the edges of the paper.

"Beautiful," he remarked, licking his lips.

He pulled a lighter from his pocket and snapped the flint. Sparks flashed and a single red flame reached for the sky. It wavered, leaning away from the wind, trying to protect itself. Preston watched with intense focus as small twists of smoke rose from Franklin's hand; dead skin on the Deathless' hand was burning.

"Somewhat like kindling, eh?" Franklin said.

He smiled at Preston and then looked back at his hand.

"Aren't you afraid that it will ignite?" Preston asked.

"Why, should I be? I am already dead, in case you haven't noticed, and I don't feel any pain. I take risks because I have nothing to lose."

"So you have no hope."

"Hope of what? Life after death? All a crock of bull if you ask me."

"I'm not talking about that. I mean, you don't have hope of regaining your soul?"

Franklin glanced around and looked directly into Preston's eyes. He laughed to himself and placed his cigarette on the tip of his curled lips. He lifted the lighter and scorched the end of the cigarette, puffing all the while. Snapping the lighter shut, Franklin leaned back and took the cigarette from his mouth. He never exhaled. He didn't have to.

"I do this out of habit," he explained. "At least, I think that's what it is. Who knows what I used to do before I became this way, but the heat and fire feels right. My lungs are dead, so I guess there is no reason not to do it."

He placed his hands behind his head and situated himself comfortably against the rocks.

"I know what you're thinking," he said.

"What's that?" Preston said.

"You think that you can save me."

Preston contemplated what Franklin said. He was thinking the very same thing, but he was afraid to bring up the topic. Franklin was still a stranger, and Preston had yet to determine whether he was trustworthy.

"I don't want it," Franklin said.

"What do you mean?" Preston asked.

"I don't want my soul back. I am not like your friend Arthur. You have to understand that not all the Deathless are alike. Some crave to relive their unknown pasts; others embrace their new lifestyles. Others yet are completely indifferent."

Franklin retrieved his lighter again from his pocket and flipped open the top. He rolled the flint back and forth in-between his fingers.

"It would be so easy," Franklin whispered.

Preston eased himself down onto the ground, giving his knees a break.

"So what group are you a part of?" he asked.

"Humph? Oh, I am part of the group that watches out for the other groups," Franklin joked. "I am a lone ranger if you catch my drift."

"Do you even care if you die?"

"I'm already dead."

"You know what I mean. You can't let him win like that. He must be stopped."

"Ha, *him*. That's where you're wrong. Prendergast is your enemy, not mine."

Franklin stopped playing with his lighter. He tossed it across the path. It landed in the teenager's lap. Ultimately surprised, Preston picked it up and looked at it.

"Read it," Franklin ordered.

Preston held the lighter between his thumb and forefinger. It was made of polished steel, cold and smooth. With a finger from his other hand he spun the object around in order to see the opposite side. There, etched deep into the case, were the letters 'F.T.B'.

"When I first saw that I figured they had to be initials," Franklin explained. "I have no idea if the lighter was even mine, but it being in my pocket felt like a sign. I looked at the letter 'F' and thought of all the names that start with it. Frederick. Ferris. Ferguson. Fitzgerald. That's when I came up with Franklin. I can't explain why, but it just sounded right. It was a feeling, almost as if something from my past was trying to tell me something."

"So you do care about your past," Preston said.

"You would think so, wouldn't you. No, I don't care at all. This lighter is as close to the past as I want to get. I am not as hopeful as the others. They all think that they are missing out on wives, children, and all manner of joyous occasions. Not me. Prendergast doesn't choose those kinds of people to work for him. He chooses tramps, lowlifes, and criminals. Take your pick. I don't know about you, but I think I am better off living out my days in this life. Maybe it's all part of a bigger plan, you know? Maybe this is punishment for my sins."

"Arthur isn't a criminal," Preston exclaimed. "He is convinced that he has a family back home. He stays with us because he feels he owes us something."

"Well, maybe I just don't want to *owe* anyone anything. Prendergast plays God. It's not natural, and I'm not sure if you should be doing the same thing. Nothing good can come from it Preston, mark my words."

Their conversation was interrupted by the sound of heavy feet on the trail. Franklin tossed his cigarette into the bushes and rose to his feet. Preston started to do the same, but Franklin held up his hand, telling him to hold still. The sound stopped. Something rustled in the bushes as a whistle rang high and long. Franklin smiled at Preston.

"Are you ready?" he asked. "Let's get a move on," he shouted towards the rest of the party.

Cain, Errol, Arthur, and Dr. Fox were already waiting for Preston and Franklin when they stepped onto the path.

"Worried that I might eat your boy, Professor?" Franklin joked.

"Should I be?" Dr. Fox said. "I have eyes on him at all times. I will certainly know if there is trouble, don't you worry about that."

The trek began in an ordinary fashion. The men walked single file, Deathless in the front and Errol at the rear. The sun was only a few degrees short of its peak, and Preston wondered if it was before noon or after. He had lost track of time, and now walked with his eyes toward the sky, trying to chart the course of the fiery sphere.

"Watch your step," Cain advised. "Get your head out of the clouds will you."

Preston's head snapped forward, and he noticed that he was now standing at the edge of steep cliff. The path rose steadily ahead of him and the sound of rushing water echoed throughout the valley. To his right was a vertical rock face that rose at least 100 feet above their heads.

"Stick close to the wall on your right," Franklin shouted.

Preston planted his hands along the cliff face. He felt brave enough to venture a glance over the edge again. The drop off to his left increased with ever step; ten feet; fifteen feet; twenty feet. The trail climbed higher and higher and before long they rose above the tree line. Preston was awestruck, gawking at the magnificent scenery as the valley floor stretched out before him. The tops of the trees looked like grass. He almost felt compelled to step out and run across the emerald field. The cliffs on the opposite side of the valley shone red in the summer sun. There was no shade anywhere in the valley, except beneath the tree line. The sun reached every corner and burned every crevice. It baked the very ground beneath their feet. Preston tried to shield his eyes, but the sun's rays reflected off every surface, making it impossible to escape their wrath. Birds floated up from the trees below them and quickly ascended above the cliffs. The sound of running water became louder and louder.

The path narrowed as they covered more ground. At the start of their hike, the trail measured nearly four feet across. Now, it was barely two feet; cut in half by centuries of rain and wind. Preston wondered how Errol was able to keep his footing on such a small surface. The Therian's shoulders alone measured more than two feet across. Preston tried to turn and look back, but his father grabbed him and spun him forward.

"Keep moving forward," he said. "It's dangerous."

Preston sensed fear and anxiety in his father's voice.

"The path bends to the right around a corner up ahead," Franklin warned. "Be careful and watch your step, as well as the man in front and back of you."

Preston was only fifteen to twenty feet behind the front of the pack. He could not see around Cain or the Deathless, and therefore he could not see the perilous bend in the path. The trail narrowed again, slightly, or at least that was what Preston thought. It could have been a trick of the sun or the heat clouding his mind, but he swore that at least six inches of the trail disappeared before he reached the bend.

"Hang on," Cain shouted back, stopping in his tracks. "Are you okay?"

Cain asked his question without turning around. In fact, he no longer had enough room to turn while standing on the ledge. To their right lay the sheer rock face, void of any rocks to hold onto, and to their left was a thirty foot drop to the treetops, and another fifteen to twenty beyond that to the valley floor. The bushy treetops looked like they would offer cushion and safety from a fall, but Preston knew better than to let his mind play tricks on him like that. A fall from this height meant certain, painful death.

"Are you okay?" Cain reiterated.

"I'm fine," Preston said, choking on his words. He hoped Cain would not detect the fear in his voice. "What does it look like up ahead?"

Cain shuffled his feet forward a few steps and stopped again. Now Preston could see where the path ended and turned to the right. It looked as though the trail emptied into time and space, dropping off into nothingness. Cain leaned against the cliff's face and swung his leg around the corner. He shook his head and dragged the back of his hand across his sweaty face.

"It doesn't look good," he shouted.

A lump formed in Preston's throat. His heart beat faster and his hands trembled.

"This is ridiculous," Dr. Fox yelled. "There must be an easier way."

"You got that right," Cain agreed. "What until you see what's up this way. If we make it out of this alive, I am going to kill Franklin. I don't even care if he's already dead."

Preston turned to face the wall to his right. He planted his forehead against the sizzling rock and closed his eyes. A rush of wind caressed the back of his neck, cooling his blood and his nerves. He heard flapping followed by the high-pitched screech of a bird. The noise startled him, but he was slow to move. He turned and saw the shadow of a very large bird pass above his head. He looked back and found his father alone on the trail.

"We have to go," Cain said. "Just follow my lead and stay close."

He eased his body around the bend and disappeared from sight. Preston was beginning to wonder if he and his father would ever see any of the others again. Maybe there was a colossal void, dark and evil, around the corner, swallowing up weary travelers. He crept along the wall, his left foot refusing to move until his right gave it a nudge.

The bend in the path was a perfect right angle, sharp and well defined. Preston grabbed hold of the corner and took a deep breath. He allowed his left ear to break the barrier first. Overwhelming amounts of noise flooded his eardrum. It sounded like the ocean, bone-breaking waves crashing hard and fast into one another. He allowed his eye to see the madness.

There he stood, teetering on the edge of safety and pure hell. Behind him lie the comforts of the descending path. In front of him roared a thunderous river and an unimaginable feat. The tree line ceased to exist as the path reached the bend; a gray river that rolled some fifty feet below them with frightening speed replaced it.

The path carried straight for the next few feet, curved slightly to the right, and then careened drastically to the left. The river filled the valley floor, from canyon wall to canyon wall, and Preston could barely make out the figures of Franklin and Arthur a few hundred yards ahead. All he knew was that they were safe; standing on what looked like the widest part of the trail. Preston finally looked down at his feet. The path barely measured one foot across at the turn, and appeared to lose more ground over the next few steps toward Cain.

"Just don't look down," Cain hollered. He motioned Preston forward with his free hand.

Preston scanned the Professor's face and found him calm. He was standing on a very wide portion of the trail and it widened even further up near Franklin and Arthur. Errol soared back and forth along the cliff face, squawking from time to time. He was clearly mocking them, and found their peril to be entertaining. Preston was not amused. The threat of injury, or even certain death, was suddenly all too real. One wrong step and he would tumble over the edge into the raging waters below. Even worse, if the river were shallow, then he would hit the riverbed and break every bone in his body. He wondered if he would even live long enough to drown.

"Come on, you're almost there!" Cain yelled.

"Easy for you to say!" Preston called back.

"This is insane," Preston thought. He took a deep breath and held it, hoping that eliminating one bodily function would allow him to focus more on using his feet for finesse. He closed his eyes and swung his left foot around the corner. He tenderly lowered his toes until he found solid ground. He let out a sigh of relief and laughed to himself. "Not too bad," he thought. Then he lowered his heel. The very back of his shoe hung over the edge of the cliff.

"Are you kidding me?!" he screamed.

"You're doing fine, just don't look down," Cain advised.

"What's wrong? What's the matter," Dr. Fox asked, nervously. "Is everything alright?"

"No! My foot doesn't even fit on the trail around the corner!"

Preston was outraged and nearly at a loss for words. How could Franklin deem this the safest route to the Deathless' hideout? Preston hugged his cheek against the wall where his father stood by, waiting. He lifted his left foot and felt the path once again, hoping that maybe his first attempt had simply hit a bad spot. His foot landed in a spot even shallower than the first. Preston swore. A shadow flashed across his body as Errol soared past.

"Do it quick," the Therian screamed as he flew by. He circled and came back. "Don't linger, it's unstable!"

Preston's eyes widened in horror as he realized that the path was actually crumbling underneath his feet. He rubbed his nose against the rock wall and forced his legs to navigate the path ahead of him. The dirt and gravel underneath his left foot was especially dry. Tiny particles of dust trickled over the edge and fell into the water below. The longer he delayed, the less earth he would have left to stand on. He looked up and saw Cain motioning for him to move. Franklin and Arthur were now running back down the path, realizing that there was a problem.

"Be careful, be careful," Dr. Fox cried.

"Quickly now!" Cain shouted.

Preston breathed deep again, filled his lungs and held them. He slid around the corner and planted his right foot just at the bend. He shuffled his left foot another few inches, and followed with his right. He was balanced on the balls of his feet. Plunging his chest against the wall, Preston shimmied a few more inches. The rock face felt like an oven. It scorched his bare skin, causing his blood to boil with anger and frustration. Another step. A small rock rolled under his left foot and made him readjust, reassess.

"You're almost–" Cain started.

The ground under Preston's right foot gave out, causing him to slip. He was caught off guard, seeing as how he half expected it to be the trail under his left foot that would cause him grief. He overcompensated for the slip and kicked furiously at the face of the cliff. He dug his nails into the rock like an ice climber and screamed in fear. Just then his left foot twisted and rolled off the edge.

"No!!" Cain and Dr. Fox shouted in unison.

Preston cracked his chin on the edge of the trail, and his body went flying. He did not even have enough time to cry, or let out a sound. He flipped over and over more times than he could count. The last thing he saw was his father's face, framed by darkness and fear. And in that instant, all he could think about was how it reminded him of his mother's death. Then the world went black.

Chapter 15

Death and War

Voices echoed throughout Preston's head. He thought he heard his name repeated over and over, but it was near impossible to decipher specific words. Suddenly, a thin band of light broke the darkness as his eyes began opening on their own accord. His lids rolled open, revealing three dark figures standing over him.

"Oh thank God," his father said.

"Just breath Preston, just breath," Errol added.

Preston's eyes and ears ached with a dull pain as they cleared. He tried to lift his head, but the weight of his wet clothes tethered him to the rocky floor beneath his back.

"Where...am I?" he asked.

"Try not to move, we need to make sure that you are okay," Cain said.

"I am fine."

"But you took quite a spill."

"Well, apparently I made it out alive."

Despite Cain's warnings, Preston tried a second time to lift his head. Excruciating pain erupted from his jaw and the back of his head, meeting somewhere in the middle of his skull. The sensation made him vomit. Wiping yellow foam from the corner of his mouth, he looked up and saw Franklin with his legs crossed only a few feet away, smoking a cigarette. The Deathless tipped his hat and continued to inhale gray smoke. Multiple hands reached for Preston's arms, but the teenager shooed them away.

"I am fine, I swear," he repeated. "Just tell me what happened."

He sat up too fast and suddenly became dizzy. He closed his eyes and covered his face with the palm of his hand. Any sort of light or movement made his migraine worse. He heard hushed whispers all around him and the sound of running water in the distance.

"You are in Zoar Valley," Franklin said. "You are safe."

"Why is it so cold?" Preston asked, shaking uncontrollably.

"Well, first of all your clothes are soaked, and secondly, you are in a cave, deep underground."

"A cave," Preston repeated. "And how–"

"I saved you, of course," Errol said.

"If you saved me, then why am I drenched?" Preston said, a smile skirting across his face.

"Let's just say I caught you at the last second. Either way, you are safe and sound, so be thankful."

"Oh, I am, I am."

Preston still felt dizzy and sick to his stomach, causing him to act silly. He had never drunk alcohol, but he assumed that being drunk would have had the same effect.

"Ugh," he groaned as he tried to stand up. He stumbled and sat back down on the floor of the cave without removing his hand from his face.

"Better let old 'One-Eye' know that we are here," Franklin said.

Preston was not sure if the Deathless was talking to him, or someone else nearby, and so he decided not to answer. The teen heard the shuffling of feet and boots tapping against stone as someone ran off in the distance. Preston finally mustered the strength to remove his hand and open his eyes. The initial burst of light centered on his forehead, causing him to recoil with pain; however, the longer he kept his eyes open, the quicker the pain subsided. His blurry vision cleared after a few seconds and he could finally see the cave with his own eyes. They sat on a massive stone floor that stretched as far as the eye could see in every direction. The ceiling hung low, allowing sunlight to drop in through large cracks and crevices. The floor was damp and covered in moss in certain areas. He noticed that there was an opening behind him, full of sunlight. The sound of water followed the light, and he assumed that the valley lie in that direction.

At second glance, he realized that many of the boulders surrounding him were not made of stone at all. In fact, they were far more than just inanimate objects. Creating a perimeter around where Preston sat was a throng of men, Deathless to be more exact. Preston counted fifteen at first, but then realized that the number was nearly double that. The opening at the other end of the cave was not as bright as the one behind him, but he noticed a group of dark figures moving toward him. The light behind them cast shadows across Preston's face, and he found it difficult to see who was now standing in front of him.

"All set," said one of the Deathless.

Franklin flicked his cigarette and rose to his feet.

"Time to go my friends," he said. "We will get Preston cleaned up, dried off, and fill up your bellies. Then you meet with Grishkat."

Errol lifted Preston and helped the teenager inch forward. He felt better with each passing second, and pretty soon he was able to walk on his own accord. They left the cave entrance and crossed over into a massive underground jungle. Walls of dirt and stone rose 100 feet into the air, while exotic flowers and trees flourished across the floor of the cavern. Deathless walked, talked, and laughed all around them. Every few feet a large stood erect, and bonfires shed light on the darker corners of the chamber. An enormous spire of solid stone rose from the center of the floor, and crested just below the ceiling. There, a large red tent seemed to call to him.

"That is Grishkat's tent," Franklin said, following Preston's eyes. "You will go there, tonight, but first let's patch you up."

The Deathless stopped and opened the flap of a tent nearby. Preston hesitated, but Franklin insisted with the help of Cain and Dr. Fox. The teen entered the tent, and over the next few hours his chin was stitched up, a roaring bonfire dried his clothes, and he feasted on smoked fish and roasted potatoes. The Deathless did not need food, but apparently Grishkat had ordered that his guest's be served a proper meal.

Many hours passed before Preston was called to the top of the spire. It was nighttime, and a full moon remained still in the cloudless sky, its radiant beams dancing along the edges of the cavern ceiling. The floor looked like a patchwork quilt of moonlight, while bonfires and tents filled in the empty spaces. All in all, the entire grotto was bright and alive like a city.

Preston sat with his hands under his legs, waiting to be called into Grishkat's tent. Torches nearby shed light on the walkway and bridge to his right, and he peaked over the edge from time to time to see the commotion below. Deathless walked to and fro, and most appeared to be happy. Laughter rose from the depths of the cave as someone threw a large piece of wood into one of the fires, causing it to burst forth with new life. The sparks climbed along the sides of the central spire. They turned to dust and ash before they reached Preston, but he swore he could feel the rush of heat.

This is adventure, he reminded himself. Caverns like this do not exist he tried to convince himself as he stared at the moon high above.

"Only in fairytales," Cain said as he exited the tent.

He smiled and nodded towards Preston.

"How did you know what I was thinking?" the boy responded.

"Because we think alike. I was thinking about how this place is pure fantasy."

Cain rested on the rock next to Preston and furled his coat. He took in a deep breath and stared at the sky.

"I have seen a great many things in my lifetime; ancient things that you won't even find in a book, and yet, the natural formation of this cave impresses me beyond measure."

"How was it formed?"

"Years, millions of years of mystery, my boy. We can only glimpse at the process by seeing the result. I have a feeling that this cave was once filled to the brim with water, and over time, the lakes and rivers receded and left us with this splendid hideout."

"Do you think my father knows about places like this?"

"I cannot say, but I'm sure that if he does, then he will take you to see them when this is all over."

"We both know that isn't true. You keep trying to make him out to be a better man than he is. I know you are his friend, but you didn't grow up in that house. You don't know what it was like."

"So you're still bitter?"

"Who isn't bitter after what we've been through? I just wish things could be back to normal, but I am starting to believe that they never will be. In fact, I don't even know what normal is anymore."

"None of us are normal. Look at Errol for instance. He is a dog, a lion, a bird, and who knows what other wild beasts, and yet we like him for who he is, for what he does. He is our friend."

"Somehow I think I might like my father a little better if he could turn into a dog."

Cain laughed out loud and Preston could not help but chuckle to himself. They both sighed and took in the midnight air.

"I can't believe no one ever found this place before the Deathless," Preston said. "It is a shame that it stayed hidden for so long."

"A shame also that we cannot enjoy it forever," Cain responded.

He slapped his hands on his knees and whistled.

"Well, it is time, they are ready for you," he said.

Preston turned to the floor and pushed a pile of gravel with his shoe. He felt nervous for the first time all night.

"Can they be trusted?" Preston asked.

Cain beamed with delight and shook Preston's shoulder.

"You remind me of a younger version of myself; always on the lookout for trouble. A word to the wise Preston; a man who looks for trouble will more than likely find it sooner or later. But more importantly, he will see it coming a mile away."

Preston relaxed his shoulders and took comfort in the Professor's words, then he rose from his resting place and tried to look confident. Cain stood and joined Preston in entering the tent. Preston was first to step through the opening and was astonished by the cleanliness and grandeur of the interior. The other tents in the cavern were exactly how he imagined a tent – cramped, built with scraps of canvas and splintered wood for support, but this structure was obviously built with greater effort and care.

The ceiling was erected with large tree limbs tied together by rope at the ends, and in the center of the tent hung three large lanterns. A massive stone table rose naturally from the floor, and stationed around its rim were six finely crafted wooden chairs. The table was plastered with papers, books, and candles. Preston noticed his father and Errol seated at the far end of the table. Another man was seated right in front of him, with his back facing Preston, and the teenager assumed by the smell of rotting skin that the man was Grishkat.

"I think we are now ready to begin," Cain said as he set himself down in the seat next to Errol. He motioned for Preston to find a seat. The teenager was not sure of decorum for the room, so he apologized and slipped into the nearest chair he could find. Now that he was facing Grishkat he could see why they gave the man the nickname, 'One-Eye'. There, where his left eye should have been, was a gaping black hole the size of a golf ball. The man's right eye, lidless and gray with decay, rolled around in its socket until it focused on Preston. Derelict strands of long gray hair cascaded down the sides of his head, and holes dotted his ears like rotten fruit.

"I have been waiting quite some time for this moment," Grishkat said, gnashing his teeth. "Seeing as how I am the oldest living or dead thing in this godforsaken place, I guess the responsibility falls on me to welcome you to our home."

The room fell quiet as Grishkat stopped to take a breath. Preston wondered if he should wait until the man finished, or if he should respond at that moment. His father coughed and winked at Preston, signaling that a response would be proper.

"Well uh, thank you Mr. um Grishkat," he stammered. "Professor I mean. We are very grateful, that you uh, have decided to help us."

His mind moved quicker than his lips, and before he knew it there was nothing left to say. The pressure of being in the spotlight squeezed down on Preston's lungs as he found it difficult to breath.

Grishkat stared at him with that unblinking eye. Preston desperately wanted to look away.

"You're welcome," Grishkat exhaled. "Now, it is time that we get down to business."

He reached with both hands under the table, and without ever removing his gaze from Preston, revealed a small package and placed it on the table. Errol and Cain leaned forward in their chairs while Dr. Fox pushed a candle aside in order to get a better view.

"This is why you are here gentlemen," Grishkat said. "But I am afraid there is much more to our story than just that."

As he continued to speak, Grishkat's shriveled fingers struggled to untie the bundle. His motor skills had failed him months before, and it took all his strength to grip the twine, let alone undo the knot. Preston, sensing the man's wavering resolve, reached with his tender, youthful fingers, towards the package. Grishkat stopped cold and stared at Preston with sudden fear.

"Don't touch it!!" he shrieked.

Grishkat's eye swayed left to right and then lowered slightly in the direction of Preston's hands. He rubbed his fingers together, dead skin rolling off the tips, and pulled the package close to his chest.

"Forgive me," he stammered, "but you mustn't touch it, no matter the circumstances. Unless...unless you wish to end up like this. This object is pure evil, and curses the body *and* mind."

Grishkat's last words were barely audible as his hands drifted up and down his body. He subconsciously touched his empty eye socket, caressing the rim. Preston reeled his hands and placed them in his lap without a word. Grishkat took a deep breath and twisted the package until it was perpendicular to his chest. It was roughly six inches in length and a few inches wide. Preston felt a weight on his heart as Grishkat began to tear apart the wrappings. His heart pounded at a feverish pace while the Deathless' hands went to work. He tore it open piece by piece, bit by bit. Scraps of shredded paper fell to the floor and landed by his feet. The other men at the table gawked. Grishkat ripped the final strand of paper and unveiled a large, old-fashioned key. It was white, with a hint of yellow, and appeared to be made of stone. The surface of the key was pristine, no marks of use of any kind. It looked like your typical level lock key, with a small protruding bit at the tip and a bow ring at the opposite end. Its angelic polish mesmerized Preston. Even in candlelight the key seemed to glow. A circle adorned the top of the key and Preston looked at the symbol closely, determining that it looked like a star or a snowflake.

"That is the key?" Cain remarked, breaking the silence of the tent. "It looks so ordinary."

Grishkat cleared his throat, demanding attention.

"This is what you have been looking for. This may very well be the most important artifact in the history of mankind. To think that archaeologists such as ourselves spend our entire lives looking for such a discovery. This is a skeleton key, conceived by the Lord of Death, made from a fractured bone of his own body. This object is nearly indestructible, untouchable, and completely unusable by mankind. It was not made for human possession. It was meant for a different master."

"The Lord of Death?" Preston asked, dumbfounded.

Grishkat raised his hand, letting his guests know that they should wait until he finished speaking. His lidless eye was drawn to the key like a moth to a flame.

"But that master shall not have it," Grishkat began again, with renewed vigor. "Do you know what this key is meant for? Do you know why it was made?"

Grishkat stood up from his chair, to the surprise of everyone around the table, and labored along the perimeter of the tent. He appeared to be lost in thought, but his legs held firm.

"Do you?!" He shouted in Cain's ear as he passed the Professor's seat.

"Ow!" Cain screeched. "We don't know anything about the damn key. That is why we are here you old coot!"

"I should have known," Grishkat continued, like a military officer on patrol. "If you had known, then you wouldn't have thought to find it. I shall tell you the story of the key and its master. Then you can decide for yourself if you want to keep on this path, for there is only one place it can lead you.

"I did not notice anything peculiar about the key when I first found it with Samuel. If you remember, Dr. Fox, you didn't even want to touch the thing. At the time I thought you were an egotistical little prat that wasn't cut out for the life of an archaeologist, so I was more than happy to keep the prize to myself, but the big wigs at the University had a different idea. They saw you as the poster boy for the future of archaeology. You were young, well spoken, and handsome; the typical private school prodigy. They gave you all of the press and let it be known that the key was your discovery. That didn't turn out so well for you, now did it."

Grishkat smirked. Dr. Fox furrowed his brow and stared cold and hard at his folded hands. Preston could not tell if his father was angry or embarrassed.

"It wasn't until I was alone in my office that night that the key called to me," Grishkat began again. "I held it in my hands and stared at it, measuring all of its intricacies. That is when it happened. I was overcome with hallucinations. The key itself passed down its entire history into my mind. As you can guess, the burden was too much for a human being to bear, and the overall experience left me scarred and broken in more ways than one. Afterward, students and faculty at the University called me 'Grishkat the Old Bat' because I kept to myself. If only they knew of the horrific things that I saw. I could never bring myself to tell anyone. In a way, I felt as though the weight of the world rested on my shoulders, and fate had determined that it would be my duty to protect the secrets of the key. Now, let me recount what the key showed me.

"The end times began millennia ago, during the first age of mankind. With the creation of our world came the creation of its destruction, the great Harbingers of the impending apocalypse. They were nameless at their creation, as true power should never be named, but mankind in its infancy gave them the titles of 'Horsemen of the Apocalypse', and together they are War, Pestilence, Judgment, and Death. You see, our doom was predetermined from the beginning. From day one of this Earth we have been living on borrowed time. It was established that they, the Harbingers, would wait to be called upon to reap what we had sown. And so, they waited patiently in a world parallel to our own.

"But two of the horsemen became tired of waiting. War and Death, brothers they are, felt that their talents were being wasted. They sat idly by and watched for countless years as humanity bred civilizations, wealth, and prosperity. When they were able, they would intercede and sabotage progress with wars and famine. But they had a bigger plan. They wanted to enslave humanity and claim this world as their own. Being siblings, the horsemen sought council with their brother Judgment and their sister Pestilence.

"First, they chose to speak to their sister. They felt that swaying her towards their cause might ease negotiations with their eldest brother. They met with Pestilence in her garden home, and told her their plan. She scoffed at their proposal, but she neither gave them her blessing nor condemned them. She simply asked them to leave her at peace and not bother her with such things. War became furious and stormed out of his sister's home while Death quietly said his farewells and began scheming for their meeting with Judgment, but his sister had deceived him. She went in secret and revealed Death's sinister plans to Judgment.

"Of the four horsemen, there has always been a leader. Judgment took the role naturally, and his brothers despised him for it. They would never show their contempt, but they knew that his decision on whether to join them or not would hinge on their fealty towards him. On the very next day, the brothers War and Death traveled the road to the Ivory Castle where Judgment lived. A massive city made of pure white stone, right at the center of their world for all to see. The brothers requested an audience with Judgment and he reluctantly granted it to them. In the grand hall, War and Death pleaded their case like children will do with their mother. They praised his accomplishments in hopes that they could influence his decision. Ultimately, Judgment was not amused. He cursed his brothers, and charged them with high treason, sentencing them to prison until the day of reckoning. He felt that they couldn't be trusted, and that the only way to ensure they would uphold their duty would be to force it upon them.

"War's anger bested him, and he unsheathed his infernal sword. He struck blow after blow upon Judgment, but the most blessed harbinger repelled his brother's attacks. Death entered the fray with intent to kill Judgment, but again the King's shield absorbed each blow until his brothers became weary. Finally, Judgment countered, striking War and Death to the ground and forcing them to surrender. With soldiers surrounding them and their older brother at full strength, the two brothers were forced to abandon hope. They were imprisoned within the Ivory Castle and restrained by powerful incantations, and shackles made from the stone of the Ivory Tower itself. Judgment was sure that he had taken all precautions against escape, and so he locked his brothers away in the bowels of his castle and returned to his duties.

"It was some time before Death, the most cunning of the horsemen, devised a plan to escape. The two brothers were locked away in separate wings of the castle, and therefore never had direct contact with one another. But they could always feel each other's presence, feel what the other one was thinking. Death decided that he needed to make an object, full of powerful dark magic that could counteract Judgment's spells. Carefully, he removed one of his ribs and went to work on fashioning it into a key. You see, Death was frighteningly clever, and he knew Judgment would be smart enough to cast different charms on his brothers to prevent them both escaping by the same means. Death created a skeleton key, powerful enough and designed with enough malice that it would open any lock ever created.

"Once the key was complete, Death freed himself and began his search for War. He crept along endless passageways and hid in the shadows. He could feel his brother's presence, but he struggled to focus on the exact location. Soon, word began to spread that one of the prisoners had escaped, and his hopes of freeing his brother appeared to be out of reach. At that instant Death entered a grand furnace room, alit with smithing fires. War was relegated to serving as Judgment's personal blacksmith. Death saw his brother's condition and began to weep. But he wasn't alone. Judgment stood by, close at hand, securing his prisoner. Death would never be able to free War, not in his weakened state. So he concealed his key, crept back into the shadows, and fled the castle.

"He decided that he would go ahead with their plans regardless, and that he would return for his brother when he gathered his strength. It has been many long years since Death entered our world. He lost the skeleton key when he arrived, and has been looking for it ever since. It sounds simple really. Finding the key so close to his home is not a coincidence. Over the years he has been regaining his strength, and therefore the connection between he and the key is slowly being restored. He could sense it nearby, but needed help filling in the final pieces of the puzzle. That is why he wanted your soul. No one ever knew that I had the key. No one except *you*."

Grishkat rested his arms on Samuel's shoulders. Preston was amazed by Grishkat's tenacity. He could not believe that a Deathless could talk, let alone breathe, for such an extended period of time.

"How does it feel to have met Death and lived to tell the tale?" Grishkat asked.

Dr. Fox froze in place and held his breath.

"Yes Samuel, that's right. You understand now the weight of my words. You thought he was Satan the first time you met him, and it was certainly an honest assumption, but he is an even shrewder adversary. Prendergast *is* Death, the Harbinger."

The room fell silent, and the only sound anyone could hear was the distant crackling of the bonfires in the cavern below. Preston finally raised his eyes and pointed them at his father. Dr. Fox looked to Cain and Errol but neither of them offered any sort of consolation. They were just as stunned as he. Dr. Fox pursed his lips and spoke.

"It makes sense now," Dr. Fox said. "The visions that I saw when he took my soul coincide with your story. There is no doubt."

"Unsettling as it may be, I always prided myself on being a trustworthy person, Grishkat said. "I only provide people with the truth, no matter how damning it may be."

Preston could not take his eyes off the key lying in front of Grishkat, even though the sight of it made him sick to his stomach.

"So you are trying to tell me that Prendergast is *Death*? As in, the Grim Reaper?" Errol asked, completely perplexed.

"He is Death, but I am not sure about the whole Grim Reaper thing. I think it is important that we think beyond mankind's representations of the Horsemen. They are far beyond our imaginations and I do not think we can even begin to conceive the full measure of their being. Prendergast is simply a human form. There is no telling what lies beneath the skin and bones."

"That would certainly explain all the Deathless working for him," Cain said. "But I still do not understand how he could lay low for such a long time."

"Simple; he chose his appearance very wisely," Dr. Fox chimed in. "You said yourself, Herman, that he is the most cunning and shrewd of the Horsemen. No doubt that he knew a wealthy, powerful industrialist would have an easy time hiding secrets."

"Precisely," Grishkat added.

Preston, quiet and reserved, continued to stare at the key. He seemed hypnotized by its story. Lying only a few feet away was a piece of Death. It was too far fetched to be real, and yet there was no denying the reality of the last few days. Deathless, Therians, and his strange power – the world was a much stranger place than he ever imagined.

"What do we do now?" Errol asked after a short spell of silence.

"We have to destroy it," Preston said, surprising everyone. "If we destroy it, then we ensure that Death fails."

"It is not that easy," Grishkat lamented. "I am afraid that destroying the key may not be enough to stop Death's plans. He will surely figure out another way to free his brother. We need to find another means to an end."

"I still say that we destroy it," Cain demanded. "If that is what Death is after, then if we destroy it, we end his quest. We need to start somewhere if we are going to stop him."

"Sadly, it is more complicated than that. Remember that I told you that the key is indestructible. What I meant to say is that it is indestructible by the hands of man. The key can still be unmade, or at least its magic removed, by someone with great power."

"One of the Harbingers, I suppose."

"You are correct."

Grishkat turned towards Errol.

"Now I have a question for you. In my research, I found multiple accounts of Therians, or shifters as historians like to call them. On more than one occasion I read stories that told the origins of your people. It appears that your lineage can be traced back to ancient Druids that once roamed the European countryside."

"I have heard such things, but I have never met a '*Drew-It*', as you call them."

"That is a shame. Did you know that Druids are the only known beings on this Earth that have access to the world of the Harbingers? Without the magic of a Druid, I am afraid that we are not going to be able to destroy this Key."

"Then what are we going to do?" Preston asked.

"As an alternative, you might *be* our key, Preston," Grishkat said, his eye now drooping to one side. "Death takes life away, but you have the ability to give it back. You are his antithesis in this world, and I don't believe that your gift or your father's deal with Death is a coincidence. You were given this power for a reason. It might be that you can defeat Death himself."

"How can one possibly destroy Death? That does not make any sense!"

"Do you deny that you have the power to return life?"

"I...I do not understand the power..."

"Well why the hell not?! You brought your father back to life, twice!"

"You do not have any proof of that."

"Oh please spare me, I am sure that everyone else in this room would attest to your ability, whether they have admitted it to you or not."

The heated discussion and Grishkat's insistence aggravated Preston. He stopped and stared around the table at his father and his friends. None of them spoke, and even worse, they all seemed very embarrassed to even make eye contact with Preston. Their body language spoke louder than their words ever could, and served to prove Grishkat right.

"I am not special," he whispered.

"Sadly, you never had a choice Preston. Do you still need hard proof?"

"I think it is *you* that wants proof. Let me guess, you figure that I will bring you back and reverse the curse of the Key?"

The fierceness in Preston's voice silenced Girshkat for a moment. He contemplated the accusation.

"You Deathless sicken me," Preston scowled. "You are *all* selfish."

"Preston please," Dr. Fox started. "Herman has been more than helpful."

Preston folded his arms and tried to slow his breathing. The tent fell silent once again. For the first time, Preston could hear the world outside. Somewhere below them a Deathless was splitting wood.

"Selfish," Grishkat repeated, grief-stricken. "How dare you say that. I understand that everything you have experienced in the last few days has been almost entirely against your will, and that you never wished upon a star for this life, but you need to understand that you are not the only one to make sacrifices."

The elderly Professor stood up and hunched over the top of his cane.

"I have sacrificed, boy have I sacrificed. Do you think I wanted this life? Do you think that I wanted to be cursed with a decaying body? I was married, you know, with kids and everything. I left it all behind after what the key did to me! I could not bear to face the world, but I knew that I had to answer to a higher calling. I took it upon myself, *un*selfishly, to protect the key and its secrets. I dedicated my days to learning everything about Death and his plan for the destruction of mankind. A weaker man would have crumbled under such pressure! Every man at this table would have given up and Death would have found the key a long time ago! So how dare you call me selfish!"

Tears emanated from Grishkat's lidless eye, and streamed down the right side of his face. It was the first time that Preston witnessed a Deathless show emotion. An epiphany struck Preston as he stood up and stared into Grishkat's eye.

"You are not Deathless," he uttered.

Dr. Fox and Cain looked at each other quizzically.

"You still have your soul, don't you?"

"Yes," Grishkat answered.

"How?"

"Who really knows," Grishkat sat back down and grimaced as he hit the chair. "The key has so much mysterious power. That is why I told you that I am cursed. Death did not take my soul, but the key mimics bits and pieces of his power."

"I am sorry." Preston collapsed into his chair, and placed his head in his hands. "I am the selfish one."

"It is quite alright. I get cranky when I get tired. We are, however, running out of time. The key is no longer a secret. Death will be coming for it, and we need a plan."

"You also need to find out what I can do."

"That would be helpful."

"Then let me try my powers on you."

"They won't work. I still have my soul, remember? You need to try it on one of the Deathless."

Preston sat back in his chair. His mind immediately thought of Arthur and his promise.

"Arthur," he whispered.

"Huh?" Grishkat grunted.

"You must be joking," Cain laughed. "That man doesn't deserve–"

"It is my decision," Preston said, cutting Cain short. "If I am going to do this, then it needs to be someone of my choosing. He has more than earned it."

"Very well," Grishkat said. "Summon this 'Arthur' and bring him here."

It took Errol only a few minutes to gather Arthur to Grishkat's tent. A few Deathless were frightened half to death in the process as Errol surveyed the cavern floor as a giant hawk.

"Welcome, Arthur is it?" Grishkat said, turning on his charm.

"Uh yes sir, thank you," Arthur stammered, nervously.

"Preston would like to speak to you."

Arthur's eyes darted around the interior of the tent. He looked from Errol's face to Dr. Fox's, and then to Preston's. He pretended not to even see Cain.

"Arthur, do you remember what you hoped I would do for you?" Preston asked.

Arthur smiled sheepishly and looked at the floor like a little boy asking his crush out on a date.

"Of course I do, but I understand why you cannot."

"Actually, maybe we can help each other. You want your soul, your life, back, and I need to find out more about my power."

"So what are you proposing?"

"Let me help you."

Arthur almost jumped out of his skin with excitement. He showered Preston and the entire present company with thanks, even Cain.

"All I need you to do is come and sit in this chair," Preston ordered.

Arthur was quick as lightning, despite his decaying muscles. Preston took a deep breath and glanced towards his father. To his surprise, he found Dr. Fox looking in the other direction. Preston thought it odd that his father would not pay attention, but he found it even more odd that he had subconsciously looked to his father for strength. He looked back down at Arthur, who was smiling and cupping his hands together as if in the midst of praying. Preston clasped both of his hands around Arthur's hands and held tight. At first nothing happened. Then he recognized the icy sting that emanated from Arthur's skin and he noted the man's soft and mushy flesh. Suddenly, a flash of cold shot up his arm and coursed throughout his entire body, stopping finally in his chest, deep inside his heart. The effect was so swift that Preston did not have time to react. Then another jolt struck his heart a second time. Then another. And another. The next storm of cold and pain struck him hardest and spread to his mind. He closed his eyes and held on tighter. Arthur was surprisingly still, but Preston had little time to consider what others may have been feeling. The next wave of cold erupted and sent images floating through his mind. He saw women gathered around a table, laughing, celebrating a birthday with gifts and cake. Then he saw a throng of children running through a dirty street, cheering as the lead boy held up a baseball high above his head. Another image showed a half-naked woman lying in bed smiling at him. The next thing he saw was a fire, and he could hear voices screaming for help. Now the waves of cold were steady and threatened to freeze his heart. Preston twisted in pain and knelt on the ground. Cain and Errol rose from their seats but Grishkat held up his hand.

"Give him more time!"

Dr. Fox still could not force himself to watch. He closed his eyes, clenched his fists and rocked back and forth in his chair. Preston let out a squeal as the cold forced its way deeper and deeper into his body. Arthur appeared to be frozen in time, lifeless; however, a flush of pink spread across his skin and his lips.

"Come on Preston. Focus!" Grishkat shouted.

Preston cried out in excruciating pain as another image flooded his mind. This time it was different. It was not like the others. A blonde-haired man lay in bed, gasping for air, calling out to someone nearby. His eyes flashed with sparks of blue and white.

"This needs to stop," Cain demanded. "You are killing him!"

"No! You mustn't interfere," Grishkat cried.

The blue light exploded from the man's mouth and eyes, and the world went dark as Preston yelled at the top of his lungs. Preston collapsed to the ground, motionless. Errol leapt over the table and landed at the boy's side. He pulled him up and began feeling for a pulse. Cain brushed passed Grishkat and pushed him out of the way.

"What the hell is wrong with you?! No wonder they called you the bat, you are absolutely bat-crazy you old fool!!"

"Look!"

Grishkat ignored Cain, and instead pointed a solitary finger at Arthur. The man was alive and well. He opened his eyes and looked around the room. He had the greenest eyes Cain had ever seen.

"It...It worked," Arthur said, in utter disbelief. "It worked!"

He looked down and saw Preston lying lifeless on the floor.

"Oh no, oh no no no!"

He scrambled to find a spot next to Errol and began prodding Preston.

"Preston wake up, wake up!"

Dr. Fox fell to ground out of nowhere and took Preston's hand. He had tears in his eyes, but he did not say a word. He seized Preston's hand and held it tight within his own. He closed his eyes and let his tears baptize their joined flesh. Preston's eyes fluttered and he drew in a long breath.

"Oh Thank God," Arthur said.

"It is okay, I am okay," Preston said, his voice hoarse.

Errol gave him some space and let him stagger to his feet on his own. It seemed as though Preston was more than happy just to breath again. He slumped into his chair, and took deep breath after deep breath. Arthur stood next to him; he removed his coat and revealed tan, muscular arms.

"What you have done for me…can never be repaid."

Arthur began sobbing and knelt at Preston's feet as if he were in the presence of royalty. Preston looked over at Grishkat and smiled.

"I guess now we know what I can do," he chuckled.

He reached down and placed his hand on Arthur's shoulder.

"So what is your name?" he asked.

"Merryl. My name is Merryl Callahan."

"Well Merryl, I have to say that you have a beautiful wife and kids."

Merryl laughed, tears in his eyes and his lip quivering. Everyone in the tent took a moment to look at Merryl and smile. They were witness to a power more beautiful than any of them could have ever imagined.

"I believe that is enough for tonight," Grishkat said, trying to contain his happiness. "I can barely focus, and you all need to get your rest. For now, we protect the Key and protect Preston."

Grishkat rose to his feet and hobbled towards the exit of the tent. Cain and Errol immediately entered a heated discussion with Merryl, while Dr. Fox sat back in his chair and rubbed his sore eyes. Preston was the only other person to get up; he felt compelled to walk with Grishkat.

"Sir," he called as he followed the Professor outside.

"Ah, Preston. You of all people need some rest."

Preston smiled and wiped the moisture from his top lip. The trail behind Grishkat smelled horrific, but for once Preston did not mind.

"I just wanted to thank you for everything," he said. "And I wanted to apologize."

"Oh well that is fine, no need, no need. However, since you will be staying here for the night, a word of caution."

Grishkat leaned on his cane and motioned for Preston to come closer. Green foam oozed from a gaping hole on the side of Grishkat's neck. Preston told himself to keep his gaze fixed on the man's one eye.

"This cavern is home to many Deathless. I can vouch for most of them, but as I get older and weaker, new recruits arrive that I am not so sure about. Word will travel fast that you are here, and word will travel even faster once they find out what you can do. Most Deathless have accepted their fate, but some desperately want their old lives back. Think about it. For them, you are a tool to help them get there. It is possible they might do anything to achieve their goal. I mean *anything*."

Preston stared deep into Grishkat's eye and thought for a second that he saw a sign of warmth, a sign of life.

"I can't thank you enough," he whispered. "You have been most generous, and for that I feel as though I have wronged you."

Preston reached into his pocket and removed the glass marble; the mist inside now black and still as the night.

"I found this in your office, and I hate to admit that I took it."

Grishkat stared at the marble with intrigue.

"I have not seen that in years," he said. "But–"

He grabbed Preston's hand and closed it around the marble.

"You may find use for it before I do. Hold onto it, Preston, and if you ever meet a Druid, make sure you show them that stone."

Grishkat smiled and winked with his one eye.

"Which means you may be waiting a very long time," he laughed.

"Thank you again," Preston said.

Grishkat nodded and turned his eye toward the bridge and the path beyond. He shuffled his feet and moved his cane without making a sound.

Chapter 16

Sleepless Nights

Preston returned to the tent that Franklin had set up close to his own lean-to, under direct orders from Grishkat. The lack of camaraderie among the Deathless refugees made Preston nervous, especially after Grishkat warned him of danger. He did not want to spend the night.

"It can get pretty dark in the middle of the night, and so we try our best to keep the fires going," Franklin said. "I hate to ask, but it would be greatly appreciated if one of you could help us out with that."

Franklin stared at Errol even though he addressed the entire group. Errol felt the pressure and decided to stand up and own it.

"I'll help you out if you want, but I don't want to be too far away from the tent," he said.

"I understand, I understand," Franklin said. "Listen, there is no reason to beat around the bush here. I am Grishkat's number one guy. If you can trust him, then you can trust me."

Franklin winked with his patch-less eye.

"I appreciate your concern for our well-being, but we can take care of ourselves," Cain said bluntly. It was obvious that he distrusted Franklin, maybe even more so than Merryl.

"Sure you can," Franklin laughed. "I heard about what happened at the Hold. You killed quite a few men."

"You mean Deathless," Cain snapped.

"Sure…Deathless," Franklin lowered his voice and looked at Merryl. "Deathless. Keep in mind that it is my job here to keep everyone safe. We've had some problems as of late, as I'm sure Grishkat has told you. Sometimes the new arrivals get some crazy ideas and they need to be dealt with. That is why I am in charge of our own little security outfit. We call ourselves the Ghosts."

"The Ghosts?" Preston said.

"What's the matter, you don't like the name? Well it wasn't my idea, I can tell you that. One of my guys thought it was good, seeing as how we work in secret without being seen, sort of like ghosts if you believe in that sort of thing."

Cain and Dr. Fox stopped short and turned to each other.

"Hang on a second," Dr. Fox said. "Herman failed to mention anything about 'problems'".

"What sort of problems are we talking about," Cain asked.

"He told me when I talked with him outside the tent," Preston chimed. "He warned me not to trust anyone. He said that some of the Deathless here became unruly, impatient, dangerous even."

"That would explain the dirty looks I've been getting all night long," Errol remarked, sneering at a handful of Deathless settled around a roaring fire to their right.

"You must realize that we are not all the same," Franklin preached. "We may not have souls, but we still retain logic and reason, some more so than others. I know a few that have abandoned all sense of their past, but I can also name a few here that want nothing ore than to go back to the way things used to be, before they were wronged by Prendergast."

"I find it curious that you only tell us this now, seeing as how we are spending the night," Cain rudely stated, spitting into a torch as he walked. The fire hissed and wavered slightly, only to return to its form.

"I already told Preston about these things before we set out on the trail," Franklin said, defending his actions. He stopped walking and tried to stop himself from wheezing. "I'm sorry if Grishkat and I deemed him to be more important than the lot of you."

"We certainly cannot debate that issue," Merryl said, with a half-hearted smile.

Franklin nodded his head, despite the sudden overwhelming exhaustion that swept over his body.

"Here's your tent, and mine is just on the other side of that boulder. I like it to be dark when I'm sleeping, but you might as well have the heat and light from the fire. Errol, I want you stationed over there. I only ask that you stay for at least half the night, then you can turn in until the morning."

Franklin lowered his voice and curled his finger at Errol.

"Keep an eye on those boys over there. They have been keeping to themselves as of late, and that is not a good sign in this place."

Errol nodded, looking at Franklin's rifle.

"Do I get a weapon?"

Franklin let out a deep, goading laugh.

"I think you have plenty of weapons, my furry friend. Now I say goodnight to you all and sleep tight."

"Goodnight," Preston said. Cain climbed into the tent without saying a word.

Errol gave Dr. Fox a look of concern and then took off toward his post. Merryl explained that he felt compelled to do his part to ensure their safety, and so he planned to walk the cavern and eavesdrop, hoping to find out some pertinent information.

Before he knew it, Preston was all alone outside the tent. He gazed into the fire nearby. The logs fueling the fire were enormous, bigger around than his waist. Little pieces of scorched timber snapped and crackled as the flames turned from yellow to orange to red and then back to yellow. There was no smoke; the wood was dry, and that surprised Preston. The cave felt so damp and cold that he wondered how the Deathless ever found dry lumber, especially logs of such significant size. The voices of Cain and Dr. Fox drifted passed him. Preston swore that he could hear the river at the other end of the cave. At that distance it sounded like a faucet turned half-open.

Preston had almost forgotten about his near death experience during the day. It was not the closeness to death that bothered him; it was the where and how, the fact that he fell over a cliff, and the only thing he saw was his father's face. It was eerily similar to the way in which his mother died, and that frightened him to death.

"Preston?"

The mention of his name jolted him back to reality.

"Psst, Preston come in here," Dr. Fox whispered. He was standing with half of his body outside the tent, motioning with his hand for Preston to move quickly.

Preston rubbed his hands together profusely over the highest arching flame. He could once again feel his fingers. Walking towards the tent, he looked across the path and saw Errol huddled near a bonfire in the distance. He was not alone. Three Deathless also sat around the fire, but none of them seemed to be sharing conversation. Errol, feeling Preston's eyes, turned and met with the boy's gaze. He gave a short attempt at a wave. Preston waved back with more exuberance, pulled back the tent flap with his free hand, and stepped inside.

"Sit down," his father ordered, moving towards the back of the tent in order to make more room. The interior was awfully cramped, and Preston wondered how Franklin ever imagined that all five of them would sleep in the space without laying on top of one another.

"What is it?" Preston asked, not sure why he was called with such urgency.

"Shhhh!"

Cain and Dr. Fox glanced back and forth superstitiously.

"Keep your voice down," Cain advised. "We need to talk."

Cain began with a diatribe about his short history with Grishkat. He repeated over and over that he trusted the Professor as an expert and genuine human being, and Dr. Fox agreed. However, the curse of the key changed the entire situation. Even if Grishkat could still be trusted, there was the matter of an army of Deathless whose alliance was still unknown. The two men disagreed on their next course of action. Cain wanted to leave right away in the middle of the night while Dr. Fox wished to once again consult with Grishkat. Ultimately, they wanted to know where Preston stood on the topic.

"It bothers me that Grishkat never mentioned Franklin. He told me not to trust *anyone* in this place, and Franklin suddenly goes out of his way to make himself appear trustworthy. That is a huge red flag. If Grishkat trusted Franklin, then he would have told me. The question is: who do we trust more – Grishkat or Franklin?"

Cain and Dr. Fox contemplated Preston's analysis.

"What little proof we have definitely supports Grishkat," Cain said. "But his connection with the Key scares me. His enthusiasm should not necessarily be mistaken as loyalty to ending Death's plans. He could be just as easily working for the other side."

"I am not ready to condemn the man," Dr. Fox remarked.

"Oh please Samuel, save the morality crap for another time."

"Listen to me. I worked with Herman for many years. Even though we never really saw eye to eye, he impressed me beyond measure with his knowledge and his goodwill."

"Well since you are such a good judge of character, how about this Franklin fellow?"

"I talked to him when we first reached the valley," Preston recalled. "I liked him at first. He told me that he did *not* want to know more about his past, that he was okay being a Deathless."

"Sounds like the type of guy that would want you out of the picture then," Cain said.

"I fear then that Grishkat himself is in danger," Dr. Fox said. "He's in over his head. Our presence here has jeopardized his vision, and if we leave, then we need to convince him to come with us."

"You think they will just let us walk out?" Cain asked.

"We are not prisoners here," Preston said, trying to convince himself.

"Don't be so naïve kid. We were prisoners the moment they found us at the University. The question is, how far are these guys willing to go to get their souls back. Word will spread about Preston's power. Arthur...I mean Merryl is out there right now making the rounds. That schmuck is probably boasting all about what you did for him."

"You leave Merryl out of this," Preston barked, raising his voice and rising to his feet. "He has been nothing but loyal and he has sworn to protect me and yet you continue to attack him."

"Calm down, calm down," Cain said. "All I am saying is that when they find out, they will take with force what you won't give willingly."

"Then it's settled," Dr. Fox quickly added. "I'm not putting you in danger anymore. We are leaving tonight."

Cain smiled while Preston felt an uneasiness tickle his stomach.

"I will grab Errol, let him know, then meet with Grishkat," Cain said.

He peeled back the opening of the tent and stepped outside. He was surprised to find Franklin sitting by the fire only a few feet away.

"Nature calls?" Franklin asked.

Cain was speechless. Dr. Fox, still sitting inside the tent, smacked his palm against his forehead and shook his head in disbelief.

"You think he heard us?" Preston whispered, his hands trembling with fear. The tickle in his stomach now made him nauseous.

"That's one thing I do not miss, no sir," Franklin joked, stirring the coals on the fire with the butt of his rifle, a cigarette pinched in-between his fingers.

"I will only be a minute," Cain said, laughing to ease the tension.

"Don't travel too far," Franklin advised, his voice trailing off as Cain hustled toward the trail. Franklin coughed and spat a wad of dead tissue into the fire. It sizzled and burned to a charred crisp within seconds.

Dr. Fox held out his hand, a sign that Preston should remain still. He stepped cautiously through the opening of the tent. The world surrounding Preston fell eerily silent as soon as the flap bounced back and hit the floor. The only sound he heard was the hiss of the fire. He held his breath again, subconsciously. The light from the fire cast a flickering rain of shadows on the wall of the tent. Preston's hands stopped trembling but his legs fell asleep, rendering him motionless. He listened intently. Another snap from the fire, followed by a tremendous pop. One of the logs must have collapsed, he thought, trying to convince himself that there was no cause for concern. He still held his breath, and swore he could hear his heart beat deep within his chest. It flooded his head with blood. The lack of oxygen caused his lightheadedness to return full force. Preston was on the verge of passing out when the flap of the tent swung open. The swiftness of the motion sucked the air from his lungs and caused him to cough. When he finally caught his breath, he realized that his father had returned and was standing at the opening.

"Grab your things, we are going," Dr. Fox said in a hurry.

Preston tried to read his father's face, but the fading light only conjured a twisted mask of shadows and darkness over his father's eyes. Preston wanted to leave as quickly as possible; he began to hate the cavern. Seizing Cain's rucksack, Preston crawled out into the cave. The air felt cold on his sweating face, and the fire provided little relief. The second thing Preston noticed was how empty the massive cavern felt. Franklin was gone. There were no voices echoing from far away. Even the fires seemed to stop making noise. Dr. Fox bolted back and forth, sneaking behind rocks and bushes. He looked frantic. Preston glanced to his right and scanned the terrain for any sign of Errol. He found the fire pit where the Therian was stationed, but it burned alone in the night air. Errol was gone. The Deathless who were gathered there were also nowhere to be found. Seeing the lonely fire unsettled Preston.

"Coast is clear," Dr. Fox stated, keeping his voice low.

A shadow passed over Preston's head and landed on top of his father. Dr. Fox let out a sharp squeal and collapsed to the ground. He struggled with the shadow, rolling across the cavern floor. Preston dropped Cain's bag and ran to his father's aid. He clawed at the shadow and was surprised to find that it was solid. His father and the dark shape rolled closer to the fire, the light illuminating the shape of the attacker. It was a Deathless.

The cavern filled with whooping and hollering. Deathless poured like water from the ledge above their tent. They shouted and screamed as loud as their rotten lungs would allow. Some carried axes and large shovels, while others held rifles high above their heads. They looked like hunters, savages, and cannibals, swooping down upon their prey. Preston searched desperately for a weapon to defend himself; a rock; a stick; a large knife jutting out of Cain's sack. He snatched the knife from its sheath just as a Deathless bore down on him. Preston closed his eyes as the Deathless plowed into him, both of them tumbling to the ground. Preston opened one eye, and then the other. The Deathless laid next to him, motionless, the handle of the curved blade protruding from his neck. The wooden knob stood erect, like a monument to Preston's triumph. The sight of it made something change inside Preston. His nausea dissipated, replaced by rage.

Dr. Fox continued to reel back and forth, wrestling his attacker. The rest of the Deathless in the cave formed a perimeter around Preston and his father. They stood at least four to five deep in a massive circle. They barked and snapped like a pack of wild dogs. Preston examined their faces as he retreated closer to the fire.

He was looking for Franklin, convinced that the Ghost had betrayed them. Dr. Fox finally won the battle with his opponent. He grabbed a jagged rock near his foot and slammed it against the Deathless' skull. The man's body went limp; his legs twitched a few times and then remained still. Dr. Fox, nearly out of breath, shifted on his feet and watched in horror as the crowd grew bigger and bigger. He ran to Preston's position and grabbed hold of his son.

"Get Back!" he shouted repeatedly.

The Deathless mocked him and shouted back. A gunshot rang out, sending a shockwave throughout the cavern, followed by silence. After the echo recoiled into the deeper bowels of the caves, Preston thought he once again could hear the sound of running water. The Deathless now acted as though they were sedated, as if the gunshot caused them to regain their sanity. One section of the crowd parted, allowing a solitary figure to step forward. The single Deathless held a rifle in his hands, the barrel still smoking; Preston could even smell the gunpowder. The man stepped forward and stood along the inner circle of the fire pit. He smiled at Preston and Dr. Fox, his lips caught on his black teeth.

"You know what we want," he gargled.

Chapter 17

He Who Brings the Night

The crowd was silent.

"Our lives were stolen from us," the Deathless with the rifle continued. "And we want them back. This doesn't have to be a fight."

"You attacked us first!" Dr. Fox screamed in outrage. "I will not stand for this. Grishkat will not stand for this!"

The crowd let out a dark, sinister laugh.

"That doting old fool," the Deathless said. "We've done his business for far too long. He never had any intentions to help us. He didn't even plan to tell us about your powers. Screw him. We do it ourselves. Get them! Bring them to the spire!"

The crowd returned to acting like wild animals again and roared as they overtook Preston and his father. Preston called for Errol, shouting with all his might, but his voice was instantly drowned out. In a flash, Preston was thrown to the ground and his hands tied behind his back. He lost sight of his father as the

Deathless stood shoulder to shoulder. Claustrophobia set in and Preston cried out that he could not breath, and he began whimpering. The fact that he could not even hear himself scream made him frenzied. The Deathless lifted his body high into the air and carried him effortlessly above their heads. He bobbed up and down like a boat on the open sea. He spotted the spire at the center of the cave, capped by Grishkat's red tent.

The Deathless cheered and danced around their prize, and when they reached the base of the spire the crowd disbursed, revealing a stone slab surrounded by torches. It looked like a tomb, and the sight of it caused Preston to lose control. He tried to kick with his legs and flail with his arms, but the ropes restricted his every move. The hands supporting his back gave way, dropping his body from a frightening height. He landed on the slab without bouncing, the solid earth absorbing all of the force. The pain was delayed as Preston instead looked feverishly for his father. He found his father unconscious, his face bruised and bloodied and his hands and feet tied. Preston's breathing was irregular as he scanned the rest of the cave looking for Merryl, Cain, or Errol. He did not see any sign of a familiar face. Another gunshot skittered across the cavern floor. The crowd subsided and waited for the owner of the rifle to speak.

"Bring out the beast!"

A handful of Deathless dragged a massive figure toward a nearby bonfire. They struggled with the weight of the creature, and it was not until it was almost on top of the fire that Preston recognized the gargantuan shape as Errol. The Therian was also unconscious and appeared to be stuck mid-transformation between man and gorilla; his face covered in jet-black hair while two yellow fangs propped open his lips.

"Unhand me you creep!" Cain shouted as two Deathless shoved him forward. It was as if the crowd had belched and flung him to the ground. He rolled over and stared helplessly at Preston.

"Are you alright?"

"What happened, where did you go?!"

"I could not find Errol, so I went after Grishkat. The bastards attacked me on my way up the spire."

"Where is Franklin?"

"No idea, but that bastard isn't the one who sold us up the river. The guy's name is Simon."

"Be quiet!" Simon shouted.

"That's him."

"Silence!" Simon shouted again. He raised his rifle and leveled it against the back of Dr. Fox's head. "You ain't in any position to argue."

Preston closed his mouth and closed his eyes. The pain spread from the back of his head down his spine.

"Wake up, Errol! Wake up!" Preston shouted.

Errol shifted his weight, but remained asleep.

"Errol!" Cain joined Preston.

Simon, now aggravated, tried to yell over Cain and Preston, but failed.

"Errol for God's sake, wake up!"

"Errol , Errol, ERR…"

FWUMP!

Something large hit the ground behind Preston. It sounded soft and wet. Preston rocked back and forth until he had enough room to crane his neck to investigate. There, lying in a crumpled heap just beyond the stone slab was the lifeless body of Grishkat, eyes wide and frozen in horror. His robes were soaked with blood as black as the night, and his head was partially separated from his body. It looked as though someone tried to saw from one side to the other but did not quite make it through the bone. The contents of Preston's stomach lurched and exploded onto the floor. He coughed and coughed, his body spewing more waste with every wretch.

"You...You...You animals! God Damn You!" Cain cried out.

"A necessary evil," Simon whispered. His smile was gone, replaced by a look of shame. It pained him to kill Grishkat, but he truly believed that it was the only way to be liberated. Preston gawked toward the ceiling of the cave and the rustling of Grishkat's tent.

"Errol, wake up..." Cain whimpered in despair.

"Shut him up," Simon ordered.

A handful of Deathless stepped forward and struck Cain with large sticks. The Professor groaned and cried out in pain. Tears formed in the corners of Preston's eyes and for a moment he felt no physical pain. Grief overcame him so fast that he no longer had time to focus on his injuries.

"What the hell is going on over here?"

The voice was familiar to Preston, but he could not determine who spoke. The Deathless opposite Simon began to move out of the way, making room for another figure to step forward. It was Merryl.

"What in God's name is going on here?"

Merryl stared in horror, mouth wide open. He scanned the cave in silence until he saw Preston lying on the stone slab, helpless, and Grishkat's shattered corpse behind. Without another word he rushed for Preston and started clawing at the boy's ties. A few Deathless motioned towards him but stopped when they saw Simon raise his rifle and pull back the bolt.

"Get away from there," Simon ordered, matter-of-fact.

Merryl ignored him and continued with untying the ropes around Preston's ankles.

"I'm going to get you out of here," he promised the boy.

"Oy!" Simon aimed the rifle high above his head and fired a warning shot.

Merryl stopped moving, stunned by the sound and ferocity of the gunshot.

"Get up, NOW!"

Simon cocked the rifle again and this time aimed steadily at Merryl's chest. Merryl rose slowly to his feet, but he did not raise his hands as Preston expected. There was a renewed sense of confidence in the man ever since his resurrection. Arthur may have been a sniveling coward, but Merryl was rugged. Finally understanding the situation, he stared right back at Simon in defiance.

"Wait a minute..." Simon lowered his rifle slightly as he read over the features of Merryl's face. "You're the one they brought with them, ain't ya? You're the Deathless that arrived yesterday."

"*Was…I was* a Deathless."

Simon's eyebrows arched in surprise and he nearly coughed up a dead lung.

"What do you mean, *was?*"

"Preston and I had a deal."

"What sort of deal?"

"One that doesn't concern you. Just know this, I am going to protect him with my life from here on out. Let him go."

Those last words were addressed to the entire crowd, and they sent a wave of uncertainty throughout the cave. It appeared as though Merryl had made some friends during his evening stroll. Simon recognized that his support was wavering and knew that he needed to act quickly.

"He your friend, ain't he?" he asked Preston, softening the tone of his voice.

Preston nodded.

"Very well."

Another gunshot rang out, completely unexpected. Preston was not even sure what had happened until he saw a short puff of smoke rising in front of Simon's face.

"Preston," Merryl whispered.

Preston turned to his left and caught the look in Merryl's eyes. He saw fear, sadness, and a moment of peace. Merryl slumped to the ground, leaning against the stone slab. He cupped a hand over his stomach as if he were suffering from a stomachache. By the time he reached the floor of the cave, his hand was soaked with blood.

"NOOO!" Preston screeched.

Merryl's lips quivered and he closed his watery eyes. He tried to say something, but blood rolled across his tongue instead of words. Cain lashed out despite the onslaught of Deathless that beat him near death. He knew that their escape depended on Errol waking up. Preston remained in shock. He could not think about anything other than Merryl's wife and children at home, waiting for him to come back to them. Those thoughts fueled his anger toward Simon.

"Get him out of here," Simon ordered, waving his hand in Merryl's direction.

Preston stared into the cold face of his dying friend. Hands entered the frames of his vision from all directions and dragged Merryl away from him. Soon there was nothing left except for a narrow trail of crimson liquid on the floor. Mixed with the dust of the rocks and dirt, the blood looked solid. Cain's shouts became less and less as his injuries finally took their toll. All Preston could hear was Errol's snoring and Cain's heavy, exhausted breathing. The world looked grim and unreal through his tear soaked eyes. Simon walked forward and lifted one foot onto the stone slab near Preston's feet.

"You are going to give us back our souls," he whispered, smiling.

"It doesn't work like that", Preston responded.

"You did it for your friend, that is all the proof we need."

"I…I won't do it."

"You don't have a choice."

"I won't!"

"Give them back!"

"You're crazy...you don't understand!"

"Give me back my soul!"

Simon dropped his rifle and lunged on top of Preston, grabbing hold of the boy's hands. The Deathless crowd held their breath and watched with painstaking anticipation. Nothing happened. Simon opened his eyes and squeezed Preston's hands.

"Do it!" he demanded in a fit of anger.

Preston was still unsure how his power worked. Simon seized Preston by the collar, lifted him up and shouted in his face. The Deathless closed his hands around Preston's once again and squeezed harder than before. He clenched his rotten teeth, forcing puss and phlegm to ooze from gaps along his mouth. Preston grimaced and tried to look away, and that is when he felt it; the cold sting that nearly froze his heart when he held Merryl's hands.

"No!" he shouted, fearful that somehow his power had turned itself on.

"Yes...Yes! I feel it!" Simon screamed, exultant.

A shiver rippled throughout Preston's body. He tried to resist, but his body was weak, and his mind scarred by Merryl's and Grishkat's deaths. An unnatural breeze sifted through his hair and traveled throughout the cave. Tents nearby flapped back and forth and the fires flickered. Another jolt of cold poison passed through his heart, bringing the first of many visions – two men in uniforms lying on the ground, tied up and unconscious. Another man stood to his right, a bandana covering his face and a revolver in his hand. It was a bank robbery.

The cavern slithered back into view as Preston's mind cleared for a moment. He looked up at Simon and saw patches of blonde hair blooming from the top of his head like flowers.

A second vision invaded the teen's mind. This time he held a knife in his hand and pointed it at a frightened woman. The young girl was terrified, tears streaming down her face. She was only half-dressed, her blouse ripped from shoulder to shoulder. She begged him to stop. Preston heard a shrill laugh break the night. Simon squeezed tighter, his face twisted with a menacing smile. Preston was no longer afraid of the cold infecting his body; instead, he was horrified to learn that he was about to let an evil man loose on the world.

The last image flooded his mind. Preston felt like he was submerged in water as he saw a blonde-haired man, finely dressed, sitting in front of a roaring fire. Preston recognized the man. It was the same exact figure that he saw in Merryl's visions. The blonde-haired man was suddenly racked with pain as a blue mist forced its way out of his body. He fell back into his seat and lay there, panting.

"Not much longer…" the man said.

Simon let go and the world came to a screeching halt. Preston was still awake, and not as tired as he was after Merryl's resurrection. Maybe his body was getting used to the power, he thought. Simon, blonde-haired and dark skinned took a step back and stared at his hands.

"It…is…beautiful!" he exclaimed.

He laughed and danced and the Deathless surrounding them cheered.

"It is all yours my friends, you have earned it! Do not leave any scraps!"

The Deathless flooded the stone slab and climbed on top of one another, trying to reach Preston. The boy did not have any time to protest or even cry out for help. Dozens of icy hands latched onto his body and began draining his life force. Visions flashed before his eyes at breakneck speed. He could not think, or even focus. The only thing he noticed other than the slowing of his heart rate was the recurring image of the blonde-haired man, who seemed to be suffering much like Preston. Something seemed strange about the man. He looked familiar, like Preston had seen him even before Merryl's visions. That is when it hit him. The man in those images was his opposite. It was Prendergast. It was Death.

"Wait…" Preston was too weak to warn anyone.

Whenever a Deathless would walk away, flesh renewed, another would take his place instantly. Preston was the fountain of youth and they all wanted a taste.

"He is…"

A Deathless screamed in Preston's ear and skipped away joyously. The boy's body was rigid at this point, freezing from the inside out; his heart rate was almost non-existent, and there were still plenty of Deathless waiting their turn at the spicket.

"He knows…" Preston whispered as his eyes rolled back into his head.

A gunshot crackled through the frigid air, startling the remaining Deathless and newly resurrected souls. They backed away, reluctantly letting go of Preston in the process. The boy felt a sudden rush of hot plasma pump through his heart. He opened his eyes and took in a deep breath. Franklin stood only a few feet away, rifle in his hands.

"Get back!" he shouted.

Franklin waved his hand over his shoulder like a marine captain ordering his troops. A handful of heavily armed Deathless appeared behind him, the Ghosts, and they steadied their weapons, ready to open fire at a moment's notice.

"All of you get the hell out of here before we kill each and every last one of you," Franklin growled. The anger in his eyes struck fear in the crowd, especially the fresh souls who realized they were no longer immortal. Even Simon looked frightened.

Preston was not sure what happened next. A massive explosion shook the entire cavern, sending a shower of rocks and other debris across the floor. When the cloud of dust and dirt settled, many men lay dead or injured, and the moon shone through a gigantic hole in the side of the cave. Preston heard shouting as armed men dressed all in black emptied into the cavern. A few of the injured men lying on the floor raised their hands and cried out for help. The first line of intruders stopped and executed the injured men on the floor without remorse, one of which was Simon. Preston, still recovering, rolled onto the floor and tried to hide behind the stone slab.

More gunshots erupted, followed by raised voices. He looked to his right and saw Franklin, accompanied by the Ghosts, crouching low behind a formation of boulders. They were taking potshots at the intruders, while Franklin shouted orders to the rest of his men to flank to the right. Suddenly, a hand wrapped itself around Preston's ankle, and he screamed in fear.

"Preston, stop!"

It was his father, broken ropes dangling from his wrists, and blood dripping from his nose and a gash above his eyes.

"We have to go!"

Preston grabbed his father's hand and together they ran for cover at the opposite end of the cave.

"I am sorry Preston, I am so sorry…" he kept repeating over and over.

Bullets hissed and snapped as the two men ran along the outer edge of the spire and headed for the river entrance.

Meanwhile, Franklin fell back behind cover and checked his ammo. Eight bullets left. Six to seven gunmen stalked toward his position, ready to kill him when he moved. One of the attackers crouched low along the stone slab, hoping to take a shot from Franklin's right flank. Something behind the man let out a deep, wicked growl. In the next instant he was flying through the air, firing wildly until he landed with a sickening splat against the cavern wall. Errol was awake. The gorilla bore down on the other gunmen, ripping them to shreds and throwing the leftovers into the air. He roared, bringing the attention of the rest of the intruders to his position.

"That's Errol!" Preston hollered. "We have to go back!"

"NO!" Dr. Fox interrupted. "We cannot take anymore risks. It is just you and me now. Come on!"

They crossed the entrance to the cave. The sound of the river could be heard in-between gunshots and yelling. They turned a dark corner only to find a blinding light in their eyes. Preston and his father fell to the ground and shielded their eyes.

"Well, well, well…" The voice sent shivers up and down Preston's spine.

"Arminius…" Dr. Fox whispered.

"These are the two he wants. Kill the rest!" Arminius ordered.

A dark figure stepped in front of the light. Preston heard a crack as his father was struck in the face and knocked unconscious. The boy tried to rise to his feet and fight back, but he slipped on the slick rock under his feet and fell to the ground. Someone or something lifted him into the air and slipped a black cloth over his head.

Arminius and his men carried both Dr. Fox and Preston into the night, leaving behind a mess of bullets and fresh blood spilled throughout Zoar Valley. Clouds rolled in from the north at a slow and steady pace. Rumbles of thunder prickled Preston's ears, but he could not watch as all the light in the world went out. All he could feel was the chill breeze that seemed to rip right through to his heart.

Chapter 18

Lifting the Veil

Street lamps passed in rapid succession as Preston stared coldly at the night sky. His body was nearly paralyzed, but his eyes and thoughts continued to flourish. He lay in the back seat of the black sedan, head pinned against the door, while his father lay crumpled in a heap on the floor. The low rumble of the car's engine groaned beneath him and sent a shudder throughout his body, making his teeth chatter. The globes of fire suspended above the road continued to pass by like comets in the cloudless sky. Preston counted the seconds between each light. One. Two. Three. Blinded one moment and shrouded in gloom the next, he was convinced that even three seconds of darkness was too much.

The car bounced and changed direction. Preston felt his weight shift and the sensation of nausea swept over him. The lights burned out and now he was counting upwards of eight seconds of darkness with no relief in sight. The vehicle slid underneath a steel archway that read *Prendergast Estate* and rocked back and forth as it accelerated uphill. Dr. Fox, stuffed like luggage next to Preston, let out a sustained groan. Preston tried to roll over, but his muscles were still too weak. More lights came into view. They were brighter and closer together than the ones on the main highway.

The car came to a hard stop at the crest of the hill, right in front of the house. A single light hung in the space above the automobile like a full moon, its rays illuminating Preston's face. The hair prickled on the back of Preston's neck and his body stiffened. The door brushing up against his head lifted clear, causing his neck to roll backwards without restraint like a newborn child. His eyes met with two pairs of black boots and cold lifeless hands. After some gentle tugging, Preston was set free and rested in the arms of one of the Deathless. He played witness as the other undead man seized hold of his father and recklessly dragged him from the floor. Preston noticed that the Deathless was anything but gentle with his father. Dr. Fox's head cracked the running board and he landed flat on his face on the pavement. He groaned again, but this time the Deathless heard him cry. The undead man cocked his leg and unloaded a swift, bone breaking kick against Dr. Fox's ribs. Preston wanted to protect his father, but understood all too well that they were now at Death's mercy. Even if he mustered the strength to make a move, he would prove no match for his captors. All he could do was watch his father suffer.

"Bring them into the dining hall," a familiar voice shouted.

Without moving his head, Preston was able to roll his eyes upwards and find Arminius standing at the top of the marble staircase. He was smiling, toothless. Preston's neck snapped back as the Deathless carrying him jerked forward. His father let out a wail as he was kicked again, but his cries were drowned out as two more cars roared up the driveway and rolled to a stop. Both vehicles stood idle, engines rumbling.

Preston, eyes facing the ceiling, took in his surroundings and searched the foyer for any signs of familiar faces. He hoped to see Errol or Cain, or even Merryl, encouraging him to have hope, but their absence killed his sense of faith.

But Preston *did* find a familiar face. The Deathless did not linger in the atrium, and they quickened their pace and made off underneath the balcony, but Preston was sure that he saw Tunnamore, Uncle Thomas, and Aunt Charlotte standing in the atrium like servants. "It can't be," he thought. Uncle Thomas' decaying face turned and looked at Preston as the teenager was carried from the atrium.

"No," he cried. "Please no."

Preston closed his eyes for an instant and when he opened them he found himself standing in a massive dining hall showered in heavenly light. A massive oak table played the centerpiece, but Preston could not take his eyes off the second floor balcony, which was obscured by dusty old drapes. Suddenly overcome with a feeling of déjà vu, he watched as the curtain blocking the balcony swayed ever so gently in an imaginary breeze. A flashback, he thought, from a dream.

His undead escorts placed him gently in a chair at the far end of the table. The little bit of life left in his body escaped when he touched the charcoal seat. A hidden power took hold of him and he began seeing things that were not really there. He saw a large glass of wine and a blonde-haired man sitting at the opposite end; a large parchment rolled out in front of him, beckoning to be read. The lights flickered and everything disappeared. Searing pain forced Preston to close his eyes.

Conversation floated into the room from his left as two more Deathless dragged their decaying feet into the dining hall. They carried Dr. Fox with them, and instead of sitting him in a chair like Preston, they let him flop to the floor like a dead fish. One of the men grabbed the back of Dr. Fox's hair and lifted him until he was on his knees. Dr. Fox clawed at the man's hands, but he could not get free. The Deathless pulled so hard that Preston could see his father's Adam's apple bob up and down with every nervous swallow. Preston could not see his father's eyes; however, he could see his father's teeth just beyond the line of his lips. They were pink, soaked with bloody foam that seeped from the corner of his mouth. The Deathless loosened his grip for a second and Dr. Fox's head creaked forward, the rest of his face now illuminated in the lights above the table. His left eye was bruised and blood spilled from a gash above his brow.

The sound of footsteps at the far side of the table caught Preston's attention. He could not only hear the taps coming closer, but he could also feel them. Something moved amidst the darkness. A head popped into view as if a spotlight had revealed a magic trick on stage. It was a man, golden locks brushing the curvature of his shoulders. The rest of his body took shape out of the darkness and the sounds of his footsteps evaporated into the night, receding into the void behind him. He stood on the edge of the world; light on one side, and pure, everlasting dark on the other. There was no longer any need for introductions. Preston knew right away who stood before him.

It was Death.

It was the Angel of Light and Dark.

"Here we are at last," Death said, smiling and standing at the edge of the table. "You have caused me a great deal of trouble, and yet, I feel as though I need to thank you."

Death's voice was unlike anything Preston had ever heard. It was deep, but fragile, and pierced the boy's head like the screech of a violin. Death stretched his right arm and turned his hand, palm towards the glass ceiling. It did not look like an ordinary hand; instead, his hand was eerily smooth without any sign of aging whatsoever, and it looked extremely pale, almost chalk-like. Death winked at Preston, and balled his hand into a tight fist, squeezing harder and harder. Darkness crept up behind him and rolled across his shoulder like smoke. It danced along his outstretched arm and finally crashed like the ocean into his hand. Preston stared in awe as Death slowly unrolled his fingers, revealing the skeleton key.

"After all these years," Death said, staring at the key in amazement. "You are finally brought to me by the most unlikely of beings. I could have never foreseen these turn of events, but I am starting to understand why mankind invests so much faith in the power of luck."

Dr. Fox grumbled and began huffing and puffing. He could not speak, and this frightened Preston.

"Did you want to say something Samuel?" Death asked.

He set the key on the table and crossed his arms across his chest. Preston was not sure who or what he should be looking at; his father, Death, or the key.

"You won't be talking anytime soon by the looks of it. My men broke your jaw," Death said. "Now, I understand that you have suffered much since meeting me, but I intend to make things right with you...the both of you. You won't need to talk tonight because I will be doing the talking *for* you. I intend to settle this little father and son quarrel once and for all, but don't worry my friend, since you have brought me to the key *and* your son, I think it is fitting that I will give you a proper, painless send off...after we hear the truth."

Preston glanced over at his father and saw the agony in his face.

"Do you want to learn the truth about your mother?" Death asked.

Preston blinked until he was sure that he was not dreaming. He retraced his memories and remembered his father telling him the truth on the train after escaping the Hold. Preston was so sure that his father had finally told him the truth. It felt so genuine, he thought.

"I...I know the truth," Preston managed to say, warmth flooding his throat and tongue.

"He speaks!" Death cried out, amused by Preston's courage to speak. "You are a tenacious little boy to have come so far and still have the strength to speak. You know who I am, and yet, you show extreme resilience, not fear. I am truly amazed! Preston, I mean the *truth*, not the story that your father has fabricated over the years. I believe you deserve to hear what really happened the night your mother died."

Dr. Fox, overcome with anger, tried to break free a second time, but the Deathless held him firmly in place. He sounded like an exhausted racehorse as he inhaled and exhaled rapidly through pursed lips. The pain from his jaw sent adrenaline surging throughout his body. Pink spittle dribbled down his chin and stained his face. Death simply laughed.

You want the truth, I know, said a voice inside Preston's head. Preston recognized Death's voice even though the Harbinger's lips were no longer moving. *I will tell you what your father has been too afraid to say.*

The voice echoed and touched every corner of Preston's mind until it faded into nothingness. Death's mouth moved again as he spoke out loud.

"You have no doubt seen the memories that your father kept locked away. I wonder how they, like the man himself, have deceived you. Your father was deranged with sadness and fear for so long that it is possible he convinced himself of a false sense of the truth. If he believed in his story for long enough, then maybe it would replace what really happened. I mean, in all reality he is the only one who can tell the story, right? She fell off the cliff and drowned in the lake, that's what he told you, but didn't you notice something odd about your dreams, your father's memories?"

I know I did, came the cold, hissing voice inside Preston's head. *Come now, I know you thought it strange.*

Death walked slowly around the side of the table towards Dr. Fox. He soundlessly traced the smooth oak surface with his ghastly finger, leaving behind a black smudge.

"It was the look on your mother's face," he said.

The image of his mother standing at the edge of the cliff invaded Preston's mind. Death drifted into the darkness, the glass ceiling exploded and turned to dust, and the shapes of the Deathless and Dr. Fox became one with the ground beneath his feet. It no longer felt like a dream; instead, Preston felt as though he was literally standing in the forest on the night his mother died. He turned and saw her standing in the open with the lake spread out endlessly behind her as a backdrop. It was picture perfect. She was beautiful, more beautiful than he remembered from before, but there was something terribly wrong. Clouds rolled in from the horizon as the world stood still, and a look of undeniable terror spread across her face. The image disappeared and the dining hall returned.

"She was frightened" Preston whispered.

"Yes!" Death announced. "She was afraid before she fell. Does it look like an accident to you?"

Dr. Fox lashed out at the Deathless holding him. His body revealed the emotions that his voice could not, and everyone in the room was forced to look at him.

"Oh, please," Death barked. "I am simply doing you a favor. I am doing what you should have done years ago."

Death stood only a few feet from where Dr. Fox knelt on the floor. The latter looked like a servant bowing to his master, but the sheer ferocity in Dr. Fox's eyes told a different story. His face was so red with anger that you could no longer detect the bloodstains on his chin or above his eye.

"Preston, your mother was afraid of your father," Death continued. "She was afraid that he was going to kill her. She found out about the contract he signed, and she also found out that the ownership of his soul was dependent on her life. If he killed her, then he could keep his soul, or so he thought. She believed this to be true."

Death paused for effect, forcing Preston to hang onto every word.

"But your father never read the contract before he signed it. Her death had no bearing on the ownership of his soul. I brought her back from the dead once, that was the deal, and I warned him that whatever happened after that was none of my concern. And yet, he didn't listen and *killed* your mother. He was fueled by fear of the unknown. He killed her in cold blood."

Preston was launched back into his father's memories. He saw his mother running through the woods, crying and shouting something that sounded like 'stay away'. Preston had experienced these memories once before, but this time he saw things differently. Everything seemed clearer this time, and there was no longer any room for interpretation or doubt. It was as if the original version of the story was full of gaps and now they were magically filled in.

"He ran her down like a beast hunting its prey," Death said.

Preston's mother kept yelling as she stumbled through the rough terrain, tripping over downed logs and patches of overgrowth. He could hear the waves crashing against the cliffs only a few hundred yards ahead.

"Your father cornered her."

She tumbled to the ground just short of the cliff. Stones and pebbles skittered over the edge and fell into the chaotic mess of fresh water below. She gathered herself and turned. Her eyes were bloodshot and tears streamed down her cheeks. She kept saying 'No' over and over again, as if warning her husband.

The world transformed again and Preston was pulled back to the dining hall by his father's tantrum. Dr. Fox howled at the top of his lungs, a noise that sounded like 'No'. He fought so hard that the Deathless was forced to take his head and smash it into the floor, pinning him there.

"He pushed her," Death said.

A pair of hands rose in front of Preston's face and reached for his mother. He was back inside the memory. She closed her eyes and fell over the edge. The rest of the vision was familiar. Preston's mother fell, eyes shut, into the angry sea below. The waves eclipsed her body instantly and she disappeared from sight. Wind blew a pile of dead leaves over the edge, and as they floated along the Cliffside her body surfaced one last time before it was swept under the current.

"No!" Dr. Fox screamed. This time there was no denying what the Professor said, despite his broken jaw. Tears, blood, and sweat pooled beneath his face on the floor. One Deathless held his head to the floor while the other gripped both of his hands behind his back. The story had upset Dr. Fox beyond contention. Bits and pieces of the dream faded until Preston realized that it was over, gone forever. He still lacked the strength to lift either his legs or his arms, but he could now turn and face his father, tears in his eyes.

"You…You killed her?" he cried.

Dr. Fox slowed his breathing and tried to speak.

"No…No…I…Saved….Her"

He was forced to stop short as blood poured from his mouth. He spat on the floor and returned to crying. Death hovered close by, waiting for his turn to speak. Preston could not say anything more. He began to hyperventilate and found it difficult to breath. He choked on his tears.

"Now you know the truth, Preston," Death said, changing his tone. It sounded as if he were trying to comfort Preston. "Your father killed your mother because he thought he could save himself. It was a rash decision made by a selfish man full of cowardice. You have been right to hate him all these years."

Death rubbed his fingers together. He wanted to touch Preston, maybe even hold his hand, but he knew that such things must wait. Preston, on the other hand, was still in shock when Death spoke again.

"I put the power of God in your hands tonight, Preston," he started. "I have provided you with ample evidence. Now, all you have to do is choose. Will you spare the life of your father, and let him keep his soul. Or, will you renounce him, and allow me to take once again what is rightfully mine."

Preston stared at his father lying on the floor. The Professor was barely conscious, but his eyes met with his son's. There was no emotion; he simply stared into space as if he had already given up. It came as no surprise that Preston now hated his father more than ever before. He became feverish with rage and wished that he had the strength to exact revenge for his mother's murder.

"All you have to do is tell me what you want," Death said, kneeling next to Dr. Fox. "Tell me…life…or death…and I will take care of the rest."

A single word crawled like a spider along the rim of Preston's mind.

"He killed your mother in cold blood, and then lied to cover it up."

The word clawed its way deeper and deeper until it found a web of old memories and infinite lies, and that is where it found the truth. It jumped and spiraled until it hovered just above Preston's tongue. One single word.

"Death," he said.

The word entered the world and immediately changed the course of history. Preston's body relaxed and his mind went blank. It was if his body was shutting itself down. Dr. Fox's expression remained emotionless while he continued to stare into his son's eyes, and Preston thought that his father looked peaceful in that moment. All of his pain and sorrow were about to end. The sentence seemed justified, seeing as how Dr. Fox brought all his misery upon himself, but Preston did not find any satisfaction in his decision. Something was not right; he was supposed to feel liberated. He finally learned the truth about his mother, and he was about to avenge her death. Then why did what happened next startle him so?

"Very well then," Death said, smiling ear to ear.

The Deathless released Dr. Fox and backed away from their master. Death seized the Professor by the throat and lifted him clear off the ground, feet dangling. Dr. Fox continued to stare into Preston's eyes. His breathing was extremely shallow, but he was still alive, even if barely. Death raised his free hand and cupped it over Dr. Fox's face. The Professor's feet kicked once as a blue mist began pouring from his mouth. It wrapped round and round Death's arm until it swirled around his body and drifted upwards towards the balcony.

Preston's watery eyes could not shake his father's gaze. His lips trembled as he witnessed the last ounce of life exit his father's body. Dr. Fox's eyes went dark, and his skin turned pale. Death lowered the Professor's body and laid him gently on the floor. He lay there just as he did in his casket only a few days before. Preston wanted to say something, but he was overcome with grief. "What have I done?" he thought.

Death stepped back and watched as Dr. Fox's soul sailed through the air and scaled the second floor balcony. It hung in the air next to the curtain, waiting for something. A soft wind, not felt by anyone in the dining hall, shifted the drape and let the soul pass through. The room fell silent once again. Preston's soft whimpers were the only sound that could be heard.

Take him away and leave us, the voice roared inside Preston's head. The voice sounded different this time, suddenly deeper and much, much stronger. The Deathless scraped Dr. Fox's body off the floor and carried him out of the dining hall. The doors shut behind them with a bang that shook the panes of glass spread across the ceiling. Preston tried to speak, but could not find the words. It seemed as though 'death' would be the last word he would ever say. Maybe it was fitting.

Now is the time that we meet face to face, Preston Fox.

Death rose to his feet and began shaking uncontrollably, his body racked with convulsions and his eyes went white. He clawed at the table, trying to stay on his feet, but the strength of the seizure sent him flying across the floor. His mouth broke open and Preston heard a sound like nothing he had ever heard before. A shadow poured from Death's mouth and instantly filled the room. The lights above the table went cold and dark, and the mysterious golden light that hung in the air was swallowed by the darkness. The room became frigid and Preston's tears froze to the sides of his face.

The shadow was thick like mist and Preston had trouble seeing anything. He was afraid that not being able to move had left him vulnerable. He tried to get his muscles to respond, but they refused. Unexpectedly, the shadow began to recede towards the balcony as if a vacuum had been turned on. It climbed higher and higher until it disappeared through the curtain. The dining hall was still shrouded in darkness.

Humans are so fragile, Death said. *I find it amazing that they can be sustained for so long by something as simple as a soul. Prendergast served his purpose, but I no longer need him as a vessel. I have been very busy as of late, and your father's soul was all I needed to regain my strength. Well, almost.*

Preston gazed up at the curtain, drawn to the voice that now emanated from behind it. A pair of black, stone-like hands clawed their way through the screen. They turned in unison and parted the curtain, and the shadow returned, enveloping the hands and clouding Preston's vision. Mist splashed on the table and the floor like a waterfall and brushed against Preston's face; it felt like diving into a frozen pond and instantly took his breath away. He heard something other than wind whistling through his ears. It sounded like steel, clanking against something hard. Two orbs of blue light pierced the darkness at the opposite end of the table. They were suspended in the shadow, only a few inches apart. They looked like eyes.

I still need your soul, Preston.

Chapter 19

The Ghosts

The darkness transformed into tentacles and folded itself in and around the blue eyes. It withdrew from the other areas of the dining hall, hording itself at the opposite end of the table. Some sort of metal glistened through the veil as light from the devilish blue eyes lit up the room. There was a person sitting across from Preston, he was sure of it, but the darkness protected the being.

You were the one thing that even I could not plan for.

The eyes moved and lifted higher and higher until the figure stood erect. Shadows dripped from Death's face, leaving behind a hairless, skeletal figure wearing a cold mask of steel. The cage affixed to his face only covered the space between his eyes and his chin. His forehead arched away from Preston, but the boy saw the bluish skin that spread thinly across Death's skull. The darkness receded further behind its master as he walked forward, revealing a suit of ebony steel that protected his entire body. The armor was light and accessible, which allowed him to move with frightening agility, and in a flash he leapt onto the table and stood above Preston.

Your soul is so very powerful.

Preston tried to move, tried to look away, but his body was ensnared. His breath froze as it rolled across his lips and floated up in front of his eyes. Goosebumps spread across his skin and he felt the pain of cold air rushing into his lungs. It hurt to breathe.

The oak table crunched underneath Death's feet as he took another step towards Preston. Ice spread across the room like a tidal wave, and Preston heard another crunch and then a crack. He rolled his eyes and saw ice climbing up the armrests of his chair, surrounding him. It spread like wild fire and burned his skin with frostbite as it clawed at his ankles and wrists. Death stood still only a few feet from Preston and crouched down low. His cold eyes pierced the essence of Preston's soul, and for a fleeting second the boy was convinced that he was already dead.

Let us see what your soul can do for me.

Two black sedans sped up the driveway and came to an abrupt stop at the foot of the main house of the Prendergast Estate. Two Deathless in service of Death approached the vehicles. The driver of the first car, a Deathless, exited and waved to his welcoming party.

"Good to see you boys again," the man remarked, burping up stomach acid.

"What are you doing here?" one of the guards asked. "If you are coming from the Valley then you need to report directly to the Hold."

The driver plucked a steel lighter from his pocket and flicked it open. He cautiously lit the yellow end of the cigarette balanced between his lips. He took a meditated drag and then released a cloud of black smoke into the night air.

"We just came from the Hold. Preston wasn't there, so we figured this was the next stop."

Three gunshots broke the silence of the night and the two guards fell to the ground without ever raising their weapons. The driver, unarmed, continued to puff on his cigarette. His passenger stepped out of the car and checked the smoking barrel of his revolver.

"Going in hot?" he asked.

The driver dropped his cigarette and stomped out the smoldering ashes. He lifted the cloak from over his face. It was Franklin.

"We go in, we get the boy, and we get the hell out," he ordered as a handful of Ghosts swarmed the steps leading up to the front door. "Kill every last one of these Bastards."

He kicked open the trunk and removed one solitary stick of dynamite. He whipped out his trusty lighter and lit the fuse. The cable flared up and sent sparks flying in every which direction. Franklin flung the stick at the front door and then knelt down close to the car for cover. Within seconds the lit fuse struck the blasting cap and the TNT spit out fire at an alarming rate. The door, which stood for centuries, crumbled, blowing debris and smoke into the atrium. The Ghosts piled in and began firing at the Deathless inside. Franklin seized his rifle, closed the trunk, and stormed up the steps.

Death had stopped his approach towards Preston when the first round of gunshots echoed from beyond the closed doors. The cold creature stared at the hallway in awe and took a step back for a moment, almost as if he was second-guessing his next move.

A rescue, eh? No matter.

Emboldened by a truth that Preston could not fathom, Death reached out once again to touch the boy. Closer and closer. But something was different, something had changed with the sound of gunfire. Then the dynamite exploded in the atrium, sending a shiver down Death's spine. His hand trembled only inches from Preston's throat. Was he suddenly afraid, Preston thought. The boy stared into Death's eyes, waiting for the ice to take him. He imagined that losing his soul would feel similar to the cold sting he felt when he brought back Merryl. Preston was about to close his eyes when he noticed a change in the amount of light sifting through the glass ceiling. It was as though a shadow had passed underneath the moon. Death's finger scratched the edge of Preston's Adam's apple as the ceiling exploded into a shower of glass. An enormous shadow landed on the table with an earth-shattering crack. The ice lifted and split along the edges like an iceberg. Death was thrown from his position above Preston to the floor to the boy's right. Preston felt warmth return to his chest and spread to his limbs. He broke free from the wintry grasp of the frozen chair and flung his body on top of the table. The shadow unraveled its gigantic wings and spread them across the room; it was Errol to the rescue.

"Preston, hurry!" he squawked.

Preston climbed onto the table as quick as possible, not taking a chance to look back towards Death. Shards of glass and ice crunched under his weight, and he cut himself more than once as he clambered towards Errol's landing. Preston reached Errol and tried to swing himself around in order to climb on top of his friend, but a drastic change in Errol's appearance made him hesitate. Errol's yellow eyes grew wide with fear, and his feathers gave way to long black fur, and his beak split into large fangs. Errol transformed into a gorilla within seconds. His muscular arms knocked Preston from the table and lunged at Death, who was only a few feet behind Preston. Death's eyes blazed with renewed vigor, and Preston felt the room grow colder and colder with every waning second. Death was faster and more powerful than Errol could have imagined. The Harbinger caught Errol by the throat, causing the lumbering behemoth to stop dead in his tracks. Errol's massive black arms fell limp at his sides as Death lifted him clear from the table.

Foolish animal!

Ice spread once again, filling the gaps of the broken table. Puffs of moisture escaped Errol's mouth as he struggled to breath. Death lifted him higher and higher and then squeezed tight. Errol's feet twitched as his soul poured from his mouth. Preston sat idle, but something woke deep inside of him. Realizing that his body burned with warmth and life even as the icy sting of death surrounded him, Preston jumped to his feet and sprinted towards the table. Errol's soul wafted slowly in the direction of its new master. Preston shouted as he ran.

"Stop!"

He plowed into Death with all his might. An explosion shook the bones of the aged house, sending Preston sailing across the room. The entire dining room was bathed in blue light that erupted from the open ceiling like a volcano reaching for the heavens. Death and Errol were thrown in opposite directions. Frozen chairs and vases shattered instantly. As the light subsided, the room was left in ruins, dust and steam filling the air. Preston, deaf and convinced that his arm was broken, still managed to get to his feet and stumbled forward.

"Errol!" he shouted in earnest.

He glanced cautiously over his shoulder as he walked, looking for any sign of Death.

"Errol!" he shouted again.

Something shifted in the rubble to his left. He stopped and started to shake, half expecting it to be Death. A large, human hand rose into the air from underneath a pile of wood and plaster. Preston started clawing at the debris. He cleared a small section by lifting a large wooden plank, and Errol coughed uncontrollably as he realized that he was still alive, his soul intact.

"Come on," Preston pleaded, pulling on Errol's uncovered arm.

The Therian screeched in pain while more gunshots filled the atrium on the other side of the doors.

"You have to get up, we need to go!"

Errol tried to remove the plaster from his legs but his body was weak.

"You...you have to go without me," he whispered in despair. "You have to get to Franklin, and get clear of this place."

"Not without you, I am not leaving you," Preston cried.

"I saved your life once, and you returned the favor. We are even. Now GO!"

The doors to the dining room broke open as two Deathless caught in a endless struggle punched and stabbed each other until they fell to the floor. Gunshots snapped and cracked in the hallway.

"GO!" Errol shouted once more.

Preston, under his own volition, jumped to his feet and took flight. He reached the door to the hallway and peaked around the corner. Deathless were spread out all over the place, taking potshots at one another and ducking behind cover. He could not distinguish the difference between Franklin's Ghosts and Prendergast's lackeys. One of the Deathless nearby turned and caught sight of Preston. At first he did not act surprised, until he realized who Preston was. The man swung around, his rifle pointed at Preston and began shouting. Preston pressed his back against the wall and started to inch his way in the opposite direction. The Deathless stomped forward and his body was instantly riddled with bullets, the final shot piercing his brain. He slumped to the floor, lifeless. Another Deathless, holding a machine gun and carrying a rifle across his back turned the corner. He was smoking a cigarette, relieved to see the boy.

"Franklin!" Preston cried out.

"Come on! We need to go!" the leader of the Ghosts shouted as tilted his head.

Preston filed in behind Franklin and together they made for the front door. There were countless bodies strewn about the floor, the stairs, and hanging from the edges of the balcony. Gunshots continued to make music throughout the house. As they reached the front door, Preston stopped and looked back one more time in the direction of the dining room. He hoped to see Errol bringing up the rear, but more importantly he prayed to God that he would not see

Death hot on their tail. Nothing was there; no movement, and no sign of life.

"Come on!" Franklin shouted with urgency.

Preston ran down the marble steps outside, taking two at a time. He landed hard at the bottom and took to the pavement. Franklin kicked open the trunk of the first car and threw his machine gun to the ground. Preston opened the passenger door and was about to climb in when Franklin stopped him.

"Whoa, hold on there son," he barked nervously. "This is not our ride out of here. Get in the other car and wait for me."

Preston did as he was ordered. As he passed Franklin messing around in the trunk he caught a glimpse of two sticks of dynamite. Preston's heart began beating faster and faster. He ran for the second car and got inside. Franklin picked up one of the sticks of dynamite and held the fuse against the end of his cigarette. The burning paper was enough to ignite the cable and send sparks bouncing into the night. Franklin dropped the stick into the trunk and ran with frightening speed for the driver side door of the second car. He jumped in next to Preston and turned the key with all his strength. He flicked the gears into drive and pushed the gas pedal to the floor. The car swung right, around the parked car, and then left again around the circular drive.

"How long until it blows?" Preston asked, turning in his seat to look.

"Get down!" Franklin roared, pushing Preston's head down. "One stick is enough to break down the door, but an entire crate is enough to permanently change the map."

Preston lifted his head slightly above the seat.

"An entire crate?" he said, shocked and excited all at the same time.

"Put your head down!" Franklin shouted with an overwhelming sense of fear.

Deathless lined the driveway, guns at the ready. They opened fire just as Preston sank to the floor of the passenger seat. Their bullets hissed and snapped, shredding glass and puncturing the interior of the car.

"Hang on!"

Franklin swerved back and forth as he tried to make the car more difficult to hit. He punched the gas pedal and steadied the car again, aiming for the front gate, which was now closed. The dynamite erupted in the trunk of the car parked outside the main house. Preston saw the light from the explosion before he heard the sound. The flash illuminated Franklin's dark face and the car lurched forward with the force of the explosion. The ground beneath them shook, sending the car corralling out of control just as it plowed into the main gate.

Chapter 20

It Was Never Meant to Be Easy

Preston covered his head and pinned himself against the floor. Franklin turned the steering wheel with ferocity as he tried to regain control of the car. The gate swung open, offering little resistance to the thousand pound battering ram. Franklin turned onto the main drive and sped off south of the city along the lakeshore. Lightning sparked out over the water as black clouds continued to roll in from the west. Once more, the moon was shrouded in darkness.

"Ok," Franklin said, breathing deep. "Pick up your head."

Preston lifted his head with caution, and slid into the passenger seat without ever removing the crystals of glass. He looked out the window and saw that they were speeding passed the Nova Steel Company's main factory houses.

"Stop!" he shouted.

"What?"

"Stop! Stop the car!"

Franklin slammed on the breaks.

"Are you out of your mind?"

"We have to get to the Hold. We have to get my father."

"What are you talking about?"

"Death took his soul because of me. It is my fault. It is my fault that he is locked up in that godforsaken place. He doesn't deserve that, and I won't let it happen. Not this time."

"Preston..."

"I am not *asking* you to come with me. I am *telling* you."

"Your father no longer matters–"

"Not to you maybe, but to me..." Preston stopped and looked at the clouds in the sky and listened to the thunder. "He is all that I have left."

Franklin gripped the steering wheel and shook his head.

"This is a bad idea," he repeated over and over.

Preston stared out over the horizon and saw the rubble of the Hold. His father was there, suffering once again because of him.

"We need him. *I* need him."

Franklin coughed and let out a long sigh. He stepped on the gas and entered the right lane while sirens echoed in the distance. Fire trucks, police cars, and ambulances were on route to the Prendergast Estate. The rest of Briercliff would be focused on the explosion for the next couple of hours. Franklin pulled into the Nova Steel Company entranceway and drove straight through the security checkpoint. The man at the gate was not even paying attention and his response was severely delayed. Luck had bought them extra time.

"You do not leave my sight and you do not do anything unless I tell you to. You got it?"

"Got it."

Preston sat up in his seat, frightened and excited all at the same time. Franklin turned in the direction of the Hold. As they rose and fell over the side of a crater, the headlamps illuminated the outline of a parked sedan just outside of the entrance to the Hold.

"Is that another car?" Preston said.

Franklin swore and pounded his fist on the dashboard. He put all of his weight on the brake pedal and the car slid to a stop.

"Give me my rifle and get out," he barked.

Franklin left the keys in the ignition, anticipating the need for a quick escape. He loaded his rifle and motioned for Preston to stay close. The two men waddled along the side of the parked car. It was dark, but the engine was still warm.

"Whoever drove that car is still here," Franklin whispered.

They stalked along the edges of the melted rubble and remaining structural beams of the old factory house. Some of the ruins were still smoldering, and the smell of the scorched earth stung Preston's nostrils. There was now a large hole in the ground where the doorway to the Hold once stood. The stairs were mostly intact, although scarred and burnt. The hole itself was pitch black. Franklin raised his rifle and felt the strength of the first few steps. They held his weight without a problem, and so he motioned for Preston to follow. The two reached the bottom landing and searched for any source of light. In the distance, the solitary light bulb hanging above the first gate still burned bright. Preston heard water dripping somewhere in the tunnels, but he kept his focus on Franklin's back. They cautiously walked forward, stopping every few feet in order to listen. The light bulb hissed above Franklin's head as they reached the gateway into the cellblock. Preston heard a loud click, and Franklin spun around, raising his rifle.

"Well, what do we have here," came a cold, calculated voice that took Preston's breath away.

He turned slowly and found Arminius Blackwood standing behind him, revolver pointed directly at his heart.

"I never thought I would see you again Franklin," Arminius smiled. "Looks like you have gone and gotten yourself trapped."

"Are you alone?" Franklin said.

Arminius laughed and laughed, then struggled to catch his breath.

"I am never alone, you know that."

"Where is my father, what did you do with him?" Preston asked, staring angrily at Arminius.

"That's why you are here? You came back for a father that doesn't even love you, a father who killed your mother and lied to you? My dear boy, you truly are touched in the head!"

"Enough, where is Dr. Fox?!" Franklin roared.

"Deep, deep in the Hold; if you dare to find him."

Arminius disengaged the hammer on his revolver and placed it back into his holster.

"No matter, my master will be here before you ever find what you are looking for," he said.

"I ought to kill you right now," Franklin growled.

"Come now Franklin. If that is what you want, then why don't you put away that filthy rifle and test me flesh to flesh. Without souls – what do we have to lose?"

Preston backed into Franklin and watched as the Ghost lowered his rifle to the ground.

"Go, get your father, and come back as quick as possible. Do not linger."

"And what about you?"

"I will be fine."

Preston looked from Franklin to Arminius one last time and then bolted into the Hold.

"The keys are hanging up at the turn!" Arminius shouted after him. "Like a moth trapped in a bottle. Oh, I love to give them hope, only to see it snatched away in an instant. Now, where were we."

Arminius seized the revolver from his holster once more, cocked the hammer, and fired. Preston froze, keys in hand, as he heard the gunshot bounce and reverberate along the iron bars surrounding him.

Franklin staggered back. The bullet ripped right through his left shoulder, rendering his arm entirely useless.

"You bastard," he groaned.

"You were always too trusting," Arminius warned. "You know me well enough by now, and yet you still believe that I will play fair."

Franklin let out a ferocious roar and charged at Arminius. The Viceroy fired off two more shots, missing Franklin's head by only a few inches each time. Franklin wrapped his right arm around Arminius and dragged his enemy to the ground. Franklin delivered blow after blow with his fist, crushing portions of Arminius's skull. The Viceroy pushed Franklin away and returned the favor with two devastating haymakers.

Preston ran as fast he could, glancing left and right, searching each and every cell for any sign of life. He turned a second corner, realizing that the Hold was much larger than he imagined.

"Wait! Wait, come back!" A voice shouted after him. It was warm, alive, and familiar; it was the voice of a young girl. Preston stopped in his tracks and spun around on his heels. He ran back in the direction of the voice and found a figure clinging to the iron bars to his left.

"Who are you, can you help me?" the girl asked.

Preston slowed his pace and tried to squint in the darkness.

"Wait a minute...Preston?!?! Is that you Preston?! Dear God I cannot believe it!"

"Emma?! What are you doing here?"

"Oh Preston, it was horrible. Some men came looking for you and your father. They...they took us away. They locked me up down here, and I haven't seen anyone since. No food, no water, nothing! I don't even know where my mother and father are. Are they here, have you seen them?"

Preston's heart sank. He recalled seeing the Deathless versions of his Uncle Thomas and Aunt Charlotte at the Prendergast Estate. There was no way they could have survived the blast.

"I...I..."

He did not know what to say to his cousin.

"Preston..." Emma started to cry. "Preston what is happening?"

"I need to find my father."

As the words left his mouth, Preston understood Arminius's sinister plan. Preston did not have enough time to rescue both his cousin Emma and his father. It seemed that Arminius would have him choose, and live with the pain of the decision.

"No," Preston whispered. "No! I am getting you both out of here."

He started shuffling through the key ring, searching for the right key to open the cell door. Emma hugged the bars and cried.

Arminius reached for his revolver on the floor, but Franklin kicked it away. The Viceroy grabbed his enemy's broken arm and pulled. The muscle came loose and tore like stitches, unraveling at the seam. The arm broke off in Arminius's hand and he began beating Franklin with it. Arminius screamed as loud as his lungs would allow while he bludgeoned his opponent. Franklin, using his good arm to block Arminius's advance, swung his leg from left to right, tripping Arminius and throwing him onto his back. He got on top of the Viceroy and clawed at his face.

"I will kill you!" he screamed.

Arminius shifted his weight and flipped Franklin over. Now Franklin lay on his back with Arminius on top.

"Good luck with that," Arminius laughed.

Preston succeeded on his fourth try, finding the correct key for Emma's cell. He pulled open the door and picked her up off the floor. She was hysterical.

"Emma, you have to listen to me. Listen to me!" he shouted as she sobbed uncontrollably.

"Yeah...yes," she stammered.

"You have to go down the tunnel from where I came. You have to get back to the entrance."

"No! No I can't do it!"

"Shhh, you can do it Emma. I have a friend waiting there for me. His name is Franklin. Tell him who you are and he will keep you safe."

"And...and what about you? What are you going to do?"

"My father is down here somewhere, and I can't leave him here."

"Your father?"

"I will explain later, just go, please just go!"

Preston gave his cousin a light shove, but she just stood there, staring at him like a dog unwilling to obey orders.

"Go!"

She turned and took off down the tunnel. Preston ran off in the opposite direction, heading further into the hellish prison. He made two more turns until he arrived at a dead end. He reached the very last cell and realized that the path had ended.

"Dammit!" he shouted, and kicked the cell door.

How could he have missed his father, he thought, or even worse, what if he was not really there and this was the final surprise Arminius had in store for him. Preston felt ashamed. He hated himself for giving up on his father, and serving him to Death on a silver platter.

Something moved in the cell behind him. Something dark shifted in the corner and Preston heard something dragging across the gritty floor. He spun around and seized the bars of the cell door in his hands.

"Father! Father, is that you?" he cried out.

The shadow shifted again, this time retreating further into the depth of the cell.

"It's me, Preston. Is that you father?"

The figure slowed its retreat, and instead crawled closer to the cell door. It fell forward into the light and looked up at Preston. It was the bruised, bloodied, and broken body of his father. Preston felt like crying, but knew he was running out of time. He went straight to work looking for the key to open the door.

Arminius pinned Franklin's arm to the ground and seized the man's throat with his other hand.

"It is always nice to have *two* hands," he joked.

Lifting Franklin's neck off the ground, Arminius started slamming the Deathless' head against the floor. Franklin was losing, and he was running out of time. He guessed that Preston would come running down the tunnel at any moment with Dr. Fox in tow. He needed to get the upper hand on Arminius and finish the fight. Arminius slammed his head against the concrete two more times and then got up and walked away. Franklin was dizzy, struggling to see straight. He heard metal scraping on something hard; Arminius had picked up his revolver.

"Such a shame that it must end this way. I was hoping that you would be able to see the boy's face when he returned, empty-handed."

Franklin sat up, but realized that his good eye was smashed in and the crack in the back of his skull had left him incredibly woozy. He sensed Arminius standing over him, gun pointed at his head. Franklin reached behind his back and found the sharp blade he was looking for.

Arminius cocked the pistol. Franklin unsheathed his blade and slashed at the air with all his strength. His aim was true. He cut through Arminius's wrist, making his opponent drop the pistol. The revolver discharged as it hit the floor, the bullet striking the wall somewhere to the right. Arminius was in shock long enough for Franklin to finish the job. He jumped to his feet, buried the blade deep into Arminius's chest, and pinned the Viceroy up against the wooden barrier in front of the gate. Arminius was still surprised by the sudden turn of events. He struggled against the knife, but he could not free it from the plank of wood behind him. Franklin stumbled forward, his eyesight returned.

"It's over Arminius."

Arminius stopped struggling and started laughing.

"You think so, don't you. It will be soon, but not yet. The boy will never rescue his father."

Arminius reached into his coat pocket, eager to retrieve something, when Franklin, overcome with rage, pulled the blade from Arminius's chest and sliced the razor sharp edge across the Viceroy's throat. The Deathless' body fell to the floor and as it hit the ground, his head rolled from his shoulders and bounced across the room – bloodless and cold.

Emma stumbled through the gate and tripped over Arminius's head. She screamed with fright and fell to the ground.

Franklin, startled to see someone other than Preston come through the door, ran to her side.

"No! Don't touch me!" she screeched.

"Calm down, who are you? Did Preston send you?" Franklin asked.

"Are...are you Franklin?"

"Yes."

"Oh, thank God. Preston told me to find you. Please, we need to get out of here."

"Not without Preston."

Franklin recognized the sound of engines on the wind drifting from the staircase.

"We are out of time," he whispered, secretly lamenting the fact.

"What do you need me to do?" Emma asked.

"Call Preston to get up here, we need to go," he ordered.

Franklin picked up his rifle as Emma scampered off down the haunting corridor. As he knelt at the base of Arminius's body, he noticed that the Viceroy held something in his right hand. The object was small, dark, and made of some sort of tarnished brass or iron. It was a key. Franklin plucked it from the lifeless fingers and held it up to the flickering light. Arminius had outsmarted them. There was no doubt that this was the key that would open Dr. Fox's cell. Franklin glanced in the direction of the bowels of the Hold and squeezed the key tight.

"There is not time," he confessed.

The Deathless Dr. Fox sat there, out of arm's reach, cocking his head like a dog. Preston was desperate.

"Give me your hand. Let me bring you back, and together we can get out of here. Please."

He pushed his chest against the door, but his father was still out of reach and showed no signs of moving closer.

"Please! Please!"

Preston was now crying, tears rolling down his cheeks. He thought about everything they had been through. About his mother, her death, and how his father suffered with the truth. The Fox family deserved better. They deserved a normal life. They deserved to be together.

"Please."

Preston whispered to his father as he sat on the floor. A voice rose from deep within the tunnels behind him. Someone was calling his name. It was Emma.

"Preston! We need to go now! They are coming!"

He wiped the tears from his cheeks and retracted his arm from the door.

"I will be back for you. I promise that I will come back for you."

He kicked the key ring and ran like the wind into the darkness. Dr. Fox crawled back into the corner of his cell and rubbed his chin.

Franklin stood on the top step of the staircase, measuring the lay of the land and searching for any signs of trouble. A single set of headlights was closing in on his position. He steadied his rifle on the ground and lined up the shot. He fired. The bullet broke the windshield but failed to hit its target. The black sedan swerved to the right and approached at a different angle. Franklin lined up his second shot and fired. The bullet skipped across the hood. He groaned and took aim a third time. This time the bullet shattered the rear window.

"Dammit!"

With one bullet left, Franklin lifted his rifle off the ground and leveled it using debris nearby. He looked down the sights and drew in a deep breath. He wished that he still had some cigarettes in his pocket, because he never missed a shot while smoking. The gunpowder ignited and the bullet whizzed through the air. It struck the driver right between his eyes, killing him instantly. The car careened to the right, hit one of the old factory furnaces and flipped over. It crashed onto the ground and rocked back and forth.
Franklin was pleased with himself, but surprised that only one car had come since they broke through the security checkpoint. Something was not right.

Preston and Emma ran up behind him.

"I found him!" Emma exclaimed.

"Good, because we need to go now," Franklin grunted. He tried not to look Preston in the eyes. He knew that the boy did not rescue his father, but the question needed to be asked.

"What about your father?" he said.

"It is too late," Preston stared at his dirty shoes with an enormous sense of guilt. "We need to get going."

"So it is over?"

"I will come back for him. I promise that I will take him from here."

Franklin nodded his head.

Just then, a loud crack sounded from the overturned car. Preston, Franklin, and Emma spun around in alarm. The rear driver side door was bent in half. Another loud bang and the door's hinges barely held. A third bang and the door soared through the air, landing behind Preston. A black mist poured from the back seat like smoke. Preston immediately had a flashback to the balcony in the dining room of the Prendergast Estate.

"Take my pack and run! Go now!" Franklin shouted, tossing his rucksack into Preston's arms.

Preston seized Emma's arm and pulled her hard and fast. They took off running in the direction of the lake. Franklin backed away slowly, realizing that it would be up to him to slow down their adversary. The mist kept pouring out of the car. Lightning struck the shoreline and the dark clouds finally opened up. Rain trickled from the sky and mixed with the dark shadows on the ground. Two blue eyes exited the vehicle and floated towards Franklin.

"I am not afraid of you!" he shouted.

That is because you think Death is final, but there are far worse things in the world. I am disappointed in you Franklin.

Franklin threw his gun at the eyes but the mist deflected it.

Your insurrection ends here.

A dark blade sliced through the shadows and separated Franklin's head from his body.

Preston and Emma ran for the cliffs. They stopped short and realized that they had made a grave mistake. The drop off from the cliff was more than 100 feet into the crashing waves below. They would never survive such a fall.

"This way!" Preston shouted over the thunderous storm clouds.

They turned left, seeking a way to head farther down the shoreline.

"Watch out!" Emma shrieked as one of the cars landed on the cliff, blocking their escape route. Preston looked back and saw Death floating toward them. Tentacles in the mist plucked scraps of steel and iron, and used them to block their path. Pretty soon Preston and Emma were cornered along the cliff with nowhere to go. Preston backed up as far as he could, his heels just over the edge of the cliff. He looked down, straining his eyes to see through the dark and the rain. He saw the crashing waves below and was overcome with a vision of his mother standing on the cliff the night she died. He fell to his knees and started shaking. Death's laugh caused Emma to almost faint. The cold, hypnotic power of the Harbinger was too much for her.

You wish to die the same way as your mother?

Preston, still shaking, glanced over the edge once more. Lightning struck a tree behind Death, setting it ablaze. The sound of the thunder was tremendous and made Emma cover her ears and start screaming.

You have nowhere to go.

The mist surrounding Death recoiled and swung around behind him. There he stood, still covered in his unworldly armor and ghastly mask; however, something was different. His body was damaged. Cracks spread across his chest plate, and little splints of ebony mail were missing from his mask. Either the blast from the dynamite or Preston's interference with Errol had revealed Death's weakness. Preston, emboldened by what he saw, stood next to his cowering cousin.

Now give me your soul!

"Never!"

One of the tentacles skittered across the ground like a spider and reached out to grab Preston, but a burst of blue light exploded between them. The dark mist evaporated instantly. Preston, without a scratch, stood in disbelief. Death roared and sent multiple tentacles after Preston. Each time they came within a few feet of where he stood, they erupted in a flash of blue light. It was as if some sort of holy power was protecting Preston. Death, now showing signs of distress and unbridled anger, sent an entire cloud of mist toward Preston. The young boy put up his arms and covered his face, fearing the worst, but once again the mist was destroyed. All that was left on the cliffside was Preston, Emma, and Death, no longer able to hide in the shadows.

What is this?! What are you?!

Preston knelt down next to Emma, grabbed her hand and lifted her up. She was weak and leaned close to his chest, but she was at least able to stand. More mist crawled its way past Death. It seemed as though it would never end. Preston looked Emma in the eyes.

"We need to jump," he whispered. "It is our only chance."

"I...I can't," she cried.

"Have faith."

He turned around and stared out across the lake. The storm above them was threatening, evil in its purest form.

You would do it? Die as your mother did?

Preston blocked out Death's taunts as more and more tentacles reached for him, and flashes of blue light broke all around him. He focused entirely on the waves crashing below him. Images of his mother flooded his mind.

"Protect us," he whispered, not knowing to whom he spoke.

He wrapped his arms around Emma and together they fell over the edge of the cliff. An enormous flash of light exploded across the shoreline as Death, in a fit of rage, tried to stop Preston. They fell, faster and faster. The rain pounded them from every angle and Preston thought he heard Emma screaming. A large shadow enveloped them before they hit the water. Preston thought it was Death and closed his eyes to the world.

Chapter 21

The Beginning of The End

"Preston! Preston! Preston, wake up!"

The voice became louder and louder until it burrowed its way deep into Preston's conscience. He heard it the first time, but his mind was still a long way away.

"Preston!" Professor Cain shouted once more.

The boy opened his eyes and stared at the black ceiling of the world. Rain prickled his face and he was forced to shield his eyes. Surprisingly, he still had the strength to move.

"Oh thank God, I thought you were a goner this time," Cain remarked, laughing to himself.

Preston lifted his head and craned his neck to see his surroundings. The smell of dead fish and water was the first thing that hit him. They were on a beach somewhere. The back of his head was caked with wet sand, and his clothes were drenched.

"What happened? Where are we? Where is Emma?" he asked.

"I am right here, no worries," Emma whispered, kneeling down next to him.

She was wrapped in a blanket and placed a hand on his chest. He could tell that she was in pain.

"Errol saved you, again," Cain professed.

Errol was sitting nearby, holding onto Franklin's rucksack. Preston finally understood. That large shadow that overcame them was not Death, but Errol as a bird, come to rescue them.

"I thought you said we were even," Preston joked, stretching his legs.

"You owe me one more time," Errol said, with very little emotion.

Other than Cain's usual jovial personality, the mood of Preston's companions was bleak. Franklin was dead, Uncle Thomas and Aunt Charlotte as well, his father was a Deathless trapped in the Hold, and Death had the key. It would seem as though they had ultimately failed. Preston looked out over the thrashing waves and realized that they were not far from his home. They were south of the city, and he could see the cliffs and shoreline along the Nova Steel Company in the distance. He wondered if Death was still standing there, cursing Preston's unfounded power and bravery.

Cain sat back and rubbed his hands together.

"So what now?" he asked. "Death has the key, and Grishkat is gone, along with all of his knowledge."

"And Death is a powerful foe," Errol added. "There is no defeating a being such as him."

"He is powerful, but he has weaknesses," Preston said. "I think *I* am his weakness. He cannot touch me. You witnessed what happened in the dining room, and the same thing happened on the cliffs."

"But what is the plan? Where to next?" Cain asked, still flabbergasted by the possibilities. "We have no direction. Do we just run and protect you for as long as possible? A storm is coming, and the key will mean that we will have two of these creatures to contend with. Death's brother may very well be more powerful than him, and what if he doesn't have any weaknesses?"

Preston looked at Emma, who was on the verge of falling asleep, and wondered how long they could survive on the run. Could he face Death alone and destroy him?

"For now we will go home," Errol said. "My home, Aurora, where my family lives."

"Family?" Cain asked. "You never mentioned having any family."

"I didn't say that it would be a welcome homecoming, but it is at least an option. They are good people, and Therians, which means some of the elders in the town may have some knowledge about the things Grishkat mentioned."

"You mean, Druids?" Preston asked.

Errol shrugged his shoulders. Preston poked at his pocket and felt the bulge of the stone that they found at the University. How could he have been so foolish as to forget about what Grishkat had told him?

"Then it is decided," Cain said, searching in the faces of the gathered company for any sign of disagreement.

"And what about her?" Errol asked, pointing at Emma.

"I am going with you," Emma said, staring into the cold wet sand. "Preston may very well be all the family I have left. I am with him...until the end..."

Overcome with grief, Emma again buried her face in her hands. Cain pulled her close and whispered in her ear. Preston got up and took Franklin's rucksack from Errol. He opened it up and dumped its contents onto the beach. There were only five objects in the pack – a knife, a spool of thread, a spoon, his lighter, and a key. Preston put the lighter in his pocket, but the key mesmerized him; it looked eerily familiar to him. Then it hit him like a ton of bricks – the key was the exact same style as the ones on the ring in the Hold. Was this the key that would have unlocked his father's cell door? Why did Franklin have it? A single tear rolled down the side of Preston's face. A bolt of lightning illuminated the sky above the lake as he placed the key in his pocket along with the lighter. He placed everything else back in the sack and slung it over his shoulder. He stooped low next to Emma and gently took her hand in his.

"Let's go," he whispered to her.

She reluctantly rose to her feet. Together, with Errol in the lead and Cain following behind, they disappeared into the darkness.

Death stood still and let the rain wash away a small portion of his pain and despair. He had lost the boy, but he still had the key. The giant bird flapped its wings as it rose into the air and soared above the black waters rolling below. The burning tree was now just a smoldering stake in the ground. Death lowered his head and let the storm turn his world upside down. The cold steel on his arms, legs, and chest melted with the rainwater and evaporated into the cold mist that swirled around him. His mask gave way to a perfect chin and perfect lips. Long strands of bright blonde hair sprung from the top of his pale, bald head. The mist retreated into the shadows, and all that was left was the naked form of Lastarr Prendergast. He remained in the elements a little while longer before walking back to the Hold.

He descended into the hole in the ground, and found the headless body of Arminius Blackwood at his feet. He lifted the head of his Viceroy and stared into the Deathless' face. Gathering up the dead man's clothes, Death stalked the tunnels, the shadows hugging him close. He turned left, then turned right, and then another right, until he reached the very end. He stood outside of Dr. Fox's cell and peered into the darkness just on the other side of the bars. The Deathless Dr. Fox rolled over and stared at his visitor. Death placed a finger on the cell door and the lock disengaged, and the door creaked as it opened. Dr. Fox rose to his feet with curiosity. The initial shock of being made Deathless was beginning to wear off.

"Who...who are you?" he asked, hesitantly.

"I am your master," Death responded carefully. "I am here to take you home."

There was something about the look in Death's eyes that calmed Dr. Fox's nerves. Maybe it was how they burned with a hypnotic sapphire light, or maybe it was the way in which his voice was welcoming, full of compassion.

"And...and who might I be? I cannot seem to remember..." Dr. Fox's voice drifted off.

"Don't you know?" Death asked, pretending as though Dr. Fox suffered from amnesia. "You are Arminius. Arminius Blackwood. My dearest, and most trusted friend."

Death offered his hand, and Dr. Fox graciously received it. They returned the way they came.

"We have much work to do," Death explained. "My brother is coming to stay with us, and we must make preparations."

About the Author

The author lives in Western New York with his wife, Justine, and his dog, Buster.